Holly Green writes historical sagas about love and war, and her books are inspired by the stories she heard from her parents when she was a child. Her father was a professional singer with a fine baritone voice and her mother was a dancer, but they had to give up their professions at the outbreak of World War Two.

Holly is from Liverpool and is a trained actress and teacher – her claim to fame being that she gave Daniel Craig his first acting experience! Holly is married, and enjoys spending time with her two delightful grandchildren.

ALSO BY HOLLY GREEN:

Workhouse series:
Workhouse Orphans
Workhouse Angel
Workhouse Nightingale

Frontline Nurses series:
Frontline Nurses
Frontline Nurses On Duty
Secrets of the Frontline Nurses

HOLLY GREEN

Frontline
Nurses

EBURY
PRESS

This edition published by Ebury Press in 2018
First published as 'Daughters of War' in 2011 by Severn House

1 3 5 7 9 10 8 6 4 2

Ebury Press, an imprint of Ebury Publishing
20 Vauxhall Bridge Road,
London SW1V 2SA

Ebury Press is part of the Penguin Random House group of companies
whose addresses can be found at global.penguinrandomhouse.com

Penguin
Random House
UK

www.penguin.co.uk

A CIP catalogue record for this book is available from the British Library

ISBN 9781785039577

Typeset in 13/16.872 pt Times LT Std
by Integra Software Services Pvt. Ltd, Pondicherry

Printed and bound in Great Britain by Clays Ltd, Elcograf S.p.A.

Penguin Random House is committed to a sustainable future for
our business, our readers and our planet. This book is made
from Forest Stewardship Council® certified paper.

MIX
Paper from
responsible sources
FSC® C018179

I am grateful to Lynette Beardwood, archivist for the FANY and Fellow of Liverpool John Moores University, for drawing my attention to the stories of Mabel Stobart and Flora Sands, and for providing me with invaluable source material about the FANY during World War One.

PART ONE – BAPTISM OF FIRE

Chapter 1

The leaves on the trees in Hyde Park were drooping in the summer heat. The Bayswater Road was busy with hansom cabs and tradesmen's vans, and in the middle of the throng one or two motorcars honked and spluttered. The air was heavy with dust and the smell of horse dung. Leonora stood aside to allow a nursemaid pushing a perambulator to pass and almost collided with a small boy bowling a hoop. Children in the charge of nannies or governesses were heading home for afternoon tea after their walk in the park. To escape the crowd and the smell Leo turned into Albion Gate and paused in the shade of a tree, gazing down across the grass to where the Serpentine glittered in the sun.

Raucous voices drew her attention to Rotten Row, where the elite of London Society were accustomed to ride or drive.

'Call yourselves women? You're a bloody disgrace!'

'Gallivanting about in uniform. Who do you think you are?'

'They're not women, they're bleeding suffragettes!'

Coming towards her was a curious little cavalcade: half a dozen mounted women in scarlet tunics and peaked caps, followed by a horse-drawn wagon with a Red Cross painted on the side. The jeers were coming from a group of workmen on the far side of the track, but, as she stood watching, Leo heard a well-dressed lady nearby remark to her companion, 'Riding astride, like men! Really, it's shameful.'

At that moment a sudden movement caught Leo's attention. One of the men stooped and picked something up from the ground, then his arm went back and a missile flew through the air. One of the horses, a nervy-looking grey, let out a squeal of pain, reared up and sent its rider crashing to the ground. Panicked, the horse broke into a canter, heading directly towards the gate where Leo stood. She realised instantly that if it galloped out into the crowded road there could be a serious accident. Acting on instinct, she stepped directly into the path of the careering beast. The horse shied violently and flung up its head but with a leap Leo grabbed the reins and used her body weight to drag it to a standstill. It stood shuddering and snorting and she caressed the sweating neck and murmured to it in a language not her own, which seemed to rise unbidden from the depths of some childhood memory.

Shouts and cries of alarm erupted around her, and above the general hubbub she heard one voice raised in fury. The rider had scrambled to her feet and turned on the man who had thrown the stone.

'You brute! If you wanted to hurt someone, why didn't you aim at me instead of the poor bloody animal?'

The language was coarse but the diction was refined and Leo found herself smiling at the contrast. The girl who had spoken was running towards her. She had lost her hat and her dark hair was coming down around her neck. Her face was flushed and her eyes glittered, but with anger rather than embarrassment.

'Well done you!' she exclaimed breathlessly as she reached Leonora. 'I must say it takes guts to face a bolting horse like that.'

'Oh well.' Leo shrugged self-deprecatingly. 'I didn't stop to think. I'm used to horses. Are you hurt?'

'Only in my self-esteem. I shall be ribbed mercilessly for coming off like that.'

'Now then, miss—' a police constable had appeared at Leo's shoulder '—better let the young woman be on her way. You did very well there to stop the horse, but we don't want any more incidents.'

Leo looked at him. 'Aren't you going to arrest the man who threw the stone? He's the cause of all the trouble.'

The constable turned his gaze to the little knot of workmen, who stared back belligerently. 'If young women who ought to know better choose to disport themselves in unsuitable clothing,' he said ponderously, 'they have only themselves to blame for the consequences.'

'But that's not ...' Leo began angrily but the policeman had already turned away.

Her companion reached out and gripped her wrist. 'Let it go. No point in making a fuss.' She smiled, and Leo found herself looking into deep blue eyes that sparkled with vitality. 'By the way, I'm Victoria Langford.'

Leo took the offered hand. 'I'm Leonora Malham Brown. How do you do?'

Victoria gathered up the reins of the now docile horse. 'I'd better get going. The others are waiting for me. She placed one foot in the stirrup, then turned back to Leo. 'It would be nice to meet again. Would you care for that?'

Leo answered without needing to think. 'Yes, I should, very much.'

Victoria swung herself into the saddle with an ease that Leo could only envy. She caught a glimpse of riding breeches under the divided skirt and was aware of the frustrating impediment of her own petticoats.

'Tomorrow? How about tea at the Grosvenor?'

'That would be lovely.'

'Four o'clock then?'

'Thank you. I'll look forward to it.'

'Thank *you*! You saved a lot of people a lot of trouble. See you tomorrow.'

She turned the horse's head towards the spot where her companions were waiting and cantered away, and as she did so a church clock nearby struck the hour. Leo started. Four o'clock! It was her grandma's At Home afternoon and she was expected to put in an appearance. The last thing she wanted was an inquisition into where she had been. She began to walk briskly towards Sussex Gardens.

No. 31 Sussex Gardens was one of a terrace of elegant Georgian houses. When Beavis, her grandma's butler, opened the door to her, Leo could tell from his expression that she was both late and looking dishevelled.

'Madam is in the drawing room,' he announced, 'and she has been asking for you.'

'Does she have guests with her?' Leo asked.

'Yes, miss. Lady Stevenage and Mrs Fawcett have called.'

'I'll just go up and take off my hat,' Leo said.

Beavis made a small bow and withdrew through the green baize door to the servants' quarters. As Leo crossed to the stairs she heard her grandma's voice from the drawing room.

'Marriage? Oh dear, I'm afraid there's very little prospect of that. The girl is too tall, too clever and too arrogant.'

Leo had no doubt that she was the girl in question. Up in her bedroom she interrogated her reflection in the dressing-table mirror. Wide amber eyes flecked with green looked back at her. There was a trace of moisture on the lashes, which she hastily brushed away. She had resolved long ago that she would not let her grandma make her cry. She had been fifteen when her father sent her back to live with the old lady and she had sensed at once that she disapproved of her. She guessed that her father had been a disappointment because, instead of staying at home and going into business to increase the family fortune, he had squandered it on an inexplicable, to his mother, passion for archaeology. Then he had compounded his sins by marrying a foreigner, a Greek woman without any social credentials. As a final dereliction of duty, when his wife died he had kept Leo with him instead of sending her back to be educated in England like her brother, Ralph, with the result that when she finally arrived at Sussex Gardens she was, in her grandma's words, a hoyden with no idea of how to behave in good society.

Too tall? Leo considered her reflection. It was true that she could look most men straight in the eye, rather than gazing up at them as they seemed to prefer. And it was true that she didn't have much of a figure. In fact she was so lacking in feminine curves that her brother had long ago nicknamed her 'beanpole'. But she was not bad-looking, even if her strong chin and well-marked cheekbones were not quite what contemporary fashion regarded as beautiful. In fact, her brother had told her that one of his friends had referred to her as 'a devilish handsome gel'. Too clever? Was she to blame for the fact that her father had kept her with him on his travels and educated her himself? So that now she could not only read Latin and Greek, she also had a good understanding of mathematics and history. She spoke French and German, which might be expected, and in addition she was fluent in demotic Greek and Turkish and could make herself understood in Italian and Arabic, though possibly not in terms suitable for a young lady. Too arrogant? It was true that she did not suffer fools gladly and had never reconciled herself to the notion that well brought-up young women were not expected to express opinions on religion or philosophy, and certainly not on politics. But she did try to keep a guard on her tongue and look suitably demure and admiring when men were talking rubbish.

She secured the last wayward strand of heavy chestnut hair with a stab of a hairpin. Anyway, what her grandma had said was untrue in one respect, at least. Tom Devenish would propose to her tomorrow, if she gave him the slightest encouragement. She stood up, straightened her dress and went downstairs. Outside the drawing room door she paused, drew as deep a breath as her corset would allow, lifted her chin and went in.

The room was furnished in the heavy Victorian style of her grandma's social heyday. Thick plush curtains in faded puce kept back the sunlight and the visitors sat on overstuffed chairs upholstered in a similar colour. An occasional table covered with a velvet cloth was loaded with china ornaments and an arrangement of dried flowers under a glass dome, while the mantelpiece bore two large ormolu vases. Above it was an oil-painting of the old lady as a young woman of twenty. Amelia Malham Brown was over sixty but she still retained traces of the delicate, fair-haired beauty that had captivated the upstart engineer, William Brown, when she was simply Amelia Malham and he was building a railway line across her father's land. It was her beauty and his money that had made her the toast of London society and her land-owning pedigree that had caused him to add her surname to his own more plebeian Brown. Now a widow of many years she had to hold court in a rather depleted fashion but Leo was well aware that she was expected to rectify that by making a good marriage.

Her grandma turned an imperious, heavy-lidded gaze towards Leo as she entered. 'Leonora, you know today is my At Home day. Where have you been?'

Leo decided that the earlier incident, suitably edited, would provide her with the cover story she needed. Hopefully, it would give the ladies enough to talk about and prevent any further probing. If her grandma were ever to uncover the fact that she had been attending one of Emmeline Pankhurst's public meetings she would be summarily dispatched to Bramwell Hall, the family home in Cheshire, where her activities would be even more circumscribed. Though there were times when she thought it might even be preferable to London. At least there she could have a horse saddled up and go for a good gallop.

'I'm sorry, Grandma,' she said. 'I was walking in the park and there was an incident – a horse bolted and for a while there was so much turmoil around the gate that I couldn't get through.' She turned to shake hands with her grandma's guests.

'Bolted, you say?' Lady Stevenage exclaimed. 'How did that occur?'

'One of those infernal machines, I expect,' Amelia put in sharply.

'They don't allow motor cars in the park, Grandma,' Leo pointed out.

Her grandma snorted. Motor cars were her favourite *bête noir.* 'Out on the road. Near enough to frighten the poor beasts with their noise.'

Leo was saved from further questions by the appearance of Beavis.

'Lieutenant Malham Brown and Mr Devenish, madam.'

The appearance of her brother aroused in Leo a familiar mixture of emotions. Ralph might have been born to wear uniform. He had gone into the Guards straight from school and had found his perfect setting, and the fact was apparent from the top of his glossy chestnut head to the shining toes of his boots. He looked, Leo thought, like a thoroughbred horse in the peak of condition and it was not lost on her that they were so much alike that people had been known to mistake them for twins, although he was the elder by two years. The sight of him always induced a thrill of admiration and pride but combined with that was another, bitterer sensation, which she was forced to admit as jealousy. Try as she might to suppress it, she could not help envying his freedom of choice and his luck at finding a destiny that suited him so perfectly, while she was so constrained and limited by circumstance and convention.

Tom Devenish provoked a different set of emotions altogether. He was handsome, independently wealthy and the heir to a baronetcy, which made him in her grandma's eyes – and those of many other society matrons – the perfect catch, and Leo knew that most people thought she was mad not to encourage him. He and Ralph had been at school together and had remained close friends, but it was an attraction of opposites. Whereas Ralph was all dash and activity, unable to stay still for more than five minutes together, Tom behaved with a restraint that Leo found disturbing. She sensed that behind the mask of gentlemanly good manners simmered emotions that he was afraid to unleash. He had a good brain, and had read Classics at Oxford, but had left with a disappointing Lower Second when all his tutors had expected a First. Since then, as far as Leo could tell, he had done nothing but hang around the fringes of the Bohemian world in London. His one interest was in art and he had shown her some exquisite sketches and watercolours, but when she had suggested he might exhibit and even sell some he had reacted with horror. 'I shouldn't dream of setting myself up against the professionals. And anyway, people don't want my kind of pictures these days.' He was charming and courteous but his courting lacking any sense of passion or urgency. Leo knew that if she married him she could look forward to a life of ease and comfort – and the prospect made her want to scream with boredom. It was only occasionally, when he and Ralph were alone together in the billiard room and she heard them laughing, that it struck her that she was hearing the real Tom Devenish.

Ralph greeted his grandma and the other ladies, then turned to Leo. 'How are you, sis?' he asked, kissing her cheek. 'Behaving yourself, I hope.'

Leo felt a sudden urge to kick him hard in the shins, as she would have done when they were growing up together. Really, Ralph could be insufferably pompous sometimes! Aloud she said demurely, 'As well as you, I expect.'

'I'm sure Leonora always behaves with the utmost propriety,' Tom said, taking her hand. *Little do you know*, she felt like muttering.

'Lieutenant Malham Brown,' Lady Stevenage interrupted, 'you are a military man. What do you think? Is there going to be a war with Germany?'

Ralph turned to her and drew up a chair and Leo's desire to kick him grew stronger. Anybody would think he was a general, or at least privy to the highest military secrets, from the way he behaved!

'I'm afraid, Lady Stevenage, that it begins to look as though we may have to teach the Kaiser a lesson. But don't disturb yourself unduly. It will be a short, sharp affair and as long as we have the Royal Navy you need have no fear of an invasion.'

'What about these rumours of trouble in the Balkans. Should we be concerned about that?'

'Just a little local difficulty. Nothing that will affect us.'

'I think you are wrong there,' Leo said. 'If fighting starts there it could spread right across Europe.'

The all looked at her as if the chair she sat on had suddenly found a voice.

Ralph raised his eyebrows. 'And why should that be? If the Bulgars and the Serbs are foolish enough to take on the might of the Ottoman Empire, I don't see why we should allow ourselves to become embroiled.'

'Because they are small countries that have lived under Turkish domination for centuries and they deserve our support,' Leo replied, ignoring her grandma's disapproving looks. 'And because Austria Hungary won't stand by and do nothing.'

'Leonora!' Her grandma's voice cut across Ralph's response. 'These are military matters and best left to those who understand them. Lady Stevenage, can I offer you another cup of tea?'

Leo lapsed into silence, glaring at Ralph, but then she caught Tom's eye and thought she saw the flicker of a smile.

Leo woke the next morning with a sense of pleasurable anticipation and for a few moments she could not remember why. Then it came to her. She was meeting Victoria Langford for tea that afternoon. For some reason she could not explain, their brief encounter the previous day had sparked a sense of new possibilities. If nothing more, the meeting offered a respite from the boredom of her normal routine. It meant telling her grandma another white lie, of course. She would want to know all about Victoria, who her family were and so on, before she would countenance any kind of relationship. But it was not a problem. Grandma was used to the idea that Leo always escaped for a walk in the afternoon and had come to accept it as preferable to the caged tiger that she became if confined to the house.

As she stepped down from the hansom cab outside the colonnaded façade of the Grosvenor Hotel in Park Lane she was aware of a commotion ahead of her. A yellow motorcar was forcing its way through the throng of horse-drawn vehicles, in the face of angry shouts and skittering hooves. It drew up outside the hotel and there were gasps from the onlookers as the driver stepped out and was seen to be a woman. It took Leo a moment to realise that it was Victoria.

Her new friend saw her and crossed the pavement to take her hand.

'I'm so glad you're here. I was afraid you might have changed your mind.'

'Oh no, no!' Leo replied breathlessly, adding before she could stop herself, 'You can drive!'

'Obviously,' Victoria said with a laugh. 'Shall we go in?'

It was apparent from the doorman's manner that Victoria was a regular and valued guest, and a pageboy was dispatched to keep an eye on the car, which was now surrounded by a small crowd of curious passers-by. When they were settled in a deep sofa in the Park Room, with its long windows overlooking the park, and Victoria had ordered tea, Leonora said, 'How did you learn to drive?'

'My father taught me, years ago. He was passionate about motorcars. Making them and driving them. He could see that they were the future. One day, he used to say, there will be more cars than horses on the streets of London.'

'You speak of him in the past tense.'

'Yes. He was killed three years ago – an accident on the racetrack.'

'How tragic!'

Victoria paused, her head slightly tilted. 'I don't know. He died doing the thing he loved. He would have preferred that to a feeble old age.'

'And it hasn't put you off motorcars?'

'Good heavens, no! I love driving. It's the most exhilarating thing I've ever experienced. I've raced myself, once or twice.'

'You've driven in motor races!'

'I was third in the Ladies Bracelet Handicap at Brooklands last year.'

'How thrilling!'

The waiter brought tea in silver pots, with a plate of delicate sandwiches and a cake-stand full of exquisite pastries. Victoria poured.

'What about you?' she asked, handing Leo a cup. 'What does your father do?'

'Strangely enough, he is dead, too. But he was a scholar and a great traveller. Archaeology was his passion.'

'How fascinating! And your mother – does she share that passion?'

'I don't remember her. She died soon after I was born.'

'I'm sorry, but it is a strange coincidence. My mother died when I was twelve, so we're both orphans. I felt as soon as we met that we had something in common. Are you an only child?'

'No, I have an older brother, Ralph. What about you?'

'Oh, I'm the only one. My mother used to say one of me was quite enough for her to cope with. It must have made things very difficult for your father, being left with two small children. Who brought you up?'

'He did. He kept us with him until Ralph was twelve. Then he was sent back to school in England, but I stayed with Father until I was fifteen.'

'So you must have seen some marvellous places.'

'Yes, it's true. One of my earliest memories is of playing in the dirt while my father unearthed treasures from the ruins of Troy.'

'What a wonderful experience. I do envy you. You must miss it now – and him.'

'Oh, I do! I do!' Leo said, shaking her head sadly.

'So who do you live with now?'

'My grandma. She has the difficult task of turning me into a lady and finding me a suitable husband.'

'Any prospects?'

'Only one – and I have no intention of marrying him.'

'Good for you!'

'And you? You're not married.'

'No fear! I'm very fortunate. My father left me well provided for so I have the freedom to do as I please. I've no desire to give all that up to become part of some man's goods and chattels.'

'You are lucky,' Leo agreed. 'My father left me money but it's in trust and I can't touch it till I'm twenty-one. So for the present I'm completely dependent on Grandma.'

'No woman should be dependent on a man or a relative for subsistence,' Victoria pronounced.

'You sound like a suffragette.'

'Well, I sympathise with their objectives. But I don't agree with their methods.'

'But how else are we ever going to convince the men in government that they have to listen to us?'

'By proving that women can be as rational and clear-headed as any man. That we're capable of organising and working together. And above all, that we are as brave and as patriotic as men. That's why I joined the FANY.'

'The what?' Leo queried, wide-eyed.

'It stands for First Aid Nursing Yeomanry.'

'Is that who you were with yesterday?'

'That's right.'

'What do you do, exactly?'

Victoria put down her cup. 'Imagine a battlefield in the aftermath of a battle. The ground is strewn with bodies. Some are dead but many are just wounded, but unable to make their own way back to the lines. Some may bleed to death unless there is someone to staunch their wounds. Now imagine a corps of mounted nurses who gallop onto the battle-field to care for them. How does that picture strike you?'

Leo laughed. 'It sounds terribly romantic but I don't know if it's practical. Is that what the FANY do?'

'It's what our founder intended. He was wounded at the battle of Omdurman and saw the need for something of the sort, so when he left the army he set about recruiting young women with a spirit of adventure and that's how the FANY was born. But you're right. It is just a romantic idea. If there ever is another war, and it looks all too likely, it won't be fought on horses but with motorcars and aeroplanes.'

'So the FANY won't be any use?'

'On the contrary. People trained in First Aid will still be needed to bring the wounded from the field of battle to the casualty stations, whether on horse-back or in motor vehicles. That will be our opportunity to show that we are worthy of taking an equal part in society with the men.'

Leonora set down her fork. 'That makes sense. But will the generals ever let you get near a battlefield?'

'They won't be able to stop us!' Victoria declared.

She beckoned a waiter for the bill and when she had paid they made their way out to where the yellow motor car stood, still encircled by a group of curious small boys.

'What kind of car is it?' Leo asked.

'A Sunbeam. I call him Sparky.'

'I thought cars were feminine, like ships.'

'Well, this one is definitely male.'

'Is this the one you drove in the race?'

'Goodness, no! This is a tourer, not a racing car. I drove Toodles, the Sunbeam racing model. Can I offer you a lift?'

Leo caught her breath. 'Would you really? I've never been in a motorcar.'

'Good Lord! Why ever not?'

'Grandma thinks they are a creation of the devil.'

'Well, she'll just have to get used to them. Jump in and I'll take you for a spin.'

In a surprisingly short time they were out on the Great West Road and racing along at a speed that took Leo's breath away.

'How fast are we going?' she yelled, clinging to her hat.

'Thirty-five miles an hour,' Victoria shouted back. 'And to think that not long ago some fool of a doctor said that the human body would not be able to withstand speeds above thirty!'

'I thought the speed limit was twenty.'

Victoria flung back her head and laughed. 'So it is, officially. But who cares?'

'I've never travelled as fast as this! It's thrilling!'

'This is nothing,' Victoria yelled. 'I touched fifty-five on the track at Brooklands.'

After another mile or two she turned the car and they headed back into London. As they drove along Knightsbridge Leo plucked up courage to say, 'Will you teach me to drive?'

Victoria looked at her and gave her the mischievous smile that she found so attractive. 'On one condition. You must join the FANY.'

'Me? Oh, I couldn't.'

'Why not?'

'My grandma wouldn't approve.'

'Are you going to let her rule your life until you're twenty-one? How old are you now?'

'Nineteen.'

'Two more years of being under her thumb – or a chance to strike out for yourself and do something exciting. It's your choice.'

Leo drew a deep breath. 'You're right. How do I join?'

Chapter 2

Leo's next encounter with her grandma was stormy. When she told her that she intended to join the FANY and explained what the initials stood for the old lady sniffed dismissively. 'Romantic nonsense!'

'It's not nonsense!' Leo retorted sharply. Then she checked herself and took a deep breath. This was exactly the sort of behaviour that gave rise to her grandma's accusation of arrogance. 'I'm sorry, Grandma. I didn't intend to be rude. But I think it is a wonderful idea.'

'Young women setting themselves up as some kind of military organisation? I can't think what their parents are thinking of. No one with any breeding would countenance it for a moment.'

'Actually, all the members are gentlewomen. That's why it's called a yeomanry. And some of them are married ladies, I believe. One or two of them have titles.' Leo was struggling to restrain her temper.

'And their husbands permit it! The world is going mad.'

'Why should a woman need her husband's permission to do anything?' Leo demanded. 'It's so unfair! Anyway, I still think it's a good idea and I'm going to join.'

'You most certainly will not! I've never heard anything so ridiculous.'

'It's not ridiculous, grandma,' Leo protested. 'It's a very respectable organisation run by women who only want to serve their country in the event of a war.'

'The best way any woman can serve her country is by doing her duty, which is to stay at home and care for her family,' Amelia snapped.

'But she may not have a family,' Leo objected. 'And anyway, I don't see that there is anything wrong with learning some First Aid. It could be useful wherever she is.'

'That is enough, Leonora,' was the response. 'I am not going to discuss the matter any further. You have heard my decision.'

Leo was about to declare that she intended to join, whatever her grandma thought, but she checked the impulse. Instead she said, as calmly as she could,

'Grandma, I'm not a child anymore. Don't you think it's time I was allowed to make some decisions for myself?'

Her grandma rose to her feet. 'When you are of age you will be able to ruin your reputation in whatever way you choose. I shall not be able to stop you. Until then, you will do as you are told or I shall pack you off to Cheshire tomorrow. You can stay there until you come to your senses.'

'I won't go. If you try to make me I shall go and stay with Victoria.'

'Go to your room at once! If you continue to defy me I shall have you locked in.'

'Then I shall open the window and shout for help. Think what a scandal that would make. It might even get into the newspapers.'

For a long moment they stared at each other in silence. Then Leo said, 'I don't want to upset you, Grandma. But this is something I am really determined to do and I can't see anything wrong with it. Please don't let us quarrel.'

Amelia held her gaze for a few seconds longer, then she turned away. 'So this is all the gratitude I get for the time and care I have lavished on you. Do as you please. If you want to ruin your reputation I can't stop you. But I don't imagine Tom Devenish will approve.'

Leo was tempted to say that she did not care whether Tom approved or not but she felt that she had won a victory and decided not to push it any further.

Five days later she presented herself at the offices of the FANY at 83, Lexham Gardens. She was interviewed by a young woman who introduced herself as Sergeant Major Ashley Smith, a tall Scot with a superb figure and a mass of curly brown hair.

'What makes you want to join the FANY?' she asked.

Leo, well briefed by Victoria, was prepared for that. 'I think it is a way of showing that women can be more than just mothers and wives – and it shows that we are ready to serve our country if the need arises.'

'Good,' Ashley Smith nodded. 'If you had said that you thought it would be fun, I should have turned you down. You must understand that if you join us you must be prepared for hard work and ready to accept discipline. Are you?'

'Yes,' Leo said, silently wondering what that would entail. She knew herself well enough to recognise that she was not good at taking orders.

'Can you ride?'

'Oh yes. I've ridden all my life.'

'Do you have a horse of your own?'

'Yes, but she's up in Cheshire, at our country place.'

'In that case you will have to hire a horse here and pay for its upkeep. You will also have to buy your uniform and first aid kit. Are you in a position to do that?'

Leo thought a moment. Her father's will had made provision for a generous allowance until such time as she inherited the money he had put in trust for her, but that was supposed to be spent on clothes and other necessaries. Well, new dresses would have to wait. 'Yes,' she said.

Ashley Smith seemed to find no further impediment to her joining and a few minutes later she paid her enrolment fee of ten shillings and signed the form that officially confirmed her membership.

From that day on, Leo's horizons, which had contracted so oppressively when she was sent back to England, began to expand again. She attended cavalry drills at the Hounslow barracks run by a sergeant major in the 19th Hussars, where her expertise on horseback quickly earned her the respect of her colleagues. On other days there were training sessions in First Aid and stretcher drill, and signalling, both in Morse Code and semaphore, and instruction from an army vet in how to care for horses. And fitted in between these were the promised driving lessons from Victoria. From being aimless and boring her life was suddenly full of purpose.

One afternoon, when she and other recruits were practising bandaging each other, someone mentioned 'Stobart's lot'. The tone was dismissive but Leo sensed a story.

'Who were Stobart's lot?' she asked Victoria.

'Not were ... are,' her friend corrected. 'Mabel Stobart was a FANY but she decided a couple of years ago that we were never going to achieve anything practical and went off and founded her own outfit – the Women's Sick and Wounded Convoy. She took a lot of FANY members with her, which is why there's a certain amount of hostility from the old hands. They're still going.'

'Were you a member then?'

'I'd just joined. If I hadn't been so new I think I might have gone with Stobart. She's an impressive character – very practical and down-to-earth. The sort of woman who gets things done.'

There was another, more pressing topic of conversation – the forthcoming camp. The Corps was to spend a week under canvas outside the town of Bourne End on the River Thames. Her grandma was horrified at the idea of women going under canvas 'like common soldiers' but her attitude to the FANY had mellowed somewhat on discovering that Leo had been telling the truth when she said that there were several titled ladies in their ranks. To Leo's regret, it was her brother Ralph who remained firmly opposed to her involvement. It hurt her deeply to find that, far from supporting her in her bid for independence, he had joined the forces of convention. As children they had always been close but increasingly she felt she hardly knew him.

Victoria had become a regular visitor to the house and it seemed natural that when Ralph was off-duty he and Tom should make up a foursome with the two girls for tennis and cards. Unfortunately, it was apparent from the start that Ralph and Victoria had taken an instant dislike to one another. Things came to a head one evening at dinner when the subject of the forthcoming camp was raised. Ralph was at his most pompous, mocking the whole idea that women might have any part to play in a future conflict.

'The battlefield is no place for a lady,' he said. 'You have no idea of the horrors you might encounter.'

'Have you?' Victoria asked bluntly.

Leo saw her brother flush. 'It is something that every soldier is prepared to face, in the defence of his country,' he said stiffly. 'It is a matter of honour.'

'And are women to have no honour?' Victoria demanded.

'Surely,' Tom Devenish said, 'a woman's honour consists in supporting her husband and providing him with heirs to carry on the struggle.'

'Well said, Tom!' Ralph exclaimed.

Victoria turned to him with a look of contempt. 'So that is all we are to you? Walking wombs. No more than hens or brood mares.'

It was Tom's turn to blush. 'Not at all. That is not what I intended to imply. I have the greatest respect for women, but the battlefield is not the right place for them.'

'Not as fighters,' Leo said, 'but surely you can't deny that there would be a use for us in caring for the wounded.'

Ralph laughed. 'Would that be before or after you had recovered from your faint?'

'And how would delicately brought-up young ladies, like yourselves, have the strength to lift a man and carry him back to the clearing station?' Tom asked.

'It's what we train for all the time,' Leo said.

'And it's what we shall be practising when we go to camp,' Victoria added.

Ralph sat back in his chair and gave a snort of laughter. 'Women under canvas! You won't last two days.'

'Don't be silly, Ralph,' Leo retorted. 'I've camped out in Egypt with Father when we were at a dig.'

'Yes, in a nice dry climate, with servants to fetch and carry for you. And men around to protect you.

You wait till you try it on your own in a muddy English field. You'll be back after the first night.'

'No we won't! You wait and see.'

'What do you think, Mr Devenish?' Victoria asked, a challenge in her look.

Tom hesitated. 'I think you're being rather brave, actually.'

Ralph turned on him. 'For heaven's sake, Tom! Whose side are you on? I expected you to have more sense.'

It was the first time Leo could remember Tom failing to back up whatever her brother said and she was shocked by the violence of Ralph's reaction. She saw Tom blanch and he turned his head away as if he had been struck.

Later, they left the two men to their brandy and cigars and retired to the drawing room. Leo's grandma had a headache and had had dinner sent up to her room, so she and Victoria were alone.

Victoria helped herself to a cigarette from the box on the table and remarked, 'I suppose you realise that the only reason Tom Devenish wants to marry you is because he can't marry your brother.'

Leo gasped. 'That's a terrible thing to say!'

'I don't see why. I've met a lot of men like that. You can't blame them. We send them off to school at the age of twelve and shut them up together where they don't see a woman for weeks on end. To them we're a race apart. They don't know how to deal with us. Is it surprising that they fall in love with other?'

'And you think that is what has happened to Ralph and Tom?'

'I'd put money on it. They may not have done anything about it. They probably aren't even fully aware of it. But that's the way things are, take my word for it.'

The following evening Leo was sitting alone in her room writing letters when Ralph came in. It seemed that he was in a more conciliatory mood. He sat down opposite her at her writing table and laid a hand on her wrist.

'Leo, I want to talk to you, seriously.'

She put down her pen. 'Yes?'

'All this galloping about in uniform pretending to be nurses is great fun, I'm sure, but you really should be thinking about your future, you know.'

'We are not "pretending". We are absolutely serious. It's time you men learned that women are good for more than just bringing children into the world.'

'You sound like that harridan Victoria.'

'She's not a harridan!'

'Well, however that may be, the fact is you can't go on behaving like this for the rest of your life. Isn't it time you thought about getting married?'

Leo sighed. 'Here we go again! Ralph, I don't want to marry Tom. I don't want to marry anyone.'

'But why not? What's wrong with Tom?'

'There's nothing wrong with him. He's kind and … and inoffensive and *dull*. He never seems to do anything. He just … hangs around in your shadow.'

Ralph's grip tightened on her wrist. 'Leo, you don't know him. Tom Devenish is the bravest, most loyal friend a man could have. He took a flogging for me, once, at Harrow.'

'A flogging!' Leo exclaimed. 'How? Why?'

Ralph sat back. 'It was all my stupid fault. I'm not proud of myself. You know what I was like at school. I never cared much for lessons and I got up to all sorts of silly japes. At the beginning of my last term the Head sent for me and told me that if I came up in front of him one more time I'd be out on my ear. I promised to behave myself but then someone challenged me to a dare, and I could never resist a dare.'

'Dare to do what?'

'Oh, it was just a silly prank. Our housemaster's wife had a little dog – a nasty yappy little white thing that bit anyone who tried to make friends with it. I got hold of some dye and dyed it red. It didn't do the dog any harm but she was furious. Mr Washington got us all in the hall and said that unless the culprit owned up he was going to punish the whole house. Of course, I knew my number was up and I was just about to get to my feet when Tom stood up and said it was him. Well, of course Washy knew it wasn't. Tom was never in trouble. But he couldn't very well call him a liar. So he asked if anyone else had been involved and Tom said, no, he'd done it all on his own.' Ralph dropped his head and put his hand over his eyes. 'And I sat there and said nothing, sis. Not a word. He thrashed Tom, right there, in front of everyone. And do you know what Tom said, when I tried to thank him afterwards? He said that he'd get over the flogging soon enough, but if I'd been expelled it might have ruined my whole life, and he couldn't let that happen.' He looked up. 'That's the sort of chap he is, Leo. That's the sort of man you're turning down.'

Leonora looked at him in silence for a moment. Then she said, 'It was a brave thing to do, and the action of a good friend, as you say. But he did it for you, Ralph. That doesn't make him a good husband for me.'

Her brother got up impatiently. 'I don't understand you! What difference does it make? Tom is a good chap and you should be grateful he's so patient. He won't hang around for ever, you know, waiting for you to come to your senses.'

'It's not a question of me coming to my senses,' Leo snapped back. 'Tom's your friend and you're in his debt. That doesn't mean I have to marry him. Do you know what Victoria says? She says he only wants to marry me because he can't marry you.'

She regretted the words as soon as they were spoken. She saw the colour drain from Ralph's face and for a moment she thought he was going to strike her. Then he flushed deep crimson.

'That's a foul thing to say! That's the foulest thing anyone has ever said to me.'

He turned and left the room without another word.

No further objections were raised to the idea of the camp, so Leo and Victoria set off in Sparky the following weekend. Leo quickly had to recognise the force of what Ralph had said at dinner that night. It rained, and the ground was soon churned to mud. In addition to making her own bed and caring for her horse, she found herself lugging buckets of water from the river and collecting bundles of firewood and peeling huge mounds of potatoes. She got used to waking to reveille at 5.30 in the morning and living on porridge that tasted of wood smoke and meat that was singed on the outside and red in the middle. She had never worked so hard in her life – and she loved every minute of it.

Chapter 3

Returning to Sussex Gardens felt like being forced back into a straitjacket. To make matters worse, she found that her grandma had enrolled her in her absence at a finishing school, which she was expected to attend every morning in order to improve her 'deportment' and polish her social skills. When she protested that this clashed with her riding lessons at the cavalry barracks her grandma threatened to stop her allowance if she refused to attend. As if this was not bad enough, Ralph had refused to speak to her since their conversation about Tom. He visited very rarely and when he did the atmosphere between them was bitter. Leo would have apologised, given the opportunity, but he made sure they were never alone together.

She had been back from camp less than a week when she opened *The Times* to read that the Bulgarians and the Serbs, in alliance with Greece, had declared war on

Turkey. By early November the Bulgarian army had reached Chataldhza, the last line of Turkish defences between them and Constantinople, and the Greeks had captured the port of Salonika.

Three days after this news arrived Victoria burst into Leo's room when she had only just finished dressing.

'Have you seen this?' She waved a copy of *The Times* under Leo's nose.

'Seen what? You're very early. I haven't had breakfast yet.'

'This!' Victoria folded the paper back and held it for Leo to see. She read, 'GALLANT YOUNG LADIES HEAD FOR WAR ZONE. The ladies of the Women's Sick and Wounded Convoy, under the direction of Mrs Mabel St Clair Stobart, set off yesterday for Bulgaria, where they intend to offer their services as nurses to the allied forces.'

Leo put the paper aside and stared at Victoria. 'They are actually going! Going to a real war, to do all those things that we are only playing at.'

Victoria nodded grimly. 'Makes you think we joined the wrong outfit, doesn't it?'

'Couldn't we go, too – we FANYs, I mean?'

'No chance. I heard someone raise the idea with Ashley Smith the other day and she turned it down flat. She said our duty was to our own people and we had to save ourselves in case we were needed here.'

'But think of the experience!' Leo said. 'Vita, do you think Mrs Stobart would let us join her?'

'I've no idea. Anyway, it's too late now. See what it says in the paper? They left yesterday.'

'How are they getting there, do you think?'

'By train I suppose. On the Orient Express.'

'Then couldn't we follow?'

'Are you serious?'

A bubble of excitement was growing in Leo's chest. She felt it almost choking her. 'If we left tomorrow ...'

'I suppose we could catch them up and offer our services. Provided Stobart is willing to take us on.'

'She could hardly turn us down, could she, after we'd come so far? And we are trained – well, you are, and I'm not exactly a novice anymore.'

'But Leo, would your grandma let you go?'

Leo's bubble burst and she felt as if all the air had gone out of her lungs. 'No, of course she won't.' For a moment she was silent. The past weeks had been a desert of boredom and frustration, and the only prospect she could see ahead of her was more of the same. Finally she said, 'I'd have to slip out without telling anyone. I could leave a note.'

'Would you really do that?'

'Yes! I know it's wicked but I want to do this so badly and if I don't break out now I'm afraid I never will. Let's do it, Vita! We may never get another chance.'

Victoria looked at her. 'I have a feeling I ought to be saying, "no, think of the danger". I ought to be sensible and responsible but ...' Leo saw the same excitement catching fire in her friend's eyes. 'To hell with it! You're right. We may never get another chance. But we must plan properly. We can't just jump on the first train. We don't even know where they were heading, exactly. The whole of the Balkans is a war zone.'

Leo nodded, forcing herself to be calm. 'Listen, my father had an old friend who works in the Foreign Office. He specialises in Eastern Europe and my father often went to him for advice when he was planning a trip. He will know the best route, if anyone does.'

'But if you tell him what we are planning to do ...' Victoria said.

'Yes, that's a point. But he's not one of those men who think women should sit at home and knit. I've met him several times and he always encouraged Father to take me with him on our travels. If I were to tell him that the FANYs are thinking of going ... that we've been invited to join the WSWC and I've been asked to seek his advice ...'

'It would be a lie.'

Leo chewed her lip. 'Only a small one.'

Victoria shook her head with a laugh. 'I'll say this for you. Once you get the bit between your teeth there's no holding you.'

The two women met again that evening at Victoria's flat in Knightsbridge.

'Did you get to see your father's friend at the FO?' Victoria asked.

'Yes. He was very sweet. I felt bad about not telling the whole truth.'

'What did he advise?'

'In one word – don't. But just the way he explained it gave me a pretty good idea what the situation is.'

'Go on.'

'Have you got an atlas?'

'It's on the table. I've been trying to get some idea of where we might be headed.'

Leo seated herself at the table and opened the map. 'Cutting out a lot of the preliminary warnings about the chaotic situation, what he said was this. He thinks that Stobart's lot might have made a mistake taking the train to Sophia. The battle front is over here, at Chataldzha, almost on the Black Sea and the Turks have cut the railway line. The only way to get there from Sophia is to go to Jamboli and then travel by road and it would take the best part of a week, because the roads are terrible and the only transport is by wagons pulled by oxen. He said, if he wanted to get there he would go by sea to Salonika and then hope to get a train from there.'

'By sea? But it would take weeks from any English port.'

'I know. But if we picked up a ship in Marseilles, that would shorten the journey enormously. I'm sure there are ships going from there to Athens and then we could find another heading for Salonika. We could take the train to Marseilles ...'

Victoria's eyes lit up. 'I've got a better idea. We'll go in Sparky.'

'Drive, all that way? Could Sparky do it?'

'Yes, given time. We couldn't take him on the Orient Express but there wouldn't be any problem about getting him on a ship as deck freight. And think how useful it would be to have a car. If we can't get a train from Salonika we could drive, and he could be used for transporting the wounded when we get to the other end.'

'How long would it take to drive to Marseilles?' Leo asked.

'Four days, three if we're lucky. Then there's the sea voyage. It's still going to take a long time.'

'But Stobart's lot have got to make arrangements when they get to Sophia. That will take time, too.

And if it really is going to take them a week to get from Jamboli to the front we might not be far behind them.'

'Better late than never, I suppose. And the war isn't going to be over quickly, by all accounts. What do you think?'

Leo grinned at her. 'Let's do it. Whatever happens, it'll be an adventure.'

'When do we start?'

'The sooner the better. Tomorrow night? I'll have to creep out when everyone has gone to sleep.'

'Agreed.'

Next day Leo collected what clothes and other things she felt were essential and transferred them to Victoria's house, telling her grandma that she was taking worn-out clothes to a charity. Meanwhile, Victoria purchased as much in the way of bandages, lint, disinfectant and other medical supplies as they could carry with them. They allowed themselves only the minimum of personal belongings, anticipating that they would wear their FANY uniforms most of the time. What they did take was packed into a large trunk and strapped to the back of the car.

Leo had one other errand, which she did not mention to Victoria. Her father had left her a brooch and two rings that had belonged to her mother. She took them to a shop in the Burlington Arcade and got what she hoped was a reasonable price for them. It seemed likely that she would be unable to access her allowance and she was determined not to have to rely on Victoria for funds.

When they met again that evening they were both in a more sober mood.

'You know, we haven't given this enough thought,' Victoria said. 'Do we really know what we are letting ourselves in for?'

'No,' Leo responded. 'Perhaps if we did we wouldn't be doing it.'

'Do you want to change your mind?'

'Not unless you do.' Leo sat down and leaned urgently towards her friend. 'It isn't just about us going off on some mad adventure, Vita. It's about proving something. Proving that we are capable of taking our own decisions, making our own way in life.'

'You're right, of course,' Victoria said. 'So let's get going while we've still got the courage. If we leave at midnight and drive all night we can be in Dover in time for the first ferry in the morning.'

'Wait for me at the corner of the road,' Leo instructed her. 'Don't bring Sparky too close or you'll wake the neighbours.'

A few minutes before twelve Leo opened her bedroom door and stood listening intently. The house was silent. She picked up the small bag containing her last-minute essentials and crept down the stairs. She did not go to the front door, knowing that Beavis would have locked and bolted it before retiring for the night, and taken the key with him. Instead, she passed through the green baize door leading to the servants' quarters and tiptoed down the stairs to the kitchen. There was a door here that led out into the basement area and she knew that the key would be hanging on a hook beside it. Her heart hammered as she put it into the lock. Maisie, the kitchen maid, slept next door and Leo prayed that she was not easily awakened. The lock turned and the door swung open. Chill, damp air replaced the warmth of the kitchen. The steps were shrouded in fog. For a moment Leo hesitated, thinking of her warm bed and the unknown hazards ahead. Then she stepped outside, closed and locked the door behind her and pushed the key back underneath it. There was no going back now, short of ringing the front door bell and begging to be readmitted. She climbed the steps to the pavement level and turned towards the corner. The fog obscured everything further than fifty yards away, so she could not see if Victoria was waiting for her in Sparky. She turned her collar up to her ears, grateful that the fog muffled the sound of her footsteps and concealed her from the view of any wakeful watcher in the windows of the houses she passed. For a brief moment she had a premonition that Victoria would not be there; that she had misunderstood the arrangements or simply changed her mind; but when she reached the corner she found Sparky parked at the side of the road, with her friend, muffled to the eyebrows, at the wheel.

Victoria held up a fur rug as Leonora climbed in beside her. 'Here, wrap yourself up in this and tie that scarf over your head. We're in for a freezing drive.'

She got out and cranked the engine and at the noise Leo expected lights to go on in all the houses, but the darkness remained complete. The roads were deserted but Victoria had to nose the car along at little more than a walking pace because of the fog. Once or twice they had to stop and peer around them to get their bearings, but eventually they found their way across Vauxhall Bridge and into the southern suburbs. Neither of them spoke much. Victoria was concentrating on the driving and the noise of the engine made conversation difficult. The slow progress gave Leo time to think, and to realise the enormity of what she was doing. She thought of the note she had left on her bedside table and her grandma's reaction when she read it and was suddenly smitten with remorse. The old lady was a martinet but after all she had only wanted what she thought was best for Leo. To run away like this was the height of ingratitude. But what was the alternative? She knew that faced with the possibility that Leo might take herself off to a foreign war, her grandma was quite capable of locking her in her room until the opportunity had passed. This was her one chance to strike out on a path of her own – and it was too late to have second thoughts. She huddled deeper into the fur and tried to stop her teeth from chattering.

Once they were clear of the city the fog cleared and they were able to see the stars. As they glided down Wrotham Hill, the Kentish Weald lay before them like a dark ocean, and Leo had a strange illusion that the car was stationary and the shadowy trees and hedges were somehow being blown past them by the wind that whipped her face. They would go on like this forever, never reaching their destination, and the dawn would never come. As they passed through the villages on their route, the noise of the engine echoed back from the houses, and Leo expected to hear windows being thrown open but no one stirred. In Maidstone a tramp sleeping in a doorway jumped to his feet and sent a stream of curses after them and at every farm they passed the noise set dogs barking frantically. By the time they reached Dover it was getting light and the first pedestrians were about, moving like ghosts, the men with their coat collars turned up round their ears and the women wrapped in shawls. But at the docks there was already a bustle of activity as the cross-channel ferry prepared to leave.

There was a delay while Victoria negotiated with officials who were reluctant to accept Sparky without prior warning but eventually the car was strapped to a wooden platform and hauled up on the ferry's deck by a crane. When Victoria was satisfied that it had been lashed firmly in position and was quite secure they were at last able to seek the warmth of the passenger cabin.

Leo blew on her fingers. 'Thank goodness! I don't think I've ever been so cold!'

'We'd better try to get a bit of sleep,' Victoria said. 'It's the only chance we'll have.'

There were few other passengers, so they both stretched out on the seats and Leo fell into an uneasy doze, interrupted mid-channel when the movement of the ship threatened to tip her onto the deck. When she next woke, it was broad daylight and they were sailing into Calais harbour.

Chapter 4

While Leo and Victoria were breakfasting in Calais, Tom Devenish was working in his studio at the top of his house in Cheyne Walk. It was a large room, ideal for his purpose, with a big north-facing sky-light, and a view from the front windows over the River Thames. He was working on a sketch of the river, with its constant traffic of barges and pleasure boats, but after a short while he threw down his pencil and turned away in a fit of despondency. It was not that the work itself displeased him. He knew that he was a skilled draughtsman. But who, he asked himself for the hundredth time, needed one more picture of the Thames, however perfect, or one more pretty watercolour of a rural scene? They added nothing to the sum total of human knowledge and there were more than enough already to decorate the walls of every house in the country.

He looked round the room. The walls were covered in sketches and watercolours, some finished, others incomplete. He had tried his hand at portraiture, too, and stacked in one corner were several sketches of Leonora, each one abandoned because, no matter how hard he tried, at some stage they all began to look like Ralph. There was only one set of pictures that he really valued. In a folder locked away in a drawer was a series of portraits of Ralph, which constituted a complete record of his development from a boy of fourteen to the present day. Ralph had never seen them and had no idea that they existed and Tom had promised himself that no one else would ever have sight of them either.

He went to the window and looked out towards the river. A tug was chugging downstream, a string of barges bobbing behind it. On the road beside the river a motorcar passed in the opposite direction, its occupants, wrapped to the ears in scarves, waving cheerily to someone on the pavement. Tom leaned his head against the glass. It seemed a perfect metaphor for his situation. Out there was life, with all its complex possibilities, but he was cut off from it, condemned forever to be an observer.

There was a tap on the door and his manservant, Peters, entered.

'Excuse me, sir. I'm sorry to disturb you but this note has just been delivered from Sussex Gardens. It's marked urgent.'

Tom slit the envelop and read, '*Leonora vanished. Come at once. Ralph.*'

When Tom arrived at the house he found Amelia Malham Brown sitting bolt upright in her morning room with a face like marble, while Ralph paced distractedly around her.

'Here's a fine thing, Tom!' he exclaimed as soon as his friend entered. 'Leo's gone off on some fool's errand, without saying a word to anyone. First thing we knew about it was when her maid went in this morning and found the bed unslept in and this note on the dressing table.'

He handed Tom a sheet of notepaper and his nostrils caught a breath of perfume which he recognised as Leonora's, though he had never been conscious of it before. He read, '*By the time you read this I shall be in France. I am going to join the Women's Sick and Wounded Convoy caring for soldiers in the Balkans. Please forgive me for going off without telling you, but I knew if I said anything you would try to stop me. Don't worry about me. Victoria is with me and I'm sure we shall not come to any harm. This is something I have to do, so please try to understand. Leonora.*'

'That damned woman!' Ralph exploded. 'Victoria, I mean. I knew she was no good for Leonora.'

'Really, Ralph,' his grandma said coldly, 'there is no need for profanity.'

'Sorry, Grandma. But if I could get my hands on that woman I'd strangle her!'

'Idle threats will not get us anywhere,' Amelia said. 'The question is, what do we do now? And to me the answer is obvious.'

Ralph turned to Tom. 'Grandma wants me to drop everything and go and find Leo. I keep telling her that I'm a serving officer. I can't just take myself off at a moment's notice. You'll have to go.'

Tom stared at him. 'Me? I've never been further than Deauville. The mere sight of the cross-channel ferry makes me feel sick.'

'Damn it, man!' Ralph exploded. 'Someone has to go. After all, you are supposed to be engaged to Leo – well, almost.'

Tom considered the dizzying prospect before him and grasped at a last hope. 'Just a minute. Has anyone been round to Victoria's flat? Are we sure they have actually left?'

'I sent Wilson, Leo's maid, round straight away,' Amelia said. 'The flat is shut up and Victoria told the hall porter that she would be away for several weeks. I don't think there is any doubt about their intentions.'

'Then I – I suppose I shall have to go.' Tom felt a vast unknown opening up before him. 'But where do I go? How do I find her? I'm not even sure I know where the Balkans are.'

'That's easily remedied,' Ralph said. 'Grandma, do you have a good atlas in the house?'

'There is a globe in the library,' the old lady replied.

'Right!' Ralph gripped Tom's arm and marched him towards the door. 'Come on. Let's go and sort out a battle plan.'

In the library Ralph led Tom over to the large mahogany table in the centre of the room, on which stood the globe.

'Now, look.' He spun it and stabbed with his forefinger at a point to the east of the Adriatic. 'There's Serbia, and there to the east is Bulgaria.'

'It's a huge area,' Tom said despondently. 'Where do you think they are heading?'

'She just says "the Balkans". I don't suppose the silly girl has any real idea of where she's going. But I suppose they must be heading for where the fighting is.'

'Which is where?'

'According to what I've heard there are two main battle fronts at the moment,' Ralph said. 'The Serbs here, in the west, around the borders of

Albania and the Bulgars right over here to the east, almost at the Dardanelles. She could be aiming for either of those, but I doubt if she'll get anywhere near them.'

'What makes you say that?'

'Well, think about it. Two unaccompanied young women, without any credentials. The authorities in Belgrade and Sophia are not going to let them get near a battlefield. My guess is they'll be turned back at the border.'

'But that means they could be back home again in a day or two,' Tom said, but his relief was short lived.

'Not if I know my sister,' Ralph responded grimly. 'She's the most obstinate creature in the universe if she's set her mind on something. She won't give up that easily. There's no way out of it, Tom. You'll have to go and find her and bring her back.' He paused and laid his hand on Tom's arm. 'You've always been a good friend, Tom. I knew I could rely on you.'

Tom felt the colour rush to his face. He took a deep breath. 'How do I get there?'

'Train is the obvious way. Leo says she will be in France by the time we read the note, so they must have taken the early ferry. Then train to Paris, I presume, and from there on the Orient Express.'

'The Orient Express!' Tom repeated. The words seemed so exotic they might belong to another world.

'It's the obvious way. Now, I'm sure Grandma has a copy of Baedecker somewhere.' He searched along the shelves. 'Ah, here we are. Let's see . . . Yes, there's a service twice a week, Sundays and Wednesdays, to Munich, Vienna, Budapest, Belgrade, Sophia and Constantinople. Today is Wednesday and the girls obviously set off at the crack of dawn, so they are probably aiming for that one. It doesn't leave till the evening. The next one is not until Sunday, but see, here? There is a service that leaves Brussels on Thursdays and an overnight sleeper from Paris that connects with it in Vienna. So if you leave tomorrow morning you can catch that.'

'To where?'

'I'd try Belgrade. It's the closest. Anyway, you might be able to pick up their trail. Two young women travelling alone is pretty unusual. If you ask when you get to Vienna someone may remember them.'

'And if they don't?'

'Take a ticket to Belgrade. And ask on the train. Ask the stewards, the porters, anyone who travels regularly on that route. And every time you cross a border, ask the frontier guards. They will have checked everyone's passports and it's quite likely they will remember the girls. If all else fails, when you get to Belgrade, go to the British Embassy. Leo and Victoria may have gone there of their own accord to ask for help getting to the front, but more likely they will have been stopped by the Serbian police and handed over.'

'In which case,' Tom said, 'surely the embassy will contact you, or your grandma.'

'If they do, I'll be able to tell them that a friend is on his way to escort the girls home.' Ralph smiled at him and Tom knew that further argument was futile. Like it or not, he was going to Belgrade.

'Just one thing,' Ralph added. 'We don't want every Tom, Dick and Harry – sorry, old chap, but you know what I mean – knowing why you are going. You know how people gossip. Obviously, you'll have to come clean with the authorities, but in general conversation it might be better to make up some other reason for the journey. Tell them you're on business or something.'

'But I know nothing about business! I wouldn't have the faintest idea why any businessman might be going to Belgrade.'

'No, true. Well, think of something else. Tell them you're a writer looking for local colour – or a jour- nalist on your way to cover the war.' Ralph looked at the clock on the mantelpiece. 'I've got to get back. The C.O. gave me a couple of hours off when the message arrived saying Leo had done a bunk, but I'll be in trouble if I don't report back soon.' He squeezed Tom's arm. 'I won't forget this, Tom. I don't know who else I could have relied on. Cheer up! You might actually enjoy the trip – and think how much credit it will give you with Leo – her white knight riding to the rescue.'

'I doubt whether she'll see it like that,' Tom said gloomily.

'Oh, she will. Once she's had a few encounters with Serbian officialdom and realised how hopeless the whole idea is. You wait. She'll be overjoyed to see a friendly face. Now, I must go. I'll pop in to your place this evening, to check that you've got everything arranged.' He headed for the door. 'Cheerio, old chap. Best of luck!'

Tom arrived in Paris in a mood of deepening gloom. He had been sick on the ferry, as usual. It had been that experience, on three summer holidays with his parents, which had convinced him that foreign travel was not for him. The prospect of several nights on a train did nothing to improve his temper. Enquiries at the booking office at the Gare de l'Est produced no result. No one recalled two unaccompanied young

English ladies travelling on the Wednesday service to Constantinople. Worse was to come. There were no vacant berths on the Orient Express leaving Brussels that day. He would have to wait for the Paris service the following Sunday. Feeling more strongly than ever that he had been sent on a wild goose chase, he booked into the Hotel Bristol for three nights.

After an excellent dinner his mood improved somewhat and he decided to explore the city. He had never been to Paris before but he had heard of the *vie de bohème* on the Left Bank and around Montmartre. Within hours he had decided that Paris was his spiritual home and he spent the next three days happily wandering around the Louvre and poking among the pictures in the narrow streets of Montmartre or the bookstalls along the banks of the Seine. It was with considerable reluctance that he set off for the Gare de l'Est on the Sunday evening.

His first sight of the train cheered him considerably. There was something about the varnished teak exterior of the *wagons lits* that inspired confidence and he was relieved to discover that although the sleeping compartments accommodated two people he apparently had one to himself. The compartment was wood-panelled and ingeniously furnished and the steward and porters punctilious in their attentions, though none of them had any recollection of seeing Leo and Victoria. In the dining car the tables were furnished with immaculate linen cloths and sparkling silver and glass and the food was distinctly superior to many meals he had eaten in English hotels, and indeed in some great country houses. Sipping a glass of excellent Chateau Lafitte as the train slid through the French countryside Tom decided that the journey might not be as unpleasant as he had feared. When he returned to his compartment the sofa on which he had reclined earlier had been turned into a bed and the covers were turned down ready for him. He unpacked his dressing case, washed in the basin in the corner of the cabin and put on his nightclothes. He settled into bed reflecting that perhaps Leo had done him a favour. He had needed shaking out of his comfortable routine. The ennui that had dogged him for months had been replaced by an unfamiliar excitement.

At the frontier with Germany and again when the train crossed into Austria he asked the border guards if any of them remembered two young ladies, but once again he drew a blank. He consoled himself, however, with the thought that Leo and Victoria had travelled on the Wednesday service, so it was likely that the men on duty were not the same. By the time they reached Vienna he had settled into a comfortable routine, but his complacency was shattered when the door to his compartment was suddenly slid open and a thick-set man a few years older than himself, with a clean-shaven, ruddy complexion and a head of unruly dark hair, came in.

'Hi,' he said, 'looks like you and I are sharing the accommodation. Hope that's OK with you.'

It took Tom a few seconds to recognise the accent as American. His first instinct was to say that it was definitely not 'OK' with him but he suppressed the urge and murmured, 'Yes, yes, of course. Come in.'

'Thanks.' The American threw his hat and his dressing case onto the rack and turned to Tom. 'By the way, I'm Maximilian Seinfeld. Call me Max.'

'Thomas Devenish,' Tom responded. 'How do you do?'

'I'm very well, Tom, thanks. Mind if I take a seat?'

'Of course not. Please make yourself at home.'

Max settled himself and produced a cigar case from an inside pocket. 'Smoke?'

'No, thanks. I don't.'

'Don't mind if I do?'

'Not at all. Go ahead.'

'You going all the way to Constantinople?'

'No, I'm getting off in Belgrade.'

'No kidding? Me too. You got business there?'

It was the sort of inquisition Tom had been dreading. 'No,' he said shortly, and in the hope of discouraging further conversation he took out his sketch pad and began to draw the scenery he saw passing outside the window.

The American seemed to take the hint, because he took out a German language newspaper and unfolded it and soon the variety and strangeness of the changing scene absorbed Tom and he covered page after page with sketches, intending to work them up into finished pictures when he had time. After a while he became aware that his work was being studied.

'Hey!' Max exclaimed. 'That's real good. You an artist?'

'I dabble a bit.'

'Professionally?'

'No. I'm just an amateur.'

'A pretty damned good amateur, I should say. Mind if I have a look?'

Half resentful of the intrusion and half flattered by the compliment, Tom handed over the pad. Max turned the pages with whistles and exclamations of approval. Finally he handed the pad back.

'You've got a real talent there. You must have a good eye to capture so much when it passes by so fast.'

'I have a good memory, that's all,' Tom said, 'for places and scenery, at least.'

'That why you're headed for Serbia? Hoping to capture some scenes from the front, perhaps?'

Tom stirred uncomfortably. He was becoming aware that beneath all the bonhomie there was a sharp intellect at work. He decided to take refuge in the fiction that Ralph had suggested to him. 'Yes, maybe. I'm a journalist, you see.'

'No kidding? Well, there's a coincidence! So am I.' Max reached into his inner pocket and produced a visiting card which announced him as a reporter for the *Baltimore Herald*. 'Which rag do you work for?'

'Rag? Oh, no, I'm ... I'm a freelance.' Tom could feel himself blushing. 'Fact is, I'm new to all this. Just trying to get a start, you know.'

'I know,' Max beamed at him. 'We've all been there. Everyone's got to start somewhere. Well, you're in luck, son. You stick to your Uncle Max. He knows the ropes and he'll see you OK.'

'That's very kind of you,' Tom murmured, his heart sinking.

'Where're you from, Tom?'

Tom had been brought up to believe that you did not interrogate casual acquaintances about their personal affairs but Max had no such inhibitions. By the time they had had dinner Tom knew all about his grandfather, who had emigrated from Germany to America and opened a delicatessen and his father who now owned twenty similar shops in a dozen different cities. In return, Max had ascertained that Tom was the only son of a baronet and had been to Harrow School.

'Guess that makes you what they call landed gentry. A pretty privileged upbringing, huh?' There was just a hint of a sneer in the voice.

'I suppose so,' Tom murmured, adding, 'Actually, I hated most of it.'

'How so?'

Tom turned his head away and looked out of the window. 'I suppose if you regard it as a privilege to be put on a pony almost before you can walk and made to get back on again no matter how often you fall off, and to be given a gun and called a sissy when you cry over the beautiful birds you have been made to shoot, and to be sent away from home at the age of six to a school where you are beaten for the slightest infringement of rules, even if you don't understand what you have done wrong – if that is a privilege then, yes, I had a privileged upbringing.'

He took out his pad and started to draw and for once Max had the tact to keep quiet.

Chapter 5

In the late afternoon, two weeks after leaving England, Leo stood beside Victoria as the ship sailed into the Thermatic Gulf and they saw the minarets and domes of Salonika appearing out of the haze. The drive through France had taken them four days, two punctures and three uncomfortable nights in run-down roadside inns; and when they had finally reached Marseilles it was to discover that there were no ships scheduled to leave for Salonika. It was only because Leo had overheard a conversation between a Greek ship-owner and one of his captains and begged his assistance that they had found themselves, with Sparky as deck cargo, first on a ship for Athens and then finally on a rusty tramp steamer heading up the coast to the Macedonian port.

'It looks more Eastern than European,' Victoria commented.

'Well, it's been Turkish for centuries,' Leo pointed out, 'but it's a great mixture, architecturally speaking. There's Greek, Roman, Byzantine, as well as Turkish influences.'

'You sound as if you've been here before!'

'I have. My father and I passed through on our way from Troy to the excavations at Mycenae.'

Victoria looked at her. 'My word, you're full of surprises. I didn't know I'd brought my own walking guide book with me!'

As the ship docked they saw that the harbour was seething with vessels, many of them warships, and the streets were crowded with men in uniform. Every building, it seemed, was draped with the blue and white colours of the Greek flag. Platoons of armed soldiers marched to and fro and when the ship's engines fell silent they heard a low rumble that seemed to come from the ground itself.

'Thunder?' Victoria queried.

Leo shook her head. 'It's too continuous for that. I think it might be gunfire, a long way off.' She shivered. For the first time war had become a present reality instead of a distant dream. She looked at Victoria and saw from her expression that the same thoughts were going through her mind.

'Oh well,' Victoria said, 'I suppose we knew what we were letting ourselves in for. I shall just be glad to get off this beastly ship. I'm sick and tired of being leered at by that first mate with the horrible teeth.'

'What makes you think we shall be any better off on shore?' Leo asked. 'Soldiers can be just as bad as sailors, I imagine. We're two women travelling alone. What did we expect?'

'A bit of common respect, I hope!' Victoria answered crisply.

Leo sighed inwardly. She was beginning to realise that sophisticated as Victoria appeared in her own setting she was dangerously naïve about the rest of the world.

When they disembarked they had to join a long line of other passengers in the Customs House. The desk was manned by soldiers in Greek uniform and it rapidly became clear that none of them spoke any language but their own, which resulted in long wrangles while the passengers ahead of them, who seemed to come from all round the Mediterranean and beyond, tried to explain their reasons for entering the city. When Leo addressed them in fluent demotic Greek they looked both relieved and bemused. What, they wanted to know, could two young English ladies be doing in war-torn Salonika?

'We are nurses,' Leo explained, stretching a point, 'and we are going to join some other English ladies to care for the wounded. We need accommodation for tonight and transport tomorrow. Are the trains still running?'

The expression of disbelief on the soldier's face changed to amusement and then to blank obstinacy. Women, he informed them, were not allowed anywhere near the front line.

'But someone has to take care of the wounded Bulgarian soldiers,' Leo persisted.

'Bulgarians? Spff!' he spat derisively.

'I don't understand,' Leo said. 'The Bulgarians are your allies, aren't they? We're all on the same side.'

The response was a shrug.

'Tell him we want to speak to his superior officer,' Victoria suggested.

Leo repeated the request and after some delay a captain arrived. He was heavy-eyed and clearly furious at having his afternoon nap disturbed. When Leo's request was relayed to him he stared at her in disbelief.

'What you suggest is quite impossible. Perhaps you do not realise it, madame, but we are in the middle of a war here. I cannot arrange for you to travel any further.'

'Very well,' Leo said. 'Can you find us somewhere to sleep tonight? We will make our own arrangements in the morning.'

68

The officer spread his hands. 'I am sorry, but the city is already overcrowded. All the good hotels have been taken over by the military. I suggest you return to your ship and book your passage back to England.'

Leo stood her ground obstinately. Her brother, or her grandma, would have told the captain that to inform her that what she wanted was impossible was the best way to strengthen her determination. 'We don't require a good hotel. We just need a roof over our heads for one night.'

The captain conferred with someone in an inner office. It was clear to Leo that he just wanted to be rid of these troublesome women. In the end, two men were ordered to escort them to an inn.

'It is not grand, you understand,' the captain said, 'but it is the best we can do.'

By this time Sparky had been unloaded from the deck of the ship and was the cause of much excited comment when it became apparent that the driver was a woman. After some discussion, one of the soldiers got up on the running board and they set off through streets crowded with men in various uniforms, Greek, Serb and Bulgarian, together with the regular occupants of this most cosmopolitan of cities. Leo recognised Muslim women in their chadors, Jewish men wearing the yarmulke,

Greek orthodox priests in beards and robes and tall black hats, and everywhere scrawny children of different complexions. She saw a group of Greek and Serbian soldiers, obviously off-duty and slightly drunk, slapping each other on the back and exchanging hats. The Bulgarians, however, kept together in tight bunches with their weapons at the ready. Allies they might be in name, she concluded, but there seemed to be no love lost in reality.

The soldiers led them through the narrow, rubbish-strewn streets of the Jewish quarter, where the daylight was almost blocked out by the tall houses, and then into the wider thoroughfares of the upper town, lined by the larger houses of the Turkish community with their red-painted facades. Eventually they came to a low, rambling building set round a series of courtyards. It had been a Turkish caravanserai but, as their guides explained, since the capture of the city it had been used first as a hospital and then, briefly, as a prison for captured Turkish soldiers. The owner, an extremely fat man, greeted them with anxious sideways looks at their escort and showed them into a large, draughty room, containing six beds. The floors were filthy, the window panes cracked and smeared with dirt and cockroaches lurked in the corners.

Leo and Victoria looked at each other and Leo read on her friend's face the same disgust she knew must be plain on her own. Suddenly they both laughed.

'Well, we'd better get busy and clean the place up,' Victoria said. 'We need brooms and scrubbing brushes. Do you think he speaks Greek?'

'Probably not,' Leo said, 'but I speak Turkish.' She turned to the man, who was lurking by the door rubbing his hands nervously. Brooms? Yes, he had brooms but no one to use them. All his staff had fled in the fighting. 'Just give them to us,' Leo said. 'We will use them ourselves.'

'Golly!' Victoria exclaimed. 'I'm terribly impressed by your command of languages. I can get by in French but the only one I'm reasonably fluent in is German.'

'Well, that will probably be the most useful one to have when we get to Bulgaria,' Leo said. 'I suppose we shall have to try to learn Bulgarian but until then I expect we'll get by somehow.'

For an hour they swept and scrubbed and by the time they had finished the rooms were, if not spotless, tolerably clean, and the worst of the draughts had been stopped up with rags. It was only then that their thoughts turned towards food. Here their host was no help at all. He had no kitchen staff and barely enough food to feed himself and his family. Most of the restaurants had closed down during the fighting and those that had not had been commandeered by the soldiers. Most shops were shut and there was a shortage of supplies. 'They are like locusts, these soldiers,' he protested. 'They eat everything.'

Victoria turned to Leo. 'Now what? I'm famished.'

'Well, we shall just have to go and forage, I suppose.' Leo's spirits sank. She was exhausted and filthy and her clothes, which were sticking to her after her exertions, were becoming clammy now that she had stopped. She was beginning to shiver and to long for a hot bath, a good meal and a soft bed – none of which were likely to be forthcoming in the foreseeable future. 'Come on. I don't know what we will find, but we'll do our best.'

As they crossed the courtyard where the car was parked Victoria said, 'Just a minute,' and lifted the bonnet.

'What are you doing?' Leo asked.

'Removing the rotor arm,' her friend replied. 'I saw a few men giving Sparky some greedy looks. I don't want to come back and find him gone.'

'Are you sure it was the car they were looking at?' Leo asked, and then regretted the words.

It was getting dark and the narrow streets of the old town were badly lit. Leo began to wonder if they would ever find their way back to the inn.

The shops were either boarded up or their windows had been shattered and the contents looted. She slipped her hand into the pocket of her uniform skirt and her fingers closed round the butt of a small revolver. It had been a gift from her father, a few months before he had sent her back to England. There had been an encounter with some local brigands and for a moment it had seemed that Leo might be abducted. On that occasion their own guides, who acted as bodyguards, had seen the aggressors off, but her father had made her take the pistol in case of future trouble and taught her how to use it. She realised now that it had been that incident that had decided him to send her away, and she had never used the weapon, but it was a comfort now to feel its weight in her pocket. She had never shown it to Victoria, unsure how she would react, and she hoped that it would never be necessary to produce it.

Light spilled onto the street ahead of them and they heard a clamour of voices. Both were coming from a restaurant whose windows were clouded with condensation. Peering in, they saw that every table was crowded with men in uniform.

'It's no good. The place is packed,' Victoria said.

'It's worth a try, though,' Leo insisted. 'It may be the only chance we get.'

She pushed open the door and stepped inside, to be greeted with a roar of catcalls and whistles. A waiter hurried over.

'Go, go! No women in here!' he exclaimed.

'We just want something to eat,' Leo pleaded. 'We're ...'

'No. You go – now! Before there is trouble.' He almost pushed them towards the door.

Victoria plucked at Leo's sleeve. 'Come on! This is no good.'

Out in the street, they plodded onwards and very soon Leo became aware of footsteps behind them. Looking round, she saw three soldiers had left the restaurant and were following them.

'Let's hurry on a bit,' she said. 'I don't like these dark streets.'

They walked faster but the men behind them drew closer and began to call out to them. The words were in a language Leo did not understand but she had recognised the uniforms as Bulgarian. From the voices it was obvious that they were drunk. Victoria grabbed her hand and they began to run, and the men gave chase, laughing gleefully. They raced round a corner and found themselves in a small square at the junction of three roads. There, Leo came to a stop, dragging Victoria to a standstill, and turned to face their pursuers.

'Well?' she demanded, in Greek. 'What do you want? Are you men, to behave like this, or animals?'

The three faced them, panting, exchanging looks and she knew instinctively that they were daring each other to be the first to attack. She closed her hand round the butt of the revolver. There was a sudden clatter of boots from one of the side streets and four Greek soldiers appeared. Leo turned to them and shouted, 'Help us, please! These men are harassing us.'

She had gambled on the hostility she had sensed between the two occupying armies and it paid off. The newcomers exchanged looks and then plunged forwards and within seconds the little square was a melee of flying fists. Leo grabbed Victoria's hand. 'Now, run for it!'

They ran until they reached the wider and better lit streets in the city centre, but here, too, all the restaurants were packed with soldiers and they did not dare repeat their experience with the first one. Finally, they found themselves standing in front of the Makedonia Palace Hotel, the grandest in the city.

'Let's try in here,' Victoria suggested.

In the foyer they were met by a flustered porter. 'No, no!' he cried in Greek. 'You cannot come in here. Do you not see the notice?' He pointed to a placard set prominently in the middle of the entrance.

'What is he saying?' Victoria asked.

'The notice says "Reserved for Officers Only".'

'Tell him we are officers. We are both ensigns in the FANY.'

'I don't think that will cut much ice,' Leo said, but she tried it anyway. The man only waved his hands in confusion. 'No, no! No ladies! Only officers.'

Beyond him they could see the glass doors of the dining room and through them tables at which uniformed officers were tucking in. The smell of food made Leo feel suddenly faint.

'Oh, I've had enough of this!' she exclaimed. 'Out of my way!'

She thrust the man aside and marched into the dining room with Victoria close behind her. She was aware of heads turning in their direction and then a complete hush as conversation died away and the clatter of knives and forks was silenced. In the hiatus, Leo suddenly realised what they must look like with their hair coming down and faces smeared with dirt. More like a pair of vagabonds than respectable ladies! No wonder the waiter had tried to turn them away.

For a moment nobody moved, and then a man in the uniform of a Serbian colonel rose from a table near the door and came towards them. He was tall and had the bearing of one used to command. Unlike most of his fellow officers, he was clean shaven, with high cheek bones and brooding dark eyes under arched brows.

He stopped and clicked his heels and said in German, 'Excuse me. I can see you are not native to this area. I'm sure you will not speak Serbian. I hope you understand German.' When they both answered in the affirmative he went on, 'Allow me to introduce myself. I am Count Aleksander Malkovic. May I ask who you are?'

'I am Leonora Malham Brown and this is my colleague, Miss Victoria Langford. We have just arrived from England.'

'From England! But, dear ladies, you must be aware that you have come to a war zone. Until a few weeks ago this city was under bombardment and the Turks were still in occupation.'

'We are perfectly aware of the situation,' Leo responded stiffly. 'That is why we are here. We have come to join the Women's Sick and Wounded Convoy. We are on our way to Chataldzha to offer our services.'

'To Chataldzha!' His lips curled in an expression that was somewhere between amusement and contempt. 'Really, that is quite impossible. That is the front line of the Bulgarian advance. The fighting there is at its fiercest.'

'Which is why that is where we are most needed,' Leo retorted.

He laughed out loud then. 'Dear ladies, I admire your courage and we are most grateful for your offer of help, but we cannot allow you to put yourselves at risk. Now, in what other way can I be of service?'

'The risk is ours, and I think you do not have the authority to stop us,' Leo said. 'But there is one way in which you can help. We need food and there seems to be nowhere in the city where we can obtain a meal.'

'But of course! Please,' he gestured towards the table he had just left, 'you must be my guests.'

Two officers courteously gave up their places and Leo and Victoria were soon tucking in to spicy meat balls in a rich tomato sauce. As they ate, the colonel made small talk, asking them about their journey and their accommodation.

'And what is this Ladies' Convoy of which you speak?' he asked at length.

Between them, they explained about the FANY and its offshoot and the aims which both organisations shared. He listened with an expression of sceptical amusement, which Leo found infuriating.

'So, why are you not travelling with the other ladies?' he asked.

'Because we did not know that they were leaving until it was too late,' Leo explained. 'We think they probably travelled by train to Sophia. Have you heard anything about them? We are sure they will be heading for the front line but we don't know exactly where to find them.'

'So you two ladies have set off entirely alone, without any clear idea of where you are going?' Leo could not decide whether the expression in his eyes was admiration or disapproval.

'We do know where we want to go,' she said firmly. 'Once we get near the front people are bound to know where the rest of the convoy is.'

He looked at her, with that inscrutable gaze. 'I have to admire your determination, even though I think your enterprise is foolhardy.'

'Then you will help us to get to Chataldzha?'

The courteous mask faded and his eyes hardened. 'I am sorry. I have explained to you that the whole idea of women anywhere near the front line is unacceptable. You have no conception of modern warfare. You imagine a romantic charge, a brief, violent conflict and then the combatants leave the field empty except for the dead and wounded. In such a battle you might have played a part, but not now. War is no longer like that. It is about guns and shells and bombs and grenades. There is no peaceful interval during which we can collect our wounded and bury our dead. Your presence would merely be a distraction to the troops, who would feel they had to protect you instead of concentrating on defeating the enemy.' He paused, as if to regain control of himself. 'Now, if you will excuse me, I shall leave you. But please feel free to use the facilities of the hotel. Coffee will be served in the lounge and I am sure some of the other officers will be happy to entertain you.'

He rose and went out through the doors into the foyer. 'Wretched man!' Victoria exclaimed bitterly. 'What arrogance!'

Leo nodded. It was true that his whole demeanour had suggested a man who was unused to having his orders questioned, and yet … and yet … 'I think he means well,' she said. 'He believes what he said.'

While they were eating some of the officers had retired to the lounge to smoke and drink the local brandy. Leo was aware of many curious looks directed towards them from the communicating doors and when they had finished their meal one of the men came through to invite them to join him and his colleagues.

They were a mixed party of Greeks and Serbs, who were clearly delighted to have some feminine company, though Leo noticed that Malkovic remained aloof, sitting apart with one or two senior officers. Conversation was impeded by the fact that the Greeks did not speak Serbian and the Serbs did not speak Greek, while some of them understood German and others French but few spoke both, so Leo was much in demand as an interpreter. After a while she found herself chatting to a Serbian major, who introduced himself as Milan Dragitch.

'Tell me, why is it that there are only Serbs and Greeks here? I have seen Bulgarian uniforms in the streets. Where are their officers?'

'In a different hotel,' he said with a grin, 'to prevent fights breaking out.'

'Why? I thought you were all allies.'

'So we are, in theory. But the Bulgars cannot forgive the fact that the Greeks took the city one day before they got here. They wanted to occupy Salonika, you see, to strengthen their claim over the whole of Macedonia. The Greeks had to let some of them in as "guests", including Prince Kyril and Crown Prince Boris, but it's an uneasy situation.'

'So I see,' Leo said.

'Is it true that you and the other lady were planning to go to the front line to nurse the wounded?'

'Not to nurse, exactly. Our function is to collect the wounded, give them essential First Aid, and then transport them back to the casualty clearing stations.'

'But that would mean going out under fire!'

'Yes, we understand that.'

'You are very brave. But the colonel will not let you go, you know.'

'I don't understand why not.'

'Sasha Malkovic is notorious for his attitude to women. He believes a woman's place is at home. He will not tolerate them anywhere near the troops. To him they are all camp followers – by which he means women of easy virtue.' He stopped and blushed. 'Forgive me, I don't mean to suggest that that could be applied to you and your friend.'

Leo smiled. 'Don't worry. I'm not easily shocked. And whatever your Colonel Malkovic says, we are still determined to get to Chataldzha.'

He frowned. 'I can't say you aren't needed. I've seen enough during the recent weeks to know that we don't have good enough systems in place for dealing with casualties. But whether it's suitable work for women …?'

'Why should men take all the risks? If they are prepared to fight and die for their country, shouldn't we women be ready to do the same? At least, surely, we should be able to prevent them dying just through the lack of basic First Aid.'

He looked at her and she had the impression that he was coming to a decision. 'Look, I probably shouldn't say this, but I might be able to help.'

'Help? How?'

'Tomorrow I am leading a detachment to reinforce the Bulgarians who are besieging Adrianople. If you and your friend want to travel with us I won't turn you away. It's not Chataldzha, but it's a good deal nearer to the front line than this is.'

Leo caught her breath. 'You would really take us with you? Thank you! Thank you so much!'

He smiled ruefully. 'I shall probably live to regret it. Just don't, for God's sake, mention it to the colonel. I should probably be cashiered.'

Leo smiled at him. 'Don't worry. We won't say a word. When do we leave? How do we get there?'

'You need to be at the station by half past six tomorrow morning. The train leaves at seven o'clock.'

By the time Leo crawled into bed everything was settled. The major was dubious about whether Sparky could go on the train but when Victoria declared that if he could not she would drive to Adrianople he agreed that it would be managed somehow.

'I'm in enough trouble already,' he said with a laugh. 'I might as well be hung for a sheep as a lamb.'

Leo remembered the look in his eyes. All through their conversation she had been aware of his gaze and known that he found her attractive – and she knew that half-consciously she had traded on the fact. It was a not an unpleasant feeling to realise that she had that power, but it was not his face that floated across her imagination as she hovered on the brink of sleep. It was the dark, imperious eyes and the arrogant mouth of Aleksander 'Sasha' Malkovic.

Chapter 6

Tom was beginning to realise that he had been extremely lucky to meet up with Max. There had been trouble at the border with frontier police who were reluctant to admit two foreign journalists. It was not until Max slipped several large denomination banknotes into his passport that they were allowed to proceed to Belgrade. He then managed to acquire, by similar means, what seemed to be the only motor car in the village, to convey them there.

In Tom's imagination the Serbian capital was like something out of a book of Russian fairy tales, all crooked wooden houses and narrow streets, and he was surprised to find an elegant city where grand houses with neoclassical façades overlooked broad thoroughfares busy with hansom cabs, shiny barouches and even trams. Nevertheless, the signs of war were everywhere. The streets were crowded with men in uniform, and refugee families in rough

peasant attire pushing handcarts loaded with possessions mingled with the smartly dressed bour-
geoisie. Accommodation was at a premium but
eventually they found rooms in the Union Hotel in
a busy street not far from the main square.

Looking at the décor of heavy wood and stained
glass, Tom commented, 'This reminds me of a gentleman's club in London, not somewhere in eastern
Europe.'

Max smiled. 'There are places like this from
Vienna to Prague. You have to remember that
Belgrade was the southern outpost of the Austro-
Hungarian Empire for many years. The Ottoman
Turks were just the other side of the Danube.'

Over dinner Max proposed that the following
morning he would introduce Tom to some of his
contacts in the newspaper world.

'You know what? There are at least a dozen
daily papers operating in this city. And my
rag has a stringer based here who should be
able to give us all the latest news. I'll see that
you get an exclusive that'll have the editor of
The Times in London begging you to join his staff.'

Tom felt the colour rising in his face. He had never
imagined that his bluff would be called in such a
direct fashion and he felt guilty at having deceived
this good-hearted man. 'Look, Max,' he said, 'I'd

better come clean – that's the American expression, isn't it? The fact is I'm not a journalist, not even an aspiring one. Let me explain ...'

He told Max in as few words as possible about Leo's disappearance, though he glossed over the exact nature of their relationship. Max listened, pursing his lips and nodding. When Tom finished he whistled softly.

'Gee whiz! What a story! Gallant young women setting off into the unknown to render aid and succour to wounded soldiers. My readers would just love that! But I understand your feelings. A lady's reputation and all that.' He sighed regretfully. 'OK, listen. With my contacts, if your fiancée has passed through here recently I'm sure we'll be able to pick up her trail. I'll ask around tomorrow, discreetly, of course. No need for anyone to know who she is. But I just ask one thing in return. If we do find her, will you let me talk to her? I could write up her story without mentioning her name, if she wants it that way. But, gee Tom, it's not something to be ashamed of. If it was my girlfriend showing that kind of guts I'd be proud!'

Tom digested this in silence for a moment. Up until then he had only viewed Leonora's disappearance as an act of foolishness that had caused her family, and himself, a great deal of inconvenience. It had never occurred to him that it was something admirable and Max's words made him see it in a whole new light. Finally he said, 'OK, Max. If we find her you can talk to her, on condition that if she doesn't want the story published, even anonymously, you will respect her wishes. Do I have your word?'

'On my honour. So, what's your first port of call here in Belgrade?'

'I thought I'd go and see the British Consul. She may have gone to him for help, or if the Serbian authorities have detained her, they will, presumably, have contacted him.'

'Good thinking,' Max said. 'I've got people to see, as I said, so I suggest we go our separate ways and meet back here for dinner. That all right with you?'

Tom had no difficulty in obtaining an interview with the British Consul but his response was not helpful.

'Terribly sorry old chap, but I haven't seen the young lady, or heard anything about her. If she and her friend were here in Belgrade I would expect to have heard a rumour, at the very least. The British community here is not large and word soon gets round if there are any new arrivals.'

'Do you think they might have been turned back at the border? We had some difficulty getting through.'

'It's quite possible that the authorities at the frontier refused to let them pass. They are very suspicious of foreigners at the moment, particularly anyone without a really valid reason for coming here. Two unaccompanied ladies trying to reach the battlefields would be bound to raise questions. Your fiancée is probably safely back home by now, unless they have decided to stop off and sample the cultural delights of Vienna.'

On leaving the Embassy Tom found his way to the Post Office and sent a telegram to Amelia Malham Brown at Sussex Gardens. *No sign of L here. Situation very unsettled. Have you any news?* That done, he found himself at a loose end. It seemed pointless to wander round the city on the off-chance that he might bump into Leo or Victoria. On the other hand, he had no wish to spend the rest of the day sitting in the hotel, so he decided that he might as well take the opportunity to explore. What he found was a city pulsating with feverish excitement. The Serbian flag was everywhere, but the shops were mainly closed, many of them boarded up. He was aware that he attracted curious glances from passers-by and once a group of soldiers elbowed him off the pavement and one of them shouted something incomprehensible at him. He began to wonder whether it would have been more sensible to stay in the safety of the hotel; but his artist's eye was caught by the unfamiliar scenes, and he wandered on along the broad thoroughfare of the Knez Mikhailov, pausing occasionally to sketch the elegant frontage of one of the grand houses that lined it. At the end of the street he found himself entering a large park, where groups of soldiers lounged under the trees and small children attended by their nursemaids ran through drifts of fallen leaves. Beyond that were the walls of Kalmegdan, the castle that crouched like a protective lion on the cliffs dominating the confluence of the Danube and the Sava River. Tom strolled through the great gateway without hindrance and found himself in another park-like space, bounded by the curtain walls. Climbing to a vantage point on these he looked down on a panorama that included the two rivers and the bridges that linked the old city to its newer outposts. He took out his sketch pad and began to draw.

He was so immersed in the scene below him that he did not notice someone climbing the steps behind him until a heavy hand was laid on his shoulder. Looking up, he found two policemen standing above him. One of them stabbed a finger at the sketch pad and said something in Serbian. At first he thought they were merely curious but then one of them took him by the arm and jerked him to his feet. He protested, but neither man spoke English and they seemed unimpressed by his British passport and began to pull him towards the steps. Their manner was becoming increasingly threatening so Tom decided that, rather than provoke a struggle he could not win, it would be best to go with them and hope that when they reached the police station, which he presumed was where they were taking him, he would find someone with whom he could communicate. To his intense humiliation he was frogmarched through the streets and finally through the doors of a forbidding-looking building and into a room where uniformed officers were sitting at desks, surrounded by civilians who all seemed to be talking and gesticulating at once. When one of the officials was free, one of Tom's captors thrust his sketch book onto the desk and poured out a lengthy explanation. The officer skimmed through the sketches and then looked up at Tom and barked a question.

'I'm sorry,' Tom responded helplessly, 'I don't understand. I'm English. Do you have anyone here who speaks English? Look,' he produced his passport again, 'British citizen – see?'

The official took the passport and peered at it curiously, then put it down without comment on top of Tom's sketch pad. Tom realised with a sinking feeling that passports were a newfangled notion that had not yet become current in Serbia, but when he moved to pick it up the man quickly snatched it out of reach. Tom felt panic beginning to churn in his bowels.

'I want to speak to someone who understands English,' he said, as calmly and clearly as he could manage. 'I don't know why I have been brought here, but I'm a British citizen and I demand to see the British Consul.'

The official looked at him without speaking for a moment, then he said something to the policemen who had brought Tom in and jerked his head towards a bench at the side of the room. One of the men took Tom's arm and pulled him towards it.

'I want my passport back!' Tom demanded, and he could hear his own voice shaking.

There was no response, other than another jerk of his arm. Defeated, he allowed himself to be led to the bench and sat down, comforting himself with the thought that perhaps the official had summoned an interpreter and was waiting for him to arrive. Minutes passed and stretched into an hour. The crowds round the desks changed but did not lessen. Eventually Tom got up and went back to the man who had taken his passport.

'What is going on? Why am I here? What are we waiting for?'

The man simply shrugged and jerked his head towards the bench. Tom contemplated walking out of the door, but a glance showed him that it was guarded by two policemen. He went back to the bench.

After another hour a man in civilian clothes entered, spoke to the official and then came over to Tom.

'You are English?'

'Yes, I am. And I've been here for over two hours. Do you mind telling me what is going on?'

The man gestured with his chin towards a door at the back of the room. 'Come, please.'

Reluctantly Tom followed him down a dusty corridor and into a room that was bare except for a wooden table and two chairs.

'Sit, please.'

Tom sat in the chair indicated and the other man seated himself on the opposite side of the table. Tom saw for the first time that he was holding the sketch pad.

'What is this?'

'It's a sketch pad. I'm an artist.'

'Why are you drawing pictures of the city?'

'Because I have never been here before. You have some fine buildings. I like to draw buildings and landscapes.'

'Why this view?'

'Because it makes a good picture. It's very picturesque. You understand "picturesque"?'

'Why are you here in Belgrade?'

That brought Tom to a standstill. Did he explain about Leonora's disappearance? Or did he stick to the story that he was a journalist? He decided that the former approach was just too complicated.

'I'm a journalist. I am travelling with an American colleague, Maximillian Seinfelt. He works for the *Baltimore Herald*. We are staying at the Union Hotel. If you contact him he will vouch for me.'

'A journalist? You have a press card?'

'I ... no. I am a freelance. I don't work for any particular paper.'

'I think you are lying. I think you are a spy. You are working for the Austrian government, preparing pictures of strategic locations for use in the event of any future hostilities.'

'No! Why would the Austrian government want my pictures? You are fighting the Turks, not the Austrians. Anyway, I'm not Austrian. I'm British. This is all a terrible mistake. I demand to see the British Consul. I spoke to him this morning. Tell him Thomas Devenish is here and ask him to vouch for me.'

The man looked at Tom for a long moment in silence. Then he said, 'Turn out your pockets, please.'

'Why?'

'Turn out your pockets.'

Tom took out his wallet and his small change, some pieces of charcoal and a pencil and the key to his hotel room. His interrogator collected them up. 'Also your watch, please.'

'Look, this is ridiculous! Why do you want my watch? How long are you going to keep me here?' The man simply looked at him and Tom reluctantly parted with his wristwatch. The interrogator got up and moved to the door. Tom rose too.

'Where are you going? What happens now?'

His interrogator shook his head. 'Wait,' he said, and went out, closing the door.

Tom made to follow him and discovered that the door was locked. He banged on it, overwhelmed by a rising tide of mingled panic and fury.

'Let me out! You have no right to keep me here. I am a British citizen and I have done nothing wrong. Fetch me the British Consul!'

He banged until his knuckles were sore and he was out of breath but there was no response. Finally he returned to his chair and sank down. Perhaps the man had gone for the consul, he told himself. Anyway, if Max returned to the hotel and found he was not there he would look for him. He would ask at the consulate. Eventually, they would locate him. He tried to console himself with these thoughts, but found little comfort in them.

He had lost track of the time, but his stomach told him that it was well past lunchtime. Before long, the pangs of hunger were overlaid by a much more urgent need to go the lavatory. He went to the door and banged again and this time a sullen-looking policeman opened it.

'Lavatory!' Tom said. 'Toilet! W.C? I need to piss!' In the end he was reduced to miming and the policeman grunted something and led him down the corridor, where he opened the door to a malodorous lavatory that consisted of little more than a hole in the ground. When Tom had relieved himself, he tried to open some sort of conversation.

'Am I going to be here much longer?' He gestured to the bare space where his watch had been. There was no glimmer of understanding in the man's eyes. 'British Consul!' Tom said, with emphasis. 'When is he coming?' In reply his arm was gripped and he was conducted back to the room and locked in again.

There was a small window high up in the wall and through that Tom saw the last of the daylight fade. At the sound of the lock turning he jumped to his feet, expecting the consul, or at the very least Max. But it was only the gloomy looking policeman, carrying a tray on which were a tin dish of stew, a lump of bread and a glass of water. The meat in the stew was mainly gristle and fat but Tom devoured it and wiped up the gravy with the bread. He could not remember when he had been so hungry. He had just finished when the guard returned and indicated with a jerk of his head that Tom should follow him. With a leaping heart Tom went to the door but instead of taking him back to the main office the man led him along the corridor, deeper into the bowels of the building, until he opened a door and Tom found himself in what was obviously a cell, a room just big enough for a plank bed with a single blanket and, in the corner, another noisome hole to serve as a toilet. Tom turned to protest but before he could speak the guard slammed the door and he heard the lock turn.

Tom sat on the bed and put his head in his hands. Only pride stopped him from sobbing like a child. He forced himself to think calmly. No British citizen could be allowed to disappear into a foreign prison without trial or explanation. But then the thought came to him that Serbia was at war, and in wartime prisoners were treated differently. They suspected him of spying. And what happened to spies in wartime? They were shot, weren't they? But not without a trial, surely. Serbia was not England, but surely even here the law held sway. Why should he assume that Max would trouble himself to discover his whereabouts? They were casual acquaintances, no more. He would probably think that Tom had found his girlfriend and taken her home. Tom curled up on the bed with his knees up to his chest and pulled the single blanket over him. It occurred to him that he had felt like this once before – alone and abandoned. Then he remembered. It was on his first night at prep school.

He thought he had not slept, but he was suddenly awoken by the sound of the door being unlocked. He sat up stiffly, rubbing his eyes, and realised that daylight was coming through the small, barred window. It was dawn – and they shot spies at dawn, didn't they? As the door opened he began to tremble violently.

In his terror he was scarcely able to recognise the figure who bounded through the door, hands outstretched.

'My dear chap!' exclaimed the consul. 'I had no idea! Whatever has been going on?'

'It's you!' Tom responded. He had been near to tears the night before, but now they almost overcame him. 'I kept asking them to send for you, but I couldn't make them understand.'

'No one notified me,' the consul said. 'Typical of these petty bureaucrats. They enjoy the feeling of having power over someone and they like to make it last as long as possible. You can thank your American friend that we've found you so quickly. He wouldn't rest until you were located, and he wouldn't let me rest either. But what has happened? How did you end up here?'

'They think I'm a spy,' Tom said. The impulse to weep was transforming itself into a helpless giggle. 'I ask you! Me, a spy!'

'But what made them think that?'

'I was drawing one of the bridges. Just sketching, you know. No ulterior motive.'

'Of course not. But you must understand, this is a country at war. Pictures of landmarks like that could be of great use to an artillery commander.'

Tom sobered up. 'Yes, I see that now. It was foolish of me. I'm sorry I have given you so much trouble.'

'My dear chap, it is I who should apologise. Depend upon it, I shall make the displeasure of His Majesty's Government very plain to the people who have held you here. Now, come along. Let's get you out of this hole. What you need is a hot bath, a change of clothes and a good breakfast.'

'I can't think of anything more wonderful,' Tom agreed.

In the outer office they found Max waiting. He greeted Tom with a hearty slap on the shoulder.

'Good to see you, buddy. You had us worried for a bit there. I was thinking we might be pulling your body out of the Danube.'

While Tom thanked him, the consul spoke to the police officer behind the desk and he produced Tom's personal belongings and a form.

'Just sign here, to say all your things have been returned,' the consul said.

'Can I have my sketch pad back, please?' Tom asked.

A look of something close to exasperation passed over the consul's face, then he turned back to the policeman, who disappeared into an inner room. After a short wait he came back with Tom's pad. Tom flipped through it and saw that all the sketches of Belgrade had disappeared. Well, that was fair enough, under the circumstances. He thanked the man and pocketed his belongings.

Outside the police station Tom tried to express his thanks to the consul, but his words were waved aside.

'What are your plans now?' the consul asked.

'I'm not sure,' Tom said hesitantly. 'I'm waiting for a telegram from home. I hope it may say that my fiancée is now safely back there.'

'I'm sure that will be the case.' Tom could see the relief on the other man's face. 'If I were you, I'd head for home too. This isn't a good place for foreigners at the moment.'

What you mean is, you want to get rid of me before I get into any more scrapes, Tom thought, and surprised himself by adding, I'll go when I'm ready, and not before.

Back at the hotel a telegram was waiting. Its contents were terse and unhelpful. *'No word from L. Keep looking. Ralph.'* Tom crumpled it in his fist and thought, Damn you, Ralph! Am I going to spend all my life sorting out your problems for you?

Admittedly, this time it was not a problem of Ralph's making but he was beginning to regret his involvement with the whole family.

Tom bathed and changed and over breakfast he showed the telegram to Max.

'OK,' the American said. 'So where do we look next?'

'Search me,' Tom said.

'Look here.' Max took a map out of his pocket and spread it on the table. 'The fighting is spread over a pretty wide area. I've been getting the latest positions from my contacts here. The Serbian First Army, under Prince Aleksander, is down here to the south. They've driven the Turks out of Kumanovo and Prilep and they are currently attacking Bitola. The Third Army is here, in Kosovo. It looks as though their plan is to force their way through

Albania to the Adriatic. So if your girls are looking for wounded soldiers to nurse, there will be plenty in either of those places. The other front is over here, to the east, around Adrianople and Chataldzha, almost to Constantinople. What I suggest is this: I'm heading down towards Kumanovo – if you want to tag along, we can make enquiries on the way, and if we draw a blank there we can go on down to Salonika. I'm told the railway is still operating between there and the Adrianople region, so we can head over there and see if we can pick up their tracks. What do you say?'

'It's very good of you to put up with me,' Tom said. 'I don't want to cramp your style, if you see what I mean.'

'Look,' Max laid a hand on his arm. 'I can smell a good story here. OK, it may never get to be published, but I want to know what happens. And I reckon you could do with an old hand like me to help you.'

'I certainly can,' Tom agreed. 'You've proved that already. If you're happy for me to "tag along" as you put it, I'll be more than grateful.'

'OK, fine!' Max sat back with a smile. 'I've got a few more loose ends to follow up here in Belgrade. I reckon I need a couple of days for that. So if it's OK with you we'll head south the day after tomorrow. Just don't go drawing any more pictures while you're waiting!'

Chapter 7

Leo woke with a start from an uneasy sleep as the train jolted to a sudden stop. It was not the first abrupt halt, for no apparent reason. For a day and a night, the train had dragged itself up through bare, uninhabited mountains and down across river valleys that must have been, in better times, fertile oases. Now they had been transformed into a featureless landscape of mud and broken trees, whose contours disappeared into a lowering sky. From time to time they had passed through villages which had been reduced to rubble by the advancing forces. In some, a few shrouded figures picked through the blackened remains, but mostly they seemed devoid of life.

'Where have all the people gone?' Victoria asked at one point.

'Fled into the mountains, perhaps,' Leo said.

'Poor souls! In this weather!' Victoria murmured.

Now, in the first light of dawn, Leo sat up, shivering. The major had very gallantly allowed them a compartment to themselves, so they had been able to stretch out on the seats. They had brought with them the down-filled sleeping bags that they had used in FANY camp and covered themselves with the car rugs as well, but the cold still penetrated. She peered out of the window and saw a flat, dun-coloured plain with no sign of a station. She yawned and was about to lie down again when the major tapped on the door of the compartment.

'Forgive me, ladies, but this is as far as we can go. The Turks have cut the line ahead to prevent reinforcements reaching Chataldzha. We have to detrain here.'

'Oh God! I can't bear it!' Victoria moaned, sitting up.

'Cheer up.' Leo responded. 'At least we seem to have arrived somewhere.'

Muzzy-headed from lack of sleep, they gathered their belongings and scrambled down onto the track, to be met by a blast of icy wind from the Rhodope Mountains to the north. All round them soldiers were descending and the howitzers and machine guns and horses and other paraphernalia of war were being offloaded, but above, or rather below, the clatter and the shouting there was another sound, a low, continuous rumble that Leo felt through the soles of her feet. Seeking its origin she raised her head and caught Victoria's arm.

'Look!'

There in the middle distance was a walled city, its domes and towers and minarets gilded by the rays of the just risen sun, like an illustration from a book of fairy tales. But the walls were surrounded by concentric circles of dark lines, one within another, and beyond them were the tents of a vast army encampment. It was from here that the noise came and, as they watched, the scene was obscured by a rolling pall of smoke.

'Adrianople,' said the major, who had followed them out of the train.

'And that noise is gunfire?' Victoria asked.

'Yes.'

'What are the dark lines all round the city?' Leo enquired.

'Trenches, ours and theirs. Some times only a hundred yards apart, I'm told.'

Between them and the city a group of horsemen could be seen cantering in their direction. The major shaded his eyes, then turned briefly to the two women. 'Excuse me. That looks like the commander of the Bulgarian forces, coming to greet us. I'll introduce you when I get a chance.'

He moved away and Leo and Victoria watched as the horsemen drew rein beside him and dismounted. When greetings had been exchanged the major shouted an order and the troops from the train began to form up into a column. Then the major came towards them, with a small man in Bulgarian uniform.

'This is General Dimitriev, the commandant of the Bulgarian forces here. General, may I present Miss Leonora Malham Brown and Miss Victoria Langford?'

The General clicked his heels and saluted and said in excellent German, 'Ladies, I am charmed to make your acquaintance, but I fear you have had a long and uncomfortable journey for no purpose. Major Dragitch tells me you are looking for some other English ladies who have bravely volunteered to nurse our soldiers. I have to tell you that I have no knowledge of any such ladies.'

Leo and Victoria exchanged looks. This was a blow.

'We think they are probably at Chataldzha,' Victoria said. 'Their purpose is to transport the wounded from the battlefield to the hospitals.'

The general shook his head. 'That is impossible. It is our policy not to allow any foreign nationals so close to the front lines. But I have a suggestion. We have our own Red Cross unit here. Perhaps you would be prepared to stay with us and help them. I am sure the nurses will be glad of extra hands.'

Once again Leo and Victoria consulted each other with a glance. Then Leo said, 'We appreciate your offer, General, and if we cannot locate Mrs Stobart and her companions we will do whatever we can to help here. But we feel we ought to try to join the others if at all possible.'

'In that case,' Dimitriev said, 'let me suggest this. Stay with us tonight, and I will telegraph to my headquarters in Sophia and try to find out if they have any knowledge of these ladies. If not, then you can decide whether to remain here or to return to Salonika. Is that agreeable to you?'

The two girls nodded in unison. 'Thank you, General,' Victoria said. 'That is very kind of you.'

A young corporal ran up, saluted and said something in Serbian to his commanding officer. Dragitch nodded and turned to Victoria. 'Your motorcar has been unloaded quite safely, you will be glad to hear.'

The general's eyebrows shot up. 'A motorcar? You have a motorcar? But how is that possible?'

When Victoria explained that they had driven from England and then shipped the car from Marseilles, Dimitriev's eyes opened wider, then he began to smile. 'Well, well! You are two indomitable young ladies, that is clear.'

By this time the unloading was complete and the column of troops was ready to move, so they set off in procession, led by the general and his entourage on horseback, with Leo and Victoria following in Sparky and behind them Major Dragitch, also mounted, and the horse-drawn limbers carrying the guns and finally the foot soldiers. As they advanced the noise of the guns filled the air with a continuous thunder and Leo's eyes stung with smoke. The air was choked with the smell of gunpowder and other even more obnoxious odours rising from the encampment that surrounded the besieged city.

The general had set up his headquarters on a slight rise, and when they reached it he insisted that the two women should make use of his tent, with the limited facilities it offered. An orderly brought them bowls of hot water to wash in, a welcome luxury after the long journey, and then they were given a breakfast of thick, sweet black coffee, dark rye bread and goat's cheese.

They had just finished eating when a young lieutenant appeared in the entrance to the tent and introduced himself as Georgi Radic, explaining that the general had instructed him to look after them.

'I understand you are nurses. Would you care to inspect our medical facilities?'

Leo was tempted to say that they lacked the experience to 'inspect' anything but before she could speak Victoria had accepted as if she found it the most natural thing in the world. As they followed Georgi out of the tent, Leo looked towards the city. Now they were closer she could see the damage to the walls and buildings that had been wrought by the guns, and the line upon line of trenches that scarred the plain.

'How long have you been besieging Adrianople?' she asked.

'Since the end of October,' he replied.

'And is there no sign of a surrender?'

'None at all, so far.'

'Things must be terrible for the ordinary people in there,' Leo said. 'How do they get food?'

'God knows! But it seems the Turks will let them starve rather than surrender.'

Leo shivered, and not just from the icy wind. She remembered what Colonel Malkovic had said, back in Salonika. 'You have no conception of modern warfare. You imagine a romantic charge, a brief, violent conflict and then the combatants leave the field and it is empty except for the dead and wounded. Modern warfare is not like that.' It was true, she admitted to herself. She had never imagined the filth, the stench, the sheer inhumanity of a war like this.

They reached a large tent set back someway from the main encampment and marked with a red cross. As they approached two stretcher bearers staggered up from the trenches, carrying a burden that left a trail of blood on the mud-churned soil. Following them into the tent Leo was brought up short by the smell – a sharp reek of disinfectant that failed to obscure the stench of blood and excrement and another sweetly cloying scent that reminded her of rotting meat. She glanced at Victoria and saw her put her hand over her mouth, struggling to repress the urge to retch. Leo swallowed hard and gritted her teeth. She had grown up with bad smells, in the back streets of Alexandria and the souks of Istanbul, though nothing as bad as this; but this, too, could be endured.

Looking ahead of her she saw two long rows of beds, all of them occupied, and at the far end of the tent a curtained-off area, into which the stretcher bearers and their load were just disappearing. A petite, dark-haired young woman in nurse's uniform came quickly up the ward to meet them and spoke in what Leo was beginning to recognise as Serbian to the lieutenant. He replied and the nurse turned to Leo and Victoria.

'Good day. My name is Sophie and I speak a little German. The lieutenant tells me you are English nurses.'

Leo felt a sudden flush of embarrassment. She was aware that they had been mis-representing themselves, or had at least allowed their hosts to assume that they were fully qualified, and they had not disillusioned them. Now, it seemed, their deception was about to be discovered. She glanced again at Victoria but she was obviously still struggling with nausea.

Leo said, 'I am afraid there is a slight misunderstanding. We are not trained nurses. But we are fully qualified in advanced First Aid. We are on our way to join some other English ladies so we may not be here for long, but while we are here we shall be glad to help in any way we can.'

Sophie frowned for a moment while she absorbed this. Then she said, 'I will explain to the doctors and ask what they wish you to do. Please wait a moment.' Just then a long drawn-out scream of agony issued from behind the dividing curtain. Leo started with shock, her hand going involuntarily to her mouth, but looking around the tent she saw no sign of reaction from the long rows of beds. This, it seemed, was not an unusual occurrence.

Sophie said matter-of-factly, 'There is a shortage of chloroform. We have to save it for the most acute cases. Excuse me.'

She moved away and Leo looked at her two companions. Victoria had turned her back and was taking deep breaths and the lieutenant, too, had gone pale. It occurred to Leo that the horror of what they were seeing was more acute for him, since he must feel that at any time he could become one of the patients undergoing whatever was happening behind that curtain.

'Lieutenant,' she said, 'there is no need for you to stay. We shall probably be here for some time and I'm sure the doctor and the nurses will look after us. There really is no point in you waiting.'

He looked at her gratefully. 'If you are really sure, *gnädige Frau*. I expect there are more useful things I could be doing.'

'Of course there are,' Leo agreed. 'Please, feel free to go.'

He saluted briefly and stumbled out of the tent, and Leo thought she heard him being sick outside. Sophie came back.

'I have spoken to the Herr Doctor and he says that, if you wish, you are welcome to stay. We are about to start doing the dressings. You can observe, or, if you like, help.'

Leo looked at Victoria, who appeared to have regained control. She nodded and Leo said, 'Thank you. We will do whatever we can.'

A second nurse, slightly older than Sophie, came up the ward pushing a trolley laded with dressings and various instruments. Sophie said, 'This is Magda. She does not speak German but I am sure she will be able to make herself understood. Perhaps—' to Victoria '—you would go with her?'

'Yes, of course,' Victoria said, her tone uncharacteristically clipped.

Magda nodded and smiled and beckoned Victoria to follow her to the first bed on the right hand side of the ward. Sophie looked at Leo. 'And we will start over here.'

The bed was occupied by a young man whose head was almost completely swathed in bandages. As they approached the one eye visible swivelled wildly from Sophie to Leo and she realised that he was frightened of what was to come. Sophie bent over him and began to undo the bandages, murmuring something in her own language.

She added in German, 'It is difficult. I am Serbian but most of these soldiers are Bulgarian. The language is similar but sometimes it is hard for them to understand me. Perhaps you could support his head for me?'

Leo slid her hand under the boy's head and felt that he was trembling. She longed to be able to reassure him. 'I wish I could speak Serbian, or Bulgarian. It makes me feel useless.'

'You speak very good German,' Sophie said. 'Better than mine. Now, I should warn you. The wound is bad. It is not a pretty sight.'

The boy cried out as she pulled away the final dressing and Leo had to hold her breath to prevent herself from doing the same. Half his face had been blown away, leaving an amorphous mess of blood and tissue, through which splinters of bone showed white. Working deftly, Sophie applied a new dressing and rebandaged the boy's head and Leo, unable to communicate in any other way, found his hand and held it tightly.

'What can be done for him?' she asked.

Sophie shrugged slightly. 'Keep the wound clean and hope that in due course it will heal. There is nothing else.'

When she had finished Sophie led the way to the next bed and Leo prepared herself for more horror, but nothing compared with that first baptism of fire. For nearly two hours she followed Sophie down the ward, supporting wounded arms and legs, handing bandages and instruments, and trying to offer some comfort in the form of smiles and handclasps. By the time they had finished she was shaking with exhaustion and delayed shock.

Their work was not over yet, however. Two order-lies appeared at the entrance carrying a huge vat of steaming soup and a basket of hard, black bread. As she ladled the soup into tin plates Sophie said, 'Perhaps you can help some of those who cannot manage by themselves?'

Leo carried a plate over to the boy with the shattered face and helped him to prop himself up on his pillow. After the first spoonful of soup a faint smile touched his lips and he whispered the only word she had so far learned of his language.

'*Dobro!*'

She smiled back at him. 'Yes, *dobro*. Good!'

When all the patients had been fed, Sophie turned to Leo with a smile. 'Now it is time for us to eat. Perhaps you would like to join us?'

Leo and Victoria followed her to the mess tent, which had been set up alongside the hospital tent. They were introduced to the two doctors, whose white coats were spattered with blood and whose faces were taut and lined with fatigue. The meal was the same soup and bread that had been served to the patients and Leo found to her surprise that she had a good appetite for it. As they ate, she turned to Sophie.

'Did you say you are a Serb? I'm wondering how you come to be serving with the Bulgarian Red Cross.'

'I am a Serb, yes,' Sophia agreed. 'But I come from Kavala in Macedonia. You will have passed through it on the train from Salonika.'

Leo nodded vaguely. The details of the journey were becoming indistinct.

'It is one of the main towns in Macedonia,' the other girl went on. 'My father was a doctor there and he allowed me to work under him at the hospital. But when the fighting started the Turks took him away to care for their wounded. I have not seen him since.'

Leo looked at her. Her hair was drawn back smoothly from a broad brow and her eyes were large and dark. For the first time Leo noticed the signs of weariness on her face and, as Sophie turned her head away, she saw that her eyelashes were dewed with tears.

'I'm so sorry,' she murmured. 'But how did that bring you here?'

'I reasoned that the Turks would have taken him with them as they retreated, so as the Bulgarian army pursued them I thought that if I went too I might perhaps catch up with him.' She forced a smile. 'It has not happened yet, but it still may.'

'I hope it will,' Leo said.

They had just finished eating when Lieutenant Radic reappeared, looking his former cheerful self.

'The general thinks that perhaps you should rest after your journey. He has placed his tent at your disposal and insists that you use it. Shall I take you back now?'

Leo looked at Victoria and saw that she appeared as drained of energy as she felt herself. She turned to Sophie. 'I'm sure you could do with more help ...'

Sophie shook her head. 'No, the lieutenant is right. You should rest. Thank you for what you did this morning.' She smiled at Leo. 'You will be a good nurse. I can see that.'

Leo thanked her but as they walked back to the general's tent the thought uppermost in her mind was that she could never, given the choice, dedicate herself to the kind of work that Sophia carried out so calmly. Once more, cruel reality had imposed itself over what she had imagined. Her grandma had been right. Her original conception had been romantic nonsense.

In the tent Victoria laid a hand on her arm. 'Leo, you were wonderful this morning. I don't think I could have faced those horrors if it hadn't been for you.'

'I didn't do anything special,' Leo mumbled.

'Yes, you did. You were so calm, so ... so stalwart. I've always thought of myself as brave, but not today.'

'I wasn't feeling very brave, either,' Leo confessed.

'That doesn't matter. You just got on with the job.'

'So did you.'

'Yes, because I didn't want to let you down.'

Leo put her arm round her. 'Well, as long as we both try not to let each other down, we'll be all right, won't we.'

Victoria looked into her eyes. 'I dragged you into this. I'm responsible. Are you furious with me?'

'Of course not!' Leo exclaimed. 'However bad it gets, I'd still rather be here than sitting at home.' She yawned suddenly. 'I don't know about you, but I feel as though I could sleep for a week.'

'Me, too. Let's take the opportunity while it's offered. At least we can have an hour or two.'

An extra bed had been set up during their absence and they lay down, fully clothed, and both fell almost immediately into the first proper sleep they had had for forty-eight hours. They were woken by the steward calling to them from outside the tent. Leo sat up and realised that two things had changed. Darkness had fallen, and the guns had stopped firing. She called out to the steward to come in and he entered carrying a bucket of steaming water.

'The general asks if you will do him the honour of joining him for dinner.'

Leo suppressed a laugh. The formality of the invitation was in such stark contrast to their circumstances that it seemed almost ludicrous. 'Please

thank the general and tell him we shall be delighted,'
she said.

They spruced themselves up as far as possible and the steward conducted them to a large tent which obviously served as an officers' mess. As they entered Leo suppressed a gasp and looked at Victoria, whose eyes expressed the same mixture of surprise and amusement. The long table was covered with spotless linen, on which highly polished cutlery gleamed in the light of candles in silver candle-sticks. Orderlies stood along both sides with white napkins over their arms. Leo was reminded of the officers' mess at the Guards' Chelsea barracks, where she had been Ralph's guest more than once. The only item that might have looked out of place there was the huge samovar which stood, glistening, in one corner. She quickly realised that the formality of the invitation had not been out of place. Although the officers present were swathed in muddy greatcoats against the cold they behaved as if they were entertaining ladies in their mess at headquarters. Indeed, they were treated with a gallant courtesy that surpassed anything Leo had experienced anywhere in England.

They were served potato soup with soured cream, and then a goulash spiced with paprika and enriched with more cream and finally pancakes with a chocolate sauce.

Victoria pushed the last of hers to the side of her plate and muttered in English, 'If I eat any more I shall burst.'

'I know what you mean,' Leo replied. 'I wonder what those poor boys in the hospital tent are getting.'

'Not this, I'm willing to bet,' her friend grunted.

When the meal was over they all adjourned outside, where they sat round a huge campfire while a soldier sang to the accompaniment of the gusla, a kind of single-stringed banjo, which produced a curious, monotonous buzzing sound. The song, too, had a limited musical range, repeating the same pattern over and over again. When it had gone on for some time, Leo leaned over to Major Dragitch and whispered, 'What is the song about, Major?'

'It is an old legend,' he whispered back. 'Every family in Serbia tells such stories, of how their ancestors fought the Turks back in the fourteenth century, or other historic battles.'

'It sounds a very sad song,' Leo murmured.'

'We Serbs have a sad history,' he replied.

Eventually the song came to an end and then, to Leo's surprise, two soldiers rose to their feet and, linking arms, began to move in a slow, shuffling dance. Immediately the gusla began again and other men rose and joined the first two, until they had formed a circle. The pace quickened and the steps became more intricate, but the dance retained an inherent solemnity that seemed in keeping with the mood of the evening. With the ending of the bombardment a great silence had fallen over the camp and the skies had cleared to reveal stars that hung huge and lambent over the frozen plain. Leo looked up and drew a long breath. The discomforts of the journey and the horrors of the day faded and she knew that what she had said to Victoria was true. She would rather be here than in the most luxurious drawing room in London.

The following morning the general appeared at the entrance to the tent.

'I have good news for you. I have a reply from the authorities in Sophia. Your friends are at Lozengrad – or Kirk-Kilisse, if you prefer the Turkish name.'

'Where is that?' Victoria asked eagerly.

'I will show you.' The general advanced to the table in the centre of the tent and unrolled a map. 'Here is Adrianople. And here is Lozengrad, to the east and slightly north, about sixty kilometres away.'

'They are not at Chataldzha then?' Leo asked.

'No, as I told you. Foreign non-combatants are not permitted so near the front line. But the casualties from Chataldzha are being taken to Lozengrad. I am told that your friends have set up a hospital there.'

'Then we must go and join them,' Victoria said. 'Only sixty kilometres. We can be there in an hour in the car.'

The general shook his head reprovingly. 'My dear lady, I could not possibly allow you to set off alone. The countryside between here and Lozengrad has been devastated by the war and there are desperate people out there. Who knows what might happen to two unprotected women? You must allow me to send an escort with you. They will not have cars, but you will find that it is impossible to travel fast over these roads.'

They both realised that it would be foolish to argue, so an hour later they set off in a cavalcade with Georgi Radic and two troopers riding ahead and two more soldiers standing on the running boards of the car. The general had insisted on providing them with a tent, which was strapped on top of the trunk carrying their possessions, and food supplies for two days.

'This is ridiculous!' Victoria muttered as they packed. 'Anybody would think we were going six hundred kilometres, not sixty. Doesn't he have any idea how fast a car can travel?'

They soon had their answer. The roads, if they could be called that, had been churned to liquid mud by the bullock wagons that were the main form of transport for the army. They had not covered more than two miles before the car stuck fast and they were glad of the power of the two burly soldiers to push them out. Another mile further on they stuck again and this time the two mounted troopers had to get off their horses and help. By the time the short winter daylight was fading they had covered less than half the distance and Georgi called a halt by a small copse of trees, whose upper branches had been ripped away by gunfire. The fallen timber was built up into a campfire, the tent was erected and a cooking pot was soon simmering for the inevitable soup. Conversation was difficult, since only Georgi spoke anything other than Serbian, but before long one of the men produced a gusla and this time Leo took comfort in the monotonous drone, which seemed to make the darkness beyond the fire less threatening. When the song finished they said their goodnights and crawled into their sleeping bags in the tent, snuggling together for warmth and comfort, while the men, except for one to keep watch, wrapped themselves in their blankets and lay down around the fire.

'I say,' Leo murmured, on the verge of sleep, 'we wanted an adventure. Well, we've certainly found one.'

Victoria chuckled softly. 'I don't know about you, Malham Brown! Here we are, miles from anywhere, half frozen, with nothing but the hard ground to lie on, and I do believe you're enjoying yourself!'

'Do you know,' Leo responded, 'I believe I am.'

Chapter 8

The two days after his arrest passed for Tom with frustrating slowness. He was half afraid to leave the hotel and when he did venture out the febrile wartime atmosphere of the city unnerved him, as it had not done before. He spent most of the time in his room, working up some of the sketches he had made from the train, being careful not to include anything that might conceivably be seen as useful to an enemy. He also tried to produce a reasonable likeness of Leonora, reckoning that it could be useful in his search, but as always he found it impossible to catch that indefinable essence that would make the picture come to life.

On their last evening in the hotel he knocked on Max's door to see if he was ready to go down to dinner and was alarmed to find him cleaning and loading a revolver.

'I didn't know you carried a gun!'

'Don't you?'

'No! No, it would be illegal in England.'

'Oh yeah. I forgot your people's funny attitude to self-protection. Believe me, I wouldn't be without this baby.'

'Have you ever used it?'

'Never needed to. But there's always a first time.'

Max reported that it was impossible to get tickets to travel by train as the whole rail network had been taken over by the military; so in the morning he and Tom loaded their belongings into the car and set off by road. It became clear very quickly that progress was going to be slow. The roads were clogged with troops moving towards the front, on foot and on horseback, and wounded being returned in slow-moving wagons drawn by oxen. By the end of the first day they had reached Nis, the second largest city in Serbia, and were lucky to find a small, bug-ridden room in an inn, where they had to share a straw-stuffed mattress on a rickety bed. The next day they headed south towards Kumanovo. As they drew nearer they encountered sights that turned Tom's stomach. They passed through village after village that had been reduced to smouldering ruins and among the blackened buildings he caught glimpses of ragged, half-burned bundles that he tried not to recognise as human bodies. The fields on either side of the road had been churned to liquid mud and half submerged in the morass were the corpses of hundreds of men and horses. Upflung arms were stretched in pointless appeal towards the heavens and blackened skulls grinned up at them from the verges. As darkness fell, the sky was reddened by the flames of further conflagrations. That night, they reached Skopje and found a scene of total devastation. All the undamaged buildings had been commandeered by the military and they were forced to spend the night in the car, parked close to the river Vardar, which ran through the centre of the city.

Tom woke, chilled and cramped, as an unwilling winter dawn broke over the town. He had suspected for the last day or two that he was coming down with a cold and now he was sure of it. His nose was streaming and his throat felt as if it had been rubbed raw with sandpaper. He crawled out of the car to stretch his legs and wandered onto the bridge that crossed the river. He looked down and immediately doubled up in a fit of convulsive vomiting. The waters of the river were choked, as if by debris brought down by flood waters and caught up against the bridge, with the headless bodies of men.

Tom's stomach was empty and he could only bring up acid bile. When the nausea eased enough to allow him to stand he staggered back to the car and woke Max.

'Go and look,' he gasped in answer to Max's sleep-fuddled queries. 'Look in the river.'

Max came back to the car after a few minutes, grey-faced but calm. 'Tom, you should draw this. The world should know what is being done here. I can write it up, but only a picture will make people see the true horror.'

'I can't!' Tom whispered.

'Yes, you can,' Max said. 'You need to do this.'

Tom dragged himself back to the bridge and forced himself to look properly at the pitiful sight below. He got out his pad and began to draw and as he did so he understood the force of what Max had said. In confronting the horror and reducing it to planes and shadows on the paper it became no less real but somehow comprehensible. As he finished a few local men appeared from the shells of their houses and came to stand by the bridge. It was evident from their behaviour that this was not the first time they had seen the slaughter below them. Max questioned them in German and translated for Tom.

'They say it happens every night. Some think it is local men, killed by the *četniks* for resisting, others that the bodies have been carried down from higher up the river. No one knows for sure who is responsible.'

'Who are the *četniks*?' Tom asked.

'Serbian irregulars in the pay of the Black Hand. Most of the local population are Albanian and the Serbs and the Albanians have always been at daggers drawn.'

'The what? It sounds like something out of a penny dreadful.'

Max gave a mirthless grunt of laughter. 'See what you mean, but they're serious enough. The proper name for the organisation is Unification or Death but they are always referred to as the Black Hand. They are ultra-nationalists and their objective, as I understand it, is to create a Greater Serbia. It seems from these guys I've just been talking to that they pretty much run things around here at the moment.' He looked down at Tom's picture. 'That has to be sent to the London *Times,* and I need to get the story out to my paper. People have to know what's going on here. Let's go find a post office or somewhere with a telephone, so I can file my copy.'

'Maybe I can send a telegram to London in case Leonora has arrived home,' Tom said. The prospect of an affirmative answer, which would allow him to return to civilization, dangled before him like a mirage in the desert.

Enquiries in the stricken town produced the information that all communications were under the control of the Black Hand, who had set up headquarters in one of the few intact buildings, which people were already calling the Black House. There they were received courteously by a Major Tankovic but told that the telephone lines between Skopje and Belgrade were down, as were those between the town and Salonika to the south. Normal postal services had ceased to operate and all messages had to be conveyed by courier and were confined to military bulletins. With little hope of success, Tom asked his usual question regarding the possible whereabouts of Leonora and Victoria and was met, as usual, with blank incomprehension. Defeated, they returned to the car and breakfasted on the last of the provisions they had brought with them from Belgrade.

'I guess the only thing we can do is press on southwards,' Max said. 'If we can get through to Salonika we should be able to contact London and the USA, and maybe pick up some news of your lady friend.'

Tom rubbed a hand over his face, feeling the stubble that reminded him he had not washed or shaved for two days. He longed with all his heart to get away from these killing fields but unless he went on with

Max the only alternative was to try to make his own way back to Belgrade. From Salonika, he told himself, he should be able to get a boat, which would take him to Italy or France – and surely, if there was no news of Leo there, he would be justified in calling off the search.

'Very well,' he said. 'Let's get on our way.'

'There's just one problem,' Max said. 'It seems there is still fighting around the town of Bitola, which is on our route. We'll have to hope that we can get around it somehow.'

As they drove south the country grew wilder and more mountainous. There was snow on the higher slopes and the road followed river valleys full of the sound of rushing water. Everywhere, there was evidence of the fighting and from several miles outside Bitola they could hear the boom of artillery and the sky ahead was lit up by flashes.

'This is crazy,' Tom said. 'We can't drive through that.'

'I know,' Max responded. 'I'm planning on finding the battlefield HQ, which must be well back from the firing line. They may be able to tell us a way round. If not, we'll have to sit it out until the fighting is over. Seems like the Serbs are making pretty short work of the Turkish forces, so it shouldn't be too long.'

They had gone just over another mile when, on the outskirts of a small village, they were waved to a standstill by a group of raggedly dressed men carrying rifles. A bearded man jerked open the driver's door and said something in what Tom presumed was Serbian. Max replied in German but the man shook his head angrily and gestured them out of the car. Max produced his press card and waved it under his nose, but he brushed it aside and repeated the gesture. When neither Tom nor Max moved, he shouted a command to the rest of his band and they found themselves at the centre of a ring of rifles.

'Better do as the man says,' Max muttered, and climbed out. 'Maybe there is someone in charge who speaks German.'

Tom got out and as he did so the bearded man climbed into the driving seat and revved the engine.

'Hey, now, whoa!' Max yelled, jumping in front of the vehicle, but the man just laughed and drove at him, forcing him to leap aside. In numb horror, Tom watched as the car disappeared up the village street.

'You can't do that!' Max yelled. 'That's theft! What are we supposed to do? Walk to Salonika? At least let us have our bags ...'

The remaining men grinned and gestured with their guns towards the road that led through the village.

'Maybe they want us to follow him,' Tom suggested, with faint hope.

'Guess there's nothing else we can do,' Max agreed.

They trudged down the village street, followed by the men, but there was no sign of the car. Tom guessed it had been hidden in one of the dilapidated barns attached to the houses. It was only a small place and they quickly reached the far end of the street, from where the road stretched ahead of them towards the sound of the guns.

Max turned towards the gang. 'Look here, fellers, we have to be somewhere. It's important. I'll pay for the car. Look, see?' He produced his wallet and waved it at them. One of them snatched it and riffled through the notes, chuckling. Then he pocketed the money, threw the empty wallet back to Max and waved his rifle towards the open road. Tom saw Max's hand go to the pocket where he carried his revolver. He grabbed his arm.

'Don't be a fool, Max! Do you want to get us both shot?'

The man who had taken the money advanced and pushed the muzzle of his rifle into Max's stomach. Tom tugged at his arm.

'It's no use, Max. Look at them. They won't think twice about shooting us. We don't have a choice. Just walk away.'

Slowly they turned and began to trudge down the road. Tom's spine crept as if slimy creatures were running up and down it and he expected at any moment to feel a bullet strike him in the back but he plodded on, pulling Max with him, and when he eventually dared to look behind him the road was empty.

'Well, now what?' Tom asked.

Max was muttering to himself. 'Sons of bitches! My car and my money. And all our gear. Fuck it! They've even got my sodding typewriter!'

For the first time it struck Tom that he had nothing but the clothes he stood up in and the satchel in which he carried his drawing materials, which was hanging from his shoulder. He felt in his pocket and was relieved to find his wallet and his passport. He looked at Max and saw that the confident swagger had disappeared, leaving him grey faced and wild eyed.

'What do we do now?' Max demanded, echoing Tom's question.

'Keep walking, I suppose. Eventually we must reach the rear echelons of the army. Then we can ask for help.'

They trudged on. It had been raining intermittently all day but now the rain seemed to have become one more hostile force in an inimical world. Icy cold, it slanted into their faces and soaked their clothes. Tom, not sure what to expect when they left Belgrade, had dressed as he would have done for a day's shooting on the moors. He was glad of his good boots but had neglected to put on gaiters and he could feel the mud and water from the roadway soaking into his trouser legs, while the rain dripped off the back of his deerstalker and ran down inside his collar. Before long, the moisture had even penetrated the cape of his tweed Inverness coat and he could feel his shirt chill and damp against his skin. His nose had dried up but now his sinuses were clogged with catarrh, and his throat was so painful he could hardly bear to swallow. Every time he took a breath there was a sharp pain in his chest. But at least he was used to long tramps in the rain, which Max obviously was not.

'I'm a city guy,' he protested. 'I've never walked more than a couple of blocks in my life. These boots are killing me.'

'Stop!' Tom said abruptly. 'Listen.'

'Listen to what?'

'There it is again. Hear it?'

Faintly, through the relentless hiss of the rain, came a sound that sent a chill of horror through Tom's already icy body. A high, thin wailing, so shrill and attenuated that it was almost beyond the range of his ears, but insistent and unceasing.

'It's the wind,' Max said.

'No, it isn't,' Tom replied, turning his head this way and that. 'It's coming from over there, behind that wall.'

He crossed to a broken stone wall at the side of the road and looked over, then turned away and flung his hand over his eyes.

'What is it?' Max demanded.

'Look!' was all Tom could say. He forced himself to lower his hand. Lying on the ground just beyond the wall was a girl, hardly more than a child, legs splayed obscenely apart, her body ripped from crotch to navel. All round her the sodden ground was stained dark with her blood and yet, incredibly, she still lived and uttered that terrible, unworldly cry.

Tom climbed over the wall and knelt beside her. Behind him he could hear Max repeating over and over again, 'Oh, my God! Oh, my God!' He found the child's hand and gripped it and the wailing stopped, although her eyes remained closed.

'What do we do? What do we do?' Max demanded.

'What can we do?' Tom said. 'God knows where the nearest hospital is, and she would be dead before we got her there.' He was remembering a day when he was about twelve years old. His father had taken him out shooting and they had come across a young fox, which had somehow escaped from the hounds, its belly ripped open and its intestines dragging. Tom had knelt by it, weeping, and his father had handed him his shotgun and said brusquely, 'Put the poor creature out of its misery.'

Tom reached behind him with his free hand. 'Give me your revolver.'

'What?'

'Give me your gun.'

He did not look round, but felt the butt of the revolver placed in his hand. His eyes were blinded by tears but he found the child's temple and put the muzzle against it. 'Don't be afraid, little one,' he whispered in English. 'Your suffering will be over in a moment.'

He pulled the trigger and felt the small body convulse once and lie still. Words came unbidden to his lips. 'Dear God, gentle Jesus, who wipes away all tears from our eyes, take her and be merciful to her.'

He got to his feet and looked round. Max was vomiting against the wall a few feet away. Tom waited until the paroxysm had passed and then said,

'We can't leave her like this, but we've nothing to dig a grave with. Help me.'

He began pulling loose stones from the wall and piling them round the child's body. After a moment Max joined him and together they created a rough cairn, which covered her from view. Max found a couple of pieces of broken branch from a tree brought down by the bombardment and tied them together with a piece of string from his pocket to form a cross, which he wedged in the top. Then they turned away and trudged on down the road.

It was almost dark by the time they reached the Serbian encampment. A sentry took them to the commanding officer's tent, where they told their story. Max demanded to know who was responsible.

'For the theft of your car? *četniks*, almost certainly. They operate almost without control in this area and your car would be a valuable prize.'

'And for the child?'

'Who can say? Retreating Turks, Albanian irregulars. There have been atrocities on all sides.'

'Not Serbs.'

'No, not Serbs.' He spoke firmly but Tom wondered how he could be so sure.

They were given food and invited to sit round the campfire with the colonel and some of his officers.

Tom could not eat, though he craved drink like a man in the desert. He had not stopped shivering since they found the child but his face burned and his head was swimming.

'Tom,' Max said, 'I admire what you did today. I couldn't have done it myself. How come you were able to?'

'I suppose,' Tom said through chattering teeth, 'it comes from having what you called "a privileged upbringing".'

He put down his mug, felt himself sway and lost consciousness.

Chapter 9

Luke Pavel swore as the ox-cart in which he was riding lurched into a pothole and the wounded man behind him moaned in pain. It was two and a half days since the train of carts carrying the wounded had left Chataldzha and they would be lucky to reach Lozengrad before dark the day after tomorrow. By that time, the man would probably be dead, along with several others. Now they were stuck again. Luke had lost count of how many times he had made the journey now, but each time the road seemed to be worse and the weather colder. He swung himself down and joined the driver, who was tugging at the heads of the oxen and yelling encouragement to them as they strained to drag the cart out of the mire. Eventually the cart jolted free and they plodded onwards. Luke climbed aboard again and looked back along the line – twelve carts, each with its cargo of wounded. There should, he thought for the hundredth time, be a better and faster way of moving them.

The driver gave a shout and pointed ahead with his ox-goad. They were approaching a junction with the road from Adrianople and far away in that direction Luke could dimly make out a cluster of moving figures. The air was heavy with moisture and the distances were shrouded in mist, making it difficult to see how many there were. He reached under his seat for his rifle.

'*Četniks*?'

The driver shrugged. 'Maybe. Probably not.'

Three mounted figures detached themselves from the group and cantered towards them and as they drew closer Luke was relieved to see that they were in Bulgarian uniform. The ox driver called to his team and they stood still.

The leading rider called out, 'Are you bound for Lozengrad?'

'Yes,' Luke shouted in reply, but his eyes were not on the rider. Behind him, out of the mist, appeared a motor car, so caked in mud that it was impossible to make out its type or colour, but a rare enough sight to suggest that it carried someone extremely important.

The rider drew rein beside them. 'My name is Lieutenant Radic. And you are?'

'Lucas Pavlovitch.' Luke used the name his father had born with, before his grandfather anglicised it. 'I'm a medical orderly, in charge of this convoy of wounded.'

'And I am charged with escorting two important guests to Lozengrad but I am anxious to get back to my unit at Adrianople. If you are going there perhaps I can leave them with you?'

The car had stopped a few yards away, and Luke's reply died in his throat as the occupants descended. A general or a visiting dignitary would have been surprising enough, but two women …! Two young women, moreover. He heard the driver beside him grunt as if he had received a blow in the stomach.

The lieutenant was saying, 'These are two ladies who have volunteered to nurse our wounded. They are going to join some others, who we believe are in Lozengrad. Do you know anything about them?'

Luke forced himself to concentrate. 'Yes, there is a new hospital run by women.'

The lieutenant looked relieved. 'Then that must be it.' He turned to the women, who had arrived at his side, and said something in a language Luke did not understand. They both nodded and one of them, the dark-haired one, smiled up at him and said something else, in the same language. Nonplussed, he jumped down from the cart and replied in Bulgarian.

'Sorry, I don't understand.' Then, seeing the look of incomprehension on her face, he reverted to his native tongue. 'Look, I'm sorry. I speak Bulgarian and English, but nothing else.'

Her companion, a tall, chestnut-haired girl who had her arm in a sling, had come to stand beside her and he saw a look of amazement on both their faces.

'You're English!' the second girl exclaimed incredulously. 'So are we!'

'No, I'm a New Zealander,' he corrected. 'But what the heck are two English girls doing in this godforsaken neck of the woods?'

They both started to laugh and the dark one said, 'Oh, it's a long story. Anyway, we could ask the same thing. What's a New Zealander doing here?'

The lieutenant broke in and said something in what Luke assumed was German and a short conversation ensued between him and the two women. Then he turned to Luke and said in his own language, 'You seem to be a compatriot of these ladies. Can I safely leave them in your care?'

Luke nodded. He spoke Bulgarian fluently but he did not feel equal to explaining the difference between a New Zealander and an Englishman. 'Is that OK with you?' he asked the women and it seemed they were both happy to agree. After a few more words of farewell and thanks Radic remounted and saluted, then turned away and trotted back towards Adrianople, with his two troopers following and the men who had been riding on the running boards of the car jogging behind him.

The dark-haired girl turned to Luke and offered her hand. 'We haven't been introduced. I'm Victoria Langford and this is Leonora Malham Brown.'

'Luke Pavel,' he answered, shaking hands with both of them. Suddenly he felt tongue-tied. His experience of women, other than his mother and his sisters, was limited and certainly did not encompass the social niceties he assumed would be expected by English ladies. He rubbed a hand through the two-week growth of beard on his chin, uncomfortably aware that he had not bathed for the same length of time. That did not, however, seem to worry them. They both began speaking at once.

'I can't believe we've actually met another Englishman – well, someone who speaks English. How on earth did you get here?'

'Have you been to Lozengrad? Is it true that there are English nurses there?'

They were interrupted by the ox driver, who waved his goad in the direction of the man in the cart and the line of similar carts behind them and demanded to know if they were going to stand around talking until the patients were all dead.

'What did he say?' Victoria asked.

'Look, I'm sorry,' Luke said. 'We have to move on. These carts are full of wounded. There's a man here who probably won't make it as far as Lozengrad, but we have to try.'

'How long will it take you to get there?' the one called Leonora asked.

'Two days, if we're lucky. Could be more.'

'That's terrible! How long ago did you leave?'

'Day before yesterday. It's a five- or six-day trek in these things.' He indicated the ox-carts.

'Good Lord! That's ridiculous.' Leonora looked at her companion. 'Vita, can't we take him in the car?'

'Of course we can,' the dark-haired girl responded. 'What is the road like from here?'

'Much the same,' Luke said. 'You might make better time in the car, but you'd need someone to push you out of the mud when you get stuck.'

The girls looked at each other. 'There isn't enough room for a wounded man and both of us, and someone to push,' Leonora said. 'And I'm not much good to you in that department at the moment.' She indicated the sling on her arm.

'What happened?' Luke asked.

'Nothing serious. Sparky back-fired when I was cranking him – Sparky's Victoria's car. It's just a sprain, but for the time being this arm is pretty useless. Look, why don't you go with Vita and the wounded man in the car and I'll come along with the rest.'

'I can't leave you here on your own,' Victoria protested.

'Yes, you can. I'll be perfectly safe, won't I, Luke?'

Luke hesitated. The driver shouted again. 'This man's in a bad way. Let's get on.'

Luke made up his mind. 'Yes, you'll be safe enough. I'd trust these men with my life. If you're sure you can cope ...'

'Of course I can. Now, let's get my things out of the car and put your wounded man in.'

In a matter of minutes Leonora had hauled her bag out of the back seat and Luke and the driver had lifted the wounded man down from the wagon. He had lost one foot and his leg was swathed in filthy bandages.

Victoria put her hand to her nose. 'What is that smell?'

Luke looked at her. 'It's easy to see you haven't had much experience of battlefield casualties. That's gangrene. And if we don't get this guy to a hospital where they can amputate his leg pretty soon it'll kill him.'

They propped the man up in the back seat of the car and covered him with a blanket.

'Wait!' Leonora said. 'We have morphine lozenges in our First Aid kits. Hold on a minute.'

She hunted in her bag and produced a packet wrapped in oilskin. Taking a lozenge from it she leaned into the car and held it to the wounded man's lips. 'What is his name?

'Milan.'

'Suck this, Milan.' She made sucking sounds with her tongue. 'Good! *Dobro! Dobro!*' The man opened his mouth and she popped the lozenge in. Then she straightened up and turned to Victoria 'Off you go. Good luck.'

Victoria put her arms round Leo. 'I hate leaving you here alone.'

'I'm not alone. I'll be fine. I'll see you in a couple of days. Now, get going.'

They watched Leonora climb up onto the leading wagon, then Luke got into the car and Victoria cranked the engine. The motor coughed into life and they were away, skidding and bouncing over the uneven surface.

For a while they drove in silence, while Luke cursed his inability to make small talk. Victoria apparently had no such inhibitions.

'Well, come on,' Victoria said. 'I'm dying to know what a New Zealander is doing with the Bulgarian army.'

'No more than I am, to know what two English ladies are doing this close to the front line,' he responded.

'You first,' she commanded.

'OK. It's pretty simple, really. I'm a Kiwi, born and bred, but my grandparents were from Thrace. My granddad had a small holding in a village called Polia, near Komotini – that's not very far from here. He had vines and olives, and grew melons and vegetables, and he and Grandma had a pretty good life, until the local Turkish landlord took a fancy to Granddad's land. He trumped up a charge, saying that Granddad owed him money and accusing him of encouraging the locals to rebel against the Turkish governor. The land was confiscated and my grandparents were forced to take the first ship they could get out of Alexandroupolis. They really wanted to get to America but they called in at Wellington on the way and decided to stay. I grew up hearing Grandma's stories of life here and the injustice they suffered at the hands of the Turks, so when I heard the Bulgars were aiming to drive the Turks out I felt I ought to come and give them a hand.'

'What did your parents think about that?'

'My dad really needs me to help out on the farm. But he's grown up listening to Grandma, too, so I think he felt it was, kind of, a family obligation. My mum wasn't too keen, though.'

'I bet! Is she from this part of the world, too?'

'No, she isn't. But she comes from an immigrant family, like us, only her forbears were Scottish. Guess that makes me a bit of a mongrel.'

'Best kind of breed,' Victoria said. 'Healthier and more intelligent than purebred dogs. So, you came to help out. What as? You're not in uniform.'

'No.' He shifted awkwardly in his seat. 'It's not for want of trying. I volunteered but I was told that only Bulgarian nationals are accepted into the armed forces. Apparently being two generations removed doesn't count. So I offered myself as a stretcher bearer. I've been taking convoys from Chataldzha to Lozengrad ever since.'

'That's funny,' she said. 'It's what we've come here to do, as well.'

He listened in amazement as she explained about her training with the FANYs, though he had to suppress a snigger when she pronounced the name. Surprise turned to admiration as she described the journey she and Leonora had made.

'Anyway,' she finished, 'it looks as if we are finally going to catch up with Mrs Stobart and her group, so we can start doing what we trained for – except that I expected to be nearer the fighting. Why isn't there a hospital closer to the front?'

He shrugged. 'Search me. I guess you'd have to ask the High Command that question.'

They drove for a while in silence. The morphia lozenge had done its work and the man in the back seat was sleeping. Victoria was concentrating on the road and he admired the skill with which she negotiated the ruts and potholes. After a bit she said, 'So your family is settled in New Zealand?'

'Oh yes. The country has been good to us. Granddad started out working on someone else's farm but he saved until he could buy a few acres of his own in the Wairarapa valley. That's just a bit north-east of Wellington. It was virgin bush when he bought it, but he saw that it was good agricultural land. He worked hard to clear it and planted fruit and vegetables to sell in the local town. Every year he bought a bit more land and cleared it and when my dad took over he expanded it still further. So now we have five hundred acres, dairy cattle, and we're starting to plant vines. My dad reckons one day New Zealand will produce wines as good as anything they make in France. We have horses, too. That's my particular interest.'

'Riding or breeding?'

'Both. There's a race track not far away at Tauherenikau and I've had one or two good wins there, but I'd like to extend my range. You know, get into the big time. I dream of breeding a horse that'll win your Epsom Derby.'

She laughed. He liked the way she tossed her head back when something amused her. 'You'll get on well with Leo. She's a brilliant horsewoman. Personally I prefer cars.' After a moment she glanced sideways at him and said, 'You don't look Bulgarian.'

'What do you mean?'

'Well, most Bulgarians are dark, aren't they?'

'But I'm not an ethnic Bulgarian. I'm Thracian. We've lived alongside the Bulgars and the Pomaks and all the others in this melting pot but according to my granddad the original Thracians came from somewhere further north and east, the Carpathians probably, and a lot of them were fair or had red hair and grey eyes.'

'Like you.'

'Yes, a lot like me, I imagine.'

She grinned. 'I bet you were called "carrots" or "ginger" at school.'

He laughed in return. There was something straightforward in her manner, without any trace of flirtatiousness, which made him feel at ease. 'Yes, sometimes. But nobody ever did it twice.'

She flashed him a merry sideways look. 'I'll remember that.'

The road here was a little better than the one from Adrianople, but even so Luke had to get out several times to extricate the car from the mud. In spite of this, they reached Lozengrad as it was getting dark and Luke directed her to the Bulgarian Red Cross hospital on the outskirts. By this time the wounded man on the back seat was awake and moaning with pain but at the hospital they were greeted with the news that every bed was occupied and the surgeons could take no more cases that day.

'OK, we'll try the hospital run by the English ladies,' Luke said. 'They have doctors, and surgeons – women surgeons but they seem to know what they are doing. We'll take him there.'

The car bounced and skidded through the narrow streets, over cobbles covered in mud, until they turned at last into a wider road where the houses were larger and set farther apart. Luke instructed Victoria to draw up outside one of them, which had clearly been a Turkish residence judging from the harem grills over the windows and the crescent above the door. As they came to a standstill two women in linen dresses with white aprons and caps came down the steps carrying a stretcher. Victoria jumped down and spread her arms ecstatically.

'Are you Stobart's lot?'

The two came to an abrupt halt and stared at her. Then one said, 'We are members of the Women's Sick and Wounded Convoy and Mrs Stobart is our commanding officer. Who are you?'

Victoria thrust out a hand. 'Ensign Langford, FANY, come to volunteer. Thank God we've found you at last!'

*

Leo watched the car disappear into the mist with a tremor at the pit of her stomach. She had assured Victoria that she would be perfectly safe and Luke had endorsed that, but now she was painfully aware that she had entrusted herself to a group of unknown men with whom she could hardly communicate. The driver of the ox-cart called to his beasts and they began to plod forwards, and Leo took the opportunity to glance sideways at him. He was a large man, unshaven and wrapped to the nose in a coat of some partly-cured animal skin, which gave off a powerful aroma, with a greasy fur cap pulled down to his eyebrows. She twisted in her seat to look back at the rest of the convoy. All the drivers were similarly dressed and it was impossible to make out any individual faces. She wondered about the wounded men who lay in the carts out of sight and for a moment forgot her own fears in pity for them. As she turned back she was aware that the driver was surreptitiously examining her, as she had been looking at him. Their eyes met and the humour of the situation overcame Leo's nervousness. She grinned and pointed to herself.

'Leo.' Over the last two days she had made a point of starting to learn Bulgarian and had found a willing teacher in Georgi Radic. She had a natural ability for languages and had already picked up a number of useful phrases. 'My name is Leo,' she repeated in Bulgarian.

His face, which was lined and seamed with dirt, cracked open in a grin, revealing broken, brown teeth. 'Bogdan! I am Bogdan.'

From then on they conversed in broken fragments, often laughing uproariously at their misunderstandings, and Leo's command of the language grew. The oxen plodded onwards, and from time to time one of the carts stuck in the mud and the men had to descend and pull and push it free. Progress was painfully slow, and Leo reckoned that they were averaging scarcely more than two kilometres in every hour. She began to understand how it was that the journey from the front line to the hospitals could take so long.

When the winter evening drew in they made camp on a slight rise that had the advantage of being marginally drier than the road and Leo was handed down from the cart with as much ceremony as a princess arriving at a ball. The oxen were out-spanned and given hay and water and there was no shortage of wood for a fire as here, as elsewhere, the progress of the fighting had brought down trees and left the landscape littered with broken branches. Soon water was boiling for coffee and the carcase of some creature that Leo took to be a goat was turning on an improvised spit.

One of the drivers came over to Bogdan and spoke urgently for a moment and the big driver turned to Leo.

'Wounded man very ill – over there. You help him?'

Leo was immediately overcome with shame. She had been warming herself at the fire and had completely forgotten that she was supposed to be here on a mission of mercy. She collected her First Aid kit and followed the driver to the cart he indicated. As they approached she felt sick with apprehension at what she might find. She knew so little, and could do so little, yet she sensed that great things were expected of her. The man was lying on a bed of straw in the bottom of the cart. There was no sign of any injury but he was obviously in the grip of a high fever, tossing and twisting and muttering to himself. Leo searched in her bag and found several sachets of aspirin powder.

She pointed to a tin mug hanging on a hook on the side of the cart and then to the cauldron of water over the fire. Bogdan nodded and went off with the mug, returning in a moment with the boiling water. Leo held it until it had cooled sufficiently and then tipped the powder into it and, with some difficulty, persuaded the patient to drink it. In mime she indicated that he should be kept warm and given water as often as possible.

Climbing down from the cart she found Bogdan waiting for her. 'I suppose I had better see if I can do anything for the others,' she said, and when his brow wrinkled with incomprehension she gestured towards the other wagons.

There were twenty of them, lying two to a cart. Several had bullet wounds, one had a broken leg which had been roughly bound with a splint, another had had a hand blown off by a grenade and the rest had been slashed by bayonets. Leo was thankful for the brief experience she'd had of dressing real wounds in the hospital tent at Adrianople but as she worked she could not help remembering an exercise at FANY camp before the war, when she had struggled to bandage the imaginary wounds of a soldier who was rather drunk and determined not to co-operate. It had been less than six months ago but it seemed now to belong to a different existence. She did what she could, changing dressings and administering the last of her precious morphine lozenges, and by the time she had finished the meal was ready.

There was no singing that night. As soon as they had eaten the men wrapped themselves in their blankets and prepared to sleep. Leo remembered with regret that her warm sleeping bag had gone in the car with Victoria but Bogdan led her back to his cart and indicated that she should climb in. On the bottom was a thick layer of clean hay and a blanket. She guessed that the hay should have been fed to some of the oxen but at that moment she felt her need was greater than theirs. She thanked him, lay down, pulled the blanket over her and slept almost at once.

The camp was astir with the dawn and, while the water boiled for more of the thick, sweet coffee that seemed to form an essential part of the diet, Leo made the rounds of her patients. The feverish man was quiet and awake, and meekly swallowed another bitter draft of aspirin powder, and the rest greeted her with husky whispers of gratitude for the 'magic pills' that had given them a few blessed hours of relief from pain. As soon as the coffee had been drunk, the oxen were in-spanned and the convoy proceeded on its way. Leo swung herself up beside Bogdan and pointed ahead.

'Lozengrad? Today?'

He shrugged. 'The Turks say ...'

'*Insh'allah*,' Leo finished for him. It was an expression she had grown up with. 'God willing.'

The hours passed. They plodded through deserted villages where only half-starved dogs and cats roamed, and sometimes the ground was strewn with the debris of battle – cartridge cases, shrapnel pieces, scraps of clothing – and the bodies of men and horses. The first time they encountered this Leo turned her horrified gaze to Bogdan.

'Why doesn't somebody bury them?'

He looked at her and shrugged. 'Who?'

There was no stop at midday, but Bogdan reached under the seat and pulled out some hard, dry bread and a flask containing a clear liquid, which caught at Leo's throat and made her cough.

'Rakia!' he said. '*Dobro!*'

The second sip revealed a pleasant hint of muscatel and sent a warm feeling through her stomach. They jogged on, taking alternate slugs from the flask and gnawing at the hard bread.

If only Grandma could see me now! Leo thought, and immediately felt a pang of guilt. There had been no opportunity to write to her, or to Ralph, and she knew they must be frantic with worry. She resolved to write as soon as she had a chance. But there was nothing she could do at that moment ... The swaying of the oxen's heads took on a hypnotic rhythm and her eyelids began to droop and she drifted into a doze, which lasted until Bogdan nudged her and pointed ahead with his ox-goad.

'Lozengrad!'

Leo jerked upright and peered forward. The rain had stopped at last and the western sky was smouldering with the sunset. There, a few miles ahead, were the walls and towers of a city – a city which, she had learned from Radic, had been one of four great fortresses guarding the approach to Constantinople and which should have been as impregnable as Adrianople. She expected to see signs of a great battle, but the land here seemed undisturbed. Vineyards stretched away on either side of the road, the vines blackened by winter frosts but undamaged and the city itself, as they drew closer, seemed intact.

Now that it was within sight, the last few miles seemed longer than ever, but as they approached the gate Leo gave a cry of delight as a car appeared and sped towards them. Minutes later she was hugging Victoria.

'You're here at last! Thank God!' her friend exclaimed. 'I'm so glad to see you. Are you all right? I've been frantic with worry. After what we saw on the way here … I kept imagining all sorts of terrible things. I should never have forgiven myself for leaving you if anything had happened.'

'I'm fine,' Leo assured her, squeezing her shoulders. 'I've been treated like royalty. How about you? Did Milan make it?'

'Yes, he did. They had to amputate his leg, of course, but he's recovering. The doctors said if we hadn't picked him up he would probably have been dead by the time he got here.'

'We did the right thing, then,' Leo said. 'Oh, this is Bogdan. He's been looking after me.'

The ox-driver raised his goad in greeting and Victoria waved in return. Then she said, 'You're to bring your patients to our hospital. The Red Cross one is full to bursting. Come on, I'll show you the way.'

They drove slowly, to allow the ox-carts to keep up with them, which gave Leo a chance to examine the buildings as they passed. She remarked on the lack of damage.

'I know,' Victoria replied. 'I was puzzled by that. Apparently the Turks abandoned it without a fight. According to Luke, Sultan Abdulhamid refused to pay for the defences of the city to be strengthened so the main line of defence was outside to the north, at a place they call Fort Bulgaria. The Bulgars came down out of the mountains expecting a big battle but when they woke up the next morning the Turkish trenches were empty and the whole army had decamped. They were able to walk into the city without firing a shot.'

Victoria drew up outside a large house where a group of nurses was waiting with stretchers. As soon as the ox-carts came to a standstill they climbed into them and the wounded men were lifted down and carried up the steps to the front door, where a tall, middle-aged lady with fine features and an air of innate authority was waiting. She spoke briefly to each stretcher party, assessing the condition of the patient, and then they were carried inside, all except for the man with the broken leg, who was directed across the road to the house opposite.

'Where is he being taken?' Leo asked.

'That's where the operating theatre is. They are probably going to deal with him straight away,' Victoria said. 'Come on. I'll introduce you.'

She led Leo to the woman at the door. 'Mrs Stobart, may I present Leonora Malham Brown? Leo, this is Mabel St Clair Stobart, the commandant.'

Stobart extended her hand. 'I'm very glad to see you here safely. I gather from Langford here that you have had quite an eventful journey.'

'Yes, you could say that,' Leo agreed. 'I'm just sorry we couldn't get here sooner.'

'It's very brave of you to come at all,' Stobart responded. 'And we shall be glad to have you. We haven't been here very long ourselves. There doesn't seem to be any way of getting to Lozengrad quickly. Now, you must excuse me. There are wounded to be dealt with, as you realise. Langford will show you round.'

'Our sleeping house is round the corner,' Victoria said. 'I'll take you there first so you can dump your bag and tidy up, then I'll show you the hospital proper. It's amazing what they have managed to do in such a short time.'

The ox-carts had lumbered away but as they turned back to the street a voice hailed them in English. 'Hey, wait up a minute.'

For a moment Leo did not recognise the lanky figure coming towards them, until Victoria said, 'Oh good, here's Luke.'

He had shaved his beard and shed the enveloping sheepskin coat, which seemed to be the uniform of all the ox-drivers, to reveal well-worn breeches and a leather jerkin.

'Good to see you, Leonora,' he said, pulling off his cap. 'Oh, is it all right for me to call you Leonora?'

'Of course it is,' she replied. There was something in his open, boyish face that made any form of formality seem ridiculous. 'Except I'd prefer just Leo.'

'Leo it is, then,' he said, shaking her hand. Then, looking at Victoria, 'See, I told you she'd be fine. Bogdan's been singing your praises. He reckons you're an angel of mercy.'

Leo felt herself blush. 'I just did what I could and handed out some morphine lozenges. It wasn't much.'

'It meant a lot to those men,' he assured her.

'Shouldn't there be a doctor or at least a nurse travelling with them?' Leo asked.

'There should,' he said, 'but there just aren't enough to man the hospitals, without sending them off on a ten-day round trip. What these men suffer is criminal but no one seems to be able to think of a better system.'

Leo caught Victoria's eye and knew that the same thought was going through both their minds, but she decided not to bring it up for the moment.

Victoria said, 'I'm just going to show Leo around, Luke. Will you be here later?'

'Sure,' he answered. 'I'll drop by to say goodbye this evening.'

'You're leaving?'

'Crack of dawn tomorrow, back to Chataldzha with supplies, but I'll be back again in ten or twelve days with another convoy.'

'Well, we'll see you before you go.'

'Of course.' He smiled. Leo looked from him to her and saw something in Victoria's face that she had not seen before.

Luke pulled his cap on and gave a mock salute. 'See you later.'

As he walked away Leo said, 'That's quite a trans-formation. He's a good-looking chap, under all that hair. You two seem to have got on very well.'

Victoria twitched her shoulders. 'You know what they say – "adversity makes strange bedfellows".' She reddened suddenly. 'If you see what I mean.'

'Oh, I see,' Leo replied, grinning. 'By the way, did you ever find out how he comes to be here?'

'Yes. I'll explain as we go. Come on.'

Chapter 10

The hospital was, as Victoria had said, a remarkable achievement by a remarkable group of women. There were sixteen of them altogether including three doctors, two nursing sisters, four trained nurses and six general duties staff, including Mrs Godfray, the chief cook.

They had taken over four houses in the same road. In the main building the ground floor was given over to out-patients and general administration. On the first floor, which was reached by a curving staircase that made carrying stretchers extremely difficult, there was a wide corridor which was lined with beds and four large rooms which also served as wards. That evening every bed was full and some of the less severely wounded men were lying on straw-filled mattresses on the floor. On the opposite side of the street there were more wards and a large, well-lit room, which was equipped as an operating theatre.

Meals for the staff were taken in a small room on the ground floor, and Leo's first impression of this was the pervading smell of sewage. She soon discovered the reason. The plumbing and sanitary arrangements in the house were rudimentary and the effluent all collected in a cesspit located immediately below the window.

The nurses' sleeping accommodation, in the house to which Victoria took her first, was the least well furnished, consisting of several rooms completely bare of anything except iron bedsteads on which were laid straw palliasses. Water had to be drawn from a pump in the yard and was so cold that it made Leo gasp. She was glad to see her warm sleeping bag on one of the beds but Victoria warned her dryly not to get too excited.

'The bed is yours for the night, but in the morning when the night staff come off duty, someone else will take it over. And don't leave any of your things lying about or they won't be there in the morning.'

'Why? You surely don't mean that one of the women is light-fingered.'

Victoria chuckled grimly. 'Of course not. But the local rats have no such moral inhibitions. They'll make off with anything, I'm told.'

'Rats!' Leo shuddered. 'Do you mean in here?'

'We should think ourselves lucky. Most of them have been got rid of but apparently when the girls first moved in the place was overrun with them. They used to run across people's faces in the middle of the night.'

'Oh, how horrible!'

That night, although she was almost too tired to stand, Leo could not sleep for a long time, jolted awake by every rustle of straw as one of the other occupants of the room turned over. But eventually exhaustion overcame fear and she slept like a child.

At six-thirty the next morning she was woken and given a linen dress like those worn by the others, with a white cap and apron. Properly dressed, she reported for duty along with Victoria. She had seen horrors at Adrianople and had struggled unaided on the road from Chataldzha; but she realised by the end of that day that she had never worked at full stretch until then. With almost a hundred patients to care for, the work of washing, feeding and changing dressings was unending but, in compensation, there was the obvious gratitude of the men. They arrived filthy and starving, with their dressings stuck to their wounds so that they had to be sponged off, and within the hour they had been washed, fed and clothed in clean nightshirts and drawers and settled into bed under sheets and blankets.

'Do they ever object to being treated by women?' Leo asked Mabel Stobart.

'Never,' was the reply. 'Instead they tell everyone how much gentler and kinder we are than the men.'

On the first evening, Mabel Stobart asked Leo to come to her office.

'Sit down, my dear,' she began. 'Now, how old are you?'

'Nineteen, ma'am.'

'I see. So you are not "of age".'

'Not quite.'

'I presume that your parents know where you are and have given their permission?'

'My parents are both dead,' Leo hedged.

'So who is your legal guardian?'

'My grandma.'

'And she has given her permission?'

Leo considered saying yes, but Mabel Stobart was not a woman to whom you told lies. 'No. I didn't tell her because I knew she would have prevented me from coming.'

Stobart regarded her thoughtfully for a moment. Then she said, 'Well, I have defied authority myself in the cause of freedom, so I cannot lecture you on the subject. And it is not practical for me to send you home unaccompanied. So you may stay. Have you written to your grandma to tell her where you are and that you are safe?'

Leo blushed. 'No. There doesn't seem to have been an opportunity.'

'Don't you think you should write now?'

'I suppose I should. But is there any way to post it?'

'Don't worry about that. The British military attaché is a good friend of ours. He will see that it gets to Sophia and is posted there. Now, no time like the present. Do you have pen and paper?'

'No, I'm afraid I haven't.'

Stobart opened a drawer and took out writing materials. 'I am going on my rounds. I shall be gone for about half an hour. You can use my desk while I am away.'

When the door closed behind her Leo sat at the desk staring at the blank sheet of paper for some time. Finally she wrote:

Lozengrad,
Nov 23rd (I think)

Dear Grandma,

I know you must be very angry with me for leaving home without telling you, but I was sure that if I told you what I intended to do you would try to stop me.

I felt, and feel, very strongly that what I am doing is right and is my duty. Women must show that they have the ability and courage and strength of purpose to be regarded on an equal footing with men.

I have joined The Women's Sick and Wounded Convoy, which is commanded by Mrs Mabel St Clair Stobart. She has set up a hospital in Lozengrad, which is the place where wounded men are sent from the front at Chataldzha. The hospital is entirely staffed and run by women, including the doctors and surgeons, and they are doing a wonderful job. The men arrive in such a terrible condition and it is amazing to see how quickly they respond to the care they receive here. I am very proud to be able to play a small part in this.

I am safe and well, so please don't worry about me, and please try to forgive me for the anxiety I must have caused you.

Give my love to Ralph.

Your affectionate granddaughter,
Leonora

There was no doubt in Leo's mind that the motor power behind the organisation of the hospital was Stobart herself. Indefatigable and always cheerful, she faced even the most intractable problems with optimism. Over the next weeks Leo often saw her faced with blank obstinacy or sullen indifference from local officials or craftsmen. *'Nema'* ('there isn't any') was a regular refrain, but Stobart would never take no for an answer and sooner or later the required equipment or stores would appear.

'How is it,' Leo asked her one day, 'that no matter how impossible things seem, you always manage to find a solution?'

Stobart smiled. 'I am firmly of the opinion that, if your motives are good, miracles occur just when you most need them.'

Luke departed on the morning after Leo's arrival, as expected, but five days later a second column of ox-carts arrived, carrying another twenty-five wounded men. Three had died on the journey, from exposure and loss of blood, and the news reminded Leo of the thought that had occurred to her earlier. She consulted Victoria and the following morning they requested a few moments of Mabel Stobart's time.

'We feel it's all wrong that men should die like that when my car is here and could be used to transport them,' Victoria began. 'We would like to suggest that we operate a kind of shuttle service, and bring the most seriously wounded back from the battlefront.'

Stobart gave her a searching look. 'Just how do you see this working? You would have to have at least one man with you, to help push the car when it gets stuck. And anyway, I couldn't send two young women on that journey on their own. Your car will hold how many? Four at the maximum. That means that you would only have room for one patient, even if he was able to sit up for the journey.'

'We've thought about that,' Leo said. 'If we wait until Luke gets here with the next convoy, he could come with us on the way back. Then I would stay at Chataldzha to help give First Aid on the spot, and that would leave two places in the car – or enough room for one man lying on the back seat.'

'You would stay there, on your own?'

'I wouldn't be on my own, would I? There is a First Aid post, and someone must dress the wounds before the men are sent here. I could help with that.'

'I'm not sure that I could agree to a single woman being left alone with all those men.'

Leo took a deep breath. 'Mrs Stobart, I'm sure there must have been times when you have had to cope with being the only woman around. Everyone respects you. I'm sure no one would harm me if they know I am under your protection.'

'And we would take it in turns,' Victoria said. 'On one journey I would drive back, and the next time Leo would and I would stay behind. And we had another idea, though I don't know if it is practical. When we arrived, the tent and other equipment we were given at Adrianople were strapped on top of the trunk behind the car. It occurs to us that it might be possible to make some kind of fixing that would allow a stretcher to be attached there instead. Then we could bring up to three patients. I know that the man on the stretcher would be exposed to the elements, but he could be well wrapped in blankets and then covered with an oilskin to keep out the wet, and at least it would only be a matter of hours, rather than days.'

'We could drive back here in a day, at the most,' Leo put in. 'That means we could bring back two or three men every other day.'

Stobart considered in silence for a moment. Then she said. 'Let us see if it is possible to attach a stretcher, as you suggest. I will talk to the local blacksmith and see what he can do. It may result in some considerable damage to your car, of course.'

'That doesn't matter,' Victoria said. 'But there is another problem. We shall need petrol. We filled up in Marseilles and of course we didn't use any getting to Adrianople but the drive here used up the best part of a tank. We have a few cans for emergencies but they won't be enough for the sort of journeys we are talking about.'

'Ah, now that may call for a miracle,' Stobart said with a grim smile. 'But we shall see what can be done.'

The blacksmith greeted the idea for the stretcher carrier with the pessimism they had come to expect. It was impossible, it could not be done. But Stobart was not to be put off, and after she and Victoria had spent most of a morning suggesting possible solutions he finally agreed to try. By the time the next convoy arrived, with Luke on the leading wagon, two sturdy brackets had been bolted onto the rear of the car, to which a stretcher could be fixed with leather straps. Luke, when faced with the idea, screwed up his face for a moment and then grinned.

'Yeah, why not? It's got to be worth a try.'

The petrol, too, was obtained more easily than they expected. The commandant of the Bulgarian Red Cross unit revealed that he had been given a store of it, in the expectation that vehicles to use it would follow later. These vehicles had never materialised, so he was happy to hand over whatever was necessary for their mission.

The next morning, the three of them set off back towards the front line. Victoria drove and Leo, in deference to Luke's long legs, let him sit beside her. It was difficult, in this position, to join in the conversation above the noise of the engine but she watched their expressions as they turned their heads to speak to each other and had an uneasy sense of exclusion. There was something in the way they looked that seemed familiar but it was not until they were half way along that she remembered why. It was the way Ralph and Tom looked at each other, when they thought no one was watching.

The weather had turned colder and the ground was partially frozen. There were still deep ruts made by the ox-carts but the car, being smaller and lighter, was able to avoid them and keep to the firmer ground. They made good time and reached the first lines of tents soon after midday. All the way the sound of the guns had grown louder and, as they approached, Luke pointed ahead to where a series of forts stood along the skyline.

'That's it. Chataldzha. The last line of defence before Constantinople.'

Between them and the forts was line after line of trenches, and behind them the gun emplacements belching flames and smoke. At frequent intervals they saw an answering puff of smoke from one of the forts and a fountain of earth sprang up as the shell hit the ground. Leo felt as if the noise was a physical force beating her about the head and when they got out of the car the ground beneath their feet shook with the explosions. Luke directed them to a large bell tent a little apart from the rest and marked with a red cross. This was the dressing station to which the wounded were brought and from where they were dispatched to Lozengrad. Inside there were no beds. The wounded men were lying on the bare ground, while orderlies in blood-spattered aprons moved among them. Luke introduced the two women to the officer in charge, a Captain Kyril Draganoff. He stared at them for a moment, then made the standard response. 'This is no place for women.'

Leo had used the previous weeks to improve her Bulgarian. 'Well, here we are, anyway,' she replied. 'So we may as well make ourselves useful.'

Draganoff looked at her as if he was contemplating putting her on a charge of insubordination, then realised that he had no authority and turned away with a shrug.

Luke said, 'Take no notice. It took him a long time to accept me but he came round in the end. Now, I'll show you my tent. You can have it, Leo, while you are here – or Victoria when it's her turn. I can bunk in with some of the others.'

'I don't like to turn you out,' Leo protested and he grinned.

'It's the only spare space, so it's that or sleep in the open – unless you fancy sharing it with me. But I warn you, it's not very big.'

There was no way of arguing with that.

They had just finished stowing Leo's few belongings into the tent when a stretcher party came up from the trenches carrying a man who was clutching his abdomen. Blood was welling between his fingers. Leo grabbed her First Aid bag and nodded to Victoria.

'Come on. Let's prove that we can be useful.'

They followed the stretcher party into the tent. Draganoff was at the far end and apparently unaware of the new arrival and all the orderlies were occupied.

'Put him down here,' Leo ordered, indicating one of the few empty spaces. The stretcher bearers obeyed and she and Victoria knelt of either side. Leo's hands were shaking as she cut away the tattered uniform. She had learned a great deal in the last few weeks and she was no longer worried about exposing any part of the male anatomy, but this was the first time she had had to deal with an emergency. She was relieved to see that the wound had obviously been made by a bullet. There was a hole from which blood welled in a steady stream but not the terrible ripping wounds that a shell or a grenade would have caused. Further investigation revealed that there was no exit wound.

'The bullet is still in there,' Leo said. 'He needs to get to Lozengrad. The Red Cross hospital has one of those new machines that see through the body – you know, what they call an X-ray machine.'

Luke looked out at the sky. 'There are still several hours of daylight left. If you can patch him up we could take him now. What do you think?'

'Yes,' Victoria said immediately, 'it's the obvious thing to do. He can go on the stretcher carrier. We can still put one or two more inside. Can you manage here, Leo, while I ask the old Dragon over there?'

Leo nodded, busy with pads and bandages, but she stored the appellation away in the back of her mind and from then on she thought of the captain as 'the old dragon'. With Luke's help she managed to staunch the bleeding and gave the man a morphine lozenge. When she looked up, Draganoff was standing nearby watching her.

'So. You are not afraid of the sight of blood?'

'No. I've seen worse sights than this. Are there any other patients that need to be transferred urgently?'

He and Victoria had agreed already that two men, both of whom probably needed a leg or a foot amputated, should go in the car, so very quickly the stretcher was strapped onto the carrier and the other two men carried out and lifted into the car, one on the back seat and the other beside the driver.

'What about you?' Leo asked Luke.

'I can ride on the running board,' he replied. 'If I get tired of hanging on I'll squeeze into the back.'

Victoria cranked the engine and the car spluttered and swayed away in the direction of the road.

'We'll be back tomorrow,' Luke called. 'See you then.'

Leo waved till they reached the road and picked up speed, then turned back to the tent. Draganoff was watching her.

'Your friends have left you behind.'

'Yes. That was always the plan. I will help here, until they return.'

'You came from Lozengrad today?'

'Yes.'

'Have you eaten?'

Leo realised abruptly that she was hungry. 'No – and nor have my friends. They should have waited for some food.'

'Too late now for them,' he said laconically. 'But for you, there is soup left from the men's dinner.'

'Can I wash my hands somewhere?' she asked, indicating the blood which still clung to them. He seemed mildly surprised at this fastidiousness but he showed her a screened off portion of the big tent where there were buckets of icy water. Then he led her to a second tent where some of the orderlies were eating and told her to help herself from a big cauldron. All that was left in the way of meat were a few fatty morsels of some animal Leo could not identify, but the broth was thick and spicy with paprika and she devoured a bowl of it with pleasure. As soon as she had finished, she returned to the main tent and set about making herself as useful as possible, ignoring the curious looks from the men, both orderlies and patients. By the time the evening meal arrived – bread, cheese and hot, sweet black coffee – they had begun to accept her as one of themselves and as they ate she answered their questions. Where had she come from? Why? What was England like? Was it true that the streets of London were paved with gold? Most of them had never been further than their own village until they were called up and it was clear that they had little sense of geography; but Leo found, as she had done ever since she arrived in the country, that they had a natural chivalry and good manners that quickly set her at ease.

Next day, as promised, Victoria and Luke returned and Leo took her turn at driving. She had enjoyed learning to drive in England, but now, as the car skidded and bounced and she wrestled with the wheel, she swore aloud and exclaimed, 'Oh, give me a horse any day!'

Luke chuckled. 'Me, too. But then, I couldn't do what you're doing, or I'd offer to take a turn.'

'You can't drive?'

'Never had the chance to learn. We haven't got any motor vehicles on the farm back home. Plenty of horses, though.'

Three times the car stuck fast and had to be manoeuvred out of the mud and the last time the engine stalled, and for a while Leo was afraid that she would not be able to start it again. Contemplating the possibility of being marooned in the middle of nowhere until the next convoy of ox-carts came along, she realised how unqualified she was for the task in hand. Victoria understood the workings of the internal combustion engine and would almost certainly know how to get the car going again, but she had never taken an interest in what went on under the bonnet. When they finally reached Lozengrad she found herself thinking that she would have preferred to stay in the camp at Chataldzha, however gruesome the conditions. Victoria, on the other hand, greeted them with relief on their return next day, exclaiming, 'This place is terrible! I didn't sleep a wink and the noise of the guns is driving me crazy!' She was only too happy to set off back with Luke and two more patients.

The weather had broken again and the road conditions had deteriorated to such an extent that it was late afternoon the following day before Victoria and Luke returned. With only an hour or two of daylight left it would have been foolish to set off with a new cargo of patients, so it was agreed that they would all stay overnight. Leo was glad to have Victoria's company, even though there was scarcely room for two to sleep in the tent.

As they settled down, Leo said, 'Do you remember what I said that night on the way from Adrianople?'

'What about?'

'You said you thought I was enjoying myself, and I said I was.'

'I remember. What about it?'

'I've realised now what a wicked thing it was to say.'

'How do you mean, wicked?'

'How could anyone enjoy the things we've seen in the last week or two?'

'So, are you telling me you regret coming? Do you want to go home?'

'No! I'd rather be here than anywhere. But not because it's fun, or an adventure. It has made me see that war isn't fun. It isn't glamorous or exciting or heroic. It's just futile and cruel. And when I get back I'm going to tell the people back home that.'

'Including your brother?'

'Especially my brother!'

Next morning Leo made the suggestion that had been in the back of her mind for a couple of days. 'Vita, you don't like being left here, do you? And I'm worried about the driving. If anything went wrong with the car I'd be completely helpless. Why don't you go with Luke and I'll stay on here?'

Victoria looked doubtful. 'It doesn't seem fair. Are you just saying it because I made a fuss the other day?'

'No, not at all. You're a better driver than I am, and I don't mind staying here. And—' with a sly grin '—I don't think Luke will mind.'

Victoria gave the familiar shrug. 'I don't see what it has to do with him. But if you're really sure ...'

'I'm sure.'

So it was decided, and as Leo had guessed, Luke seemed more than happy with the new plan. They collected the three most serious cases and set off.

While the car took those most in need of immediate treatment, the convoys of ox-carts continued to lumber back and forth with the rest and Leo had to help load them. The process almost reduced her to tears. The men were so stoical in the midst of pain; so uncomplaining about the conditions they had to endure, that it made her want to shout with anger on their behalf. She raged futilely against the faceless officials that allowed this state of affairs to continue; at the politicians who sent these men into battle as if they were no more than senseless animals; against the waste and stupidity of war. But there was nothing she could do except wrap her patients as warmly as possible and ensure that they had water to drink on the journey.

The wet weather continued unabated and the ground around the dressing tent, churned up by the ox-carts and by the hooves and droppings of the animals, became a sea of mud and dung. Leo had relinquished her linen dress and white cap and apron and reverted to her FANY uniform of boots and breeches under a divided skirt, but by bedtime the skirt was muddy to the knees and heavy with moisture. There was nowhere in the tent to hang it to dry and when she came to put it on next morning the damp had seeped up to the waist. Leo stood holding it for a moment, looking down at herself. Her boots came to the knee and her tunic ended in mid-thigh. In between all that was visible was a few inches of riding breeches. Surely, she thought, there was nothing indecent about that. She hesitated a moment longer, then threw the wet skirt into a corner and headed for the mess tent and breakfast.

The first person she met was Captain Dragonoff. He looked her up and down for a moment and then grunted, 'I told you this was no place for petticoats.' She was uncomfortably aware of the stares of the other men but none of them commented and before long she was too busy to notice.

Victoria and Luke did not return that evening and Leo tried to calm her anxiety by telling herself that there was probably a simple explanation. Perhaps there had been some problem that had delayed them in Lozengrad. Maybe the road had just become completely impassable due to the weather. It had rained all day and she had been glad of the new freedom of movement that discarding the heavy skirt had given her. It stirred some distant memory that she could not quite put her finger on.

Most of her time was spent in the dressing tent but she was also called upon frequently to help with patients as the stretcher bearers struggled up from the trenches. She had a waterproof cape and her cap, but by the end of the day her hair had come down and hung heavy and damp on her shoulders. At bedtime she tried ineffectually to dry it with an already damp towel and realised that it was not just wet. It was matted with mud and blood and it was impossible to get a comb through it. She had a pair of scissors in her First Aid bag. She found them and sat for a moment, hesitating. Then, seized by a sudden revulsion, she hacked at the lank tresses until she was left with a rough crop about two inches long all over. Shaking her head, she felt a sudden lightness and the memory that had evaded her all day became clear. She grinned to herself as she imagined the reaction of her grandma. She would be scandalised, and so would Ralph. Well, she didn't care. But as an afterthought she gathered up the discarded locks and bound them into a switch with a piece of bandage. After all, she reasoned, she would be going home one day and it could be made into a hairpiece to cover her embarrassment. She ran a comb through what remained of her hair and climbed into her sleeping bag.

Next morning Draganoff looked at her and nodded. 'So, now you understand why this is no place for a woman.' Leo was not sure whether this was a sign of disapproval or the reverse but he said no more so she got on with her work.

She was eager to see how Victoria would react to her transformation, so she was doubly pleased when the car chugged and spluttered into view. Rather than drive through the treacherous mud around the tent Victoria parked on the road and she and Luke climbed out and began to trudge up to where Leo was waiting. They were laughing together at something and when Victoria slipped Luke caught her round the waist and continued to hold onto her rather longer than, in Leo's opinion, was strictly necessary.

'Sorry we didn't get back yesterday,' Victoria called. 'Couldn't get Sparky to start and I had to spend most of the day with my head under the …' Then she took in Leo's changed appearance and her hand went to her mouth. 'Leo! What has happened? Who did that to you?'

'No one did it,' Leo said, laughing. 'I did it myself. I got tired of trying to keep it dry. What do you think?' The two arrivals had reached her by this time and she could see that Victoria was shocked. 'Oh, come on, Vita! You're a progressive woman. I didn't expect you to disapprove.'

'But, Leo, you look like a boy! Honestly, with your hair like that and those breeches, you could be mistaken for one.'

'So what?' Leo asked and turned to Luke to see his reaction.

He was grinning broadly. 'Well, I'm really pleased to meet you, Mr Brown,' he said, extending his hand. 'I used to know your sister slightly, but I guess she's had to leave.'

Leo shook his hand, laughing. 'Oh, she'll be back. I'm just deputising for her till the weather gets better.'

'But don't you feel terribly – exposed?' Victoria asked.

'No, it feels wonderful. It reminds me of when I was much younger. When I used to travel with my father, when I started to – well, grow up – he thought in some places I might be at risk as a girl, so he used to dress me as a boy. I'd forgotten until today how marvellous it feels not to have a skirt dragging round my ankles and all that hair weighing my head down. You should try it, Vita.'

Victoria seemed to have got over her initial shock but nothing would persuade her to follow Leo's example.

By evening, having watched her and Luke together over supper, Leo had graver matters on her mind. When they were both in their sleeping bags she said, 'Vita, are you serious about Luke?'

'I don't know what you mean.'

'Yes, you do. He obviously likes you and you seem to like him. But is it serious?'

'Don't be silly! We get on well together, which is just as well since we have to spend a lot of time in each other's company. What makes you think it's anything more than that?'

'Well, you have to admit it's not usual for a young woman to spend so much time alone with a man.

'Whose fault is that? I thought you were beyond all that Victorian moralising.'

'You're a fine one to talk! Look at the way you reacted to my hair cut.'

'At least I'm not trying to masquerade as a man.'

'Nor am I. And it doesn't matter to me if you and Luke are having an affair ...'

'We are not having an affair!'

'What I'm trying to say is this. I think Luke is sweet on you, and I think he is probably quite naïve about this sort of thing. I mean, I don't know what life is like in New Zealand but I bet he's never met anyone like you before, so don't lead him on. I just don't want him to get the wrong idea. I should hate to see him hurt.'

Victoria was silent for a moment. Then she said, 'I am not leading him on, and anyway it's none of your business. So just leave it, will you?'

She turned her back and shrugged her sleeping bag up round her ears, leaving Leo unhappily aware that she had opened a rift between them that might take some time to heal.

Chapter 11

Over the next days Leo developed a routine. Up at 6.30, breakfast of black, sweet coffee, bread and cheese, or sometimes a kind of porridge, then the day spent in the endless task of dressing wounds and washing and feeding the patients, dinner and then bed. Most of the time she was cold, wet and often hungry, but that was insignificant compared with the suffering all around her. Dragonoff, perhaps because he saw her as more conscientious or more intelligent than the men under his command, or perhaps because she was neater and more nimble-fingered, began to teach her some more advanced techniques, including how to suture a wound. In civilian life he had been, she learned, the doctor in charge of a hospital in Sophia and his dour manner was his defence against the horrors he had to deal with every day.

Victoria and Luke came and went and each time they returned Leo thought she saw signs of greater intimacy between them. Once or twice she tried to tease her friend about it but Victoria always put her off with a shrug or a sarcastic remark. The convoys of ox-carts continued to plod off towards Lozengrad and the places of those who had gone were immediately filled by new casualties. The battle was at a stalemate and no one could see how it would come to an end.

The only unusual occurrence was the arrival of a Turkish prisoner at the dressing tent. He had been caught trying to burrow into one of the Bulgarian saps to lay a mine and in the ensuing fight had received a bayonet wound that had laid his scalp open. No one knew why he had been brought in instead of being dispatched on the spot, which was the usual practice, but there were rumours that he was a spy and was being held for questioning. Casualties had been heavy that day and there was hardly room in the tent for another man, so the stretcher bearers set him down outside while one of them searched for a space. The man was mumbling and protesting in Turkish, convinced that he was about to be killed, and struggling with the remaining bearer in an effort to rise. Leo, hearing the noise, went out to him and stooped beside the stretcher.

'It's all right,' she said in Turkish. 'You're quite safe here. No one is going to harm you. Lie still and

I will fetch some bandages to dress your wound. What is your name?'

'Kemal,' he mumbled.

'Don't be afraid, Kemal. I will be back in a moment.' She nodded to the stretcher bearer. 'It's all right. You can leave him to me.'

The man subsided and she turned away to go back into the tent. As she did so, she heard hoof beats and glanced round to see a company of Serbian cavalry headed by an officer on a magnificent grey horse cantering into the camp. She went into the tent, collected a tray with the necessary equipment and returned to find the Turk staggering to his feet. The cavalry company had halted a short distance away and the officer was leaning down from his saddle to consult a Bulgarian sergeant. Leo's first thought was that the Turk was attempting to run away. Then he raised his arm and something metallic caught the light, and she saw that he had pulled a pistol from the waistband of his baggy trousers and was aiming it at the officer. She was too far away to reach him before he could pull the trigger, so she acted instinctively.

'Kemal!' she shouted in Turkish. 'Look out!'

It was enough to distract him for the crucial second. He swung round, looking for the expected assailant, and before he could recover himself Leo's shoulder hit him in the midriff with all the weight of her body behind it. He collapsed onto the ground with her on top of him. Leo had grown up skirmishing with the local children in the dust of whatever archaeological dig her father had been engaged in and she had learned early to give as good as she got. For a breathless moment they struggled, the Turk trying to throw her off and she trying to seize hold of the arm that held the gun. Then a booted foot was placed on the man's wrist, a pistol was pointed at his head and a strong hand gripped Leo's arm and helped her to rise. A young Serbian lieutenant was grinning down at her.

'Well done, lad! It looks as if you've just saved the colonel's life. You can leave this bastard to me now. The colonel wants to speak to you.'

Leo looked round in a panic to where the officer still sat his horse. Should she explain, tell him who she really was? The lieutenant gave her a friendly shove. 'Go on. He won't eat you.'

She stumbled over to stand by the flank of the grey horse and found herself looking up into the searching dark eyes of Colonel Aleksander Malkovic. For a moment neither of them spoke as Leo cudgelled her brain for words of explanation and excuse. Then he smiled and said, 'Well, boy, it seems I owe you my life. What is your name?'

He had not recognised her. Relief flooded through her. She cleared her throat. The damp weather and the exhaustion of the previous days had roughened her voice and given it a convincing hoarseness. 'Leo, sir. Leo Brown.'

His smile widened. 'Leo? A young lion cub indeed! But you are not Serbian, or Bulgarian. What are you, German?'

'No, sir. English.'

'English! What is an English boy doing here in the middle of all this?' Before Leo could reply he went on, 'This is not the time to talk. You acted very bravely just now and you should be rewarded. Come to my tent before dinner. We will talk then.'

He clicked to his horse and trotted away, followed by the rest of his company. Behind her Leo heard the report of a pistol. She swung round in time to see the lieutenant holstering his weapon. The Turk lay lifeless at his feet.

'There was no need for that,' Leo protested angrily.

The man laughed. 'Don't be so soft! He tried to shoot the colonel. What did he expect – a medal? Anyway, why wasn't he searched before he was left here?' He stooped and took the pistol from the dead man's hand and held it out to Leo. 'Here, you deserve this – trophy of war.'

Leo's first instinct was to refuse, remembering her father's pistol which she kept in her knapsack, but then it occurred to her that any young man would accept the gift with enthusiasm. She took it and muttered her thanks and the lieutenant ran to his horse, vaulted into the saddle and cantered off after his superior officer.

Leo spent the day in a misery of indecision. Should she simply ignore the summons and hope Malkovic would forget about her? But suppose he sent for her? What excuse could she give? Would it be better to make a clean breast of things and try to pass it off as a joke? She imagined herself saying, 'Don't you recognise me? We met at the hotel in Salonika.' But she remembered what Dragitch had said that evening. 'Sasha Malkovic is notorious for his attitude to women at the front. He regards them all as no better than camp followers.' If she revealed herself now, he would be furious with her for deceiving him. He would certainly order her back to Lozengrad. He might even have her arrested and put on a ship back to London. Did he have the authority to do that? Perhaps not, but it was too much to risk. All these questions plagued her as she went about her work but deep down she knew that it did not matter what answer she came to. Nothing would prevent her from seeing Sasha Malkovic again, even if she had to disguise her sex to do it.

When her duties were finished for the day she begged some warm water from one of the cooks and washed herself as best she could. Running a comb through her shorn hair she wished she could see herself, but she had no mirror. Victoria had said she looked like a boy, and the resemblance had been good enough to fool the lieutenant and Malkovic, apparently. She had to rely on that. She was reminded of Shakespeare's *Twelfth Night*. *'What country, friend, is this?' 'This is Illyria, lady.'* Wasn't Illyria supposed to be somewhere in the Balkans?

She was still hesitating when a voice from outside the tent called, 'Brown? Are you in there?' and she went out to find the lieutenant waiting for her. He conducted her through the camp to the colonel's tent, which had been set up a little away from the rest, in the shelter of a ruined building. Malkovic was sitting behind a folding table, studying maps by the light of a hurricane lamp. He looked up when the lieutenant announced her.

'Ah, there you are. Come in. Thank you, Michaelo, you can go.'

The lieutenant saluted and left, dropping the tent flap behind him, and she was alone with the man whom she had disliked on first meeting and whose face had haunted her dreams ever since. He stood up, stretching as if he had spent too long at his desk, and looked down at her. There was a smile at the corner of the arrogant lips and a glint in his eye that she found unsettling. Had he recognised her from the beginning, and was he teasing her now?

'So,' he said, 'my English lion cub. What language shall we converse in? I regret I do not speak English. You speak a little Serbian, obviously.'

'A little,' Leo agreed. 'I speak Bulgarian better.'

He shrugged. 'There is little difference. I think we shall understand each other. Tell me, how old are you?'

She had given that some thought. Too young and he might send her away, too old and the deception would be difficult to sustain. She cleared her throat and dropped her voice to its lowest register. 'Seventeen, sir.'

The glint in his eyes grew to a sparkle of amusement and she knew he had assumed that she would lie about her age. 'If you say so.' He turned away to the table where a bottle of wine stood beside two silver goblets. He filled them and handed one to Leo.

'*Prost!*'

'*Prost!*' she responded and drank. It was the first wine she had tasted for several weeks and as the warmth spread through her belly she began to relax. He indicated a folding chair that stood in front of the desk.

'Sit.'

She sat and he resumed his former place behind the table.

'So,' the dark eyes studied her, 'what brings a young English gentleman to care for wounded Bulgarian soldiers?'

She had thought about this, too, and decided that Luke's story, with suitable alterations, would serve very well. 'My grandparents were from Macedonia, sir. They were driven from their land by the Turks and fled to England. I grew up hearing their story, so when I heard that you and the Bulgars were driving the Turks out of the country I decided to volunteer to help. I wanted to join the army but they told me I was too young. So I volunteered as a medical orderly.'

'And how do you come to speak Turkish?'

This was more difficult but she decided that in this case truth was the best policy. 'My father was very interested in archaeology and he worked for a time helping Herr Dorpfeld at Troy. He took me with him.'

'That is a big leap, for the son of Macedonian peasant farmers,' Malkovic commented.

Leo drew herself up in an attitude of hurt pride that was only partly assumed. 'My grandparents may have been peasants, as you call them, but they were both very intelligent. When they reached England they became prosperous merchants and my father was well educated. He was also a very clever man.'

'You say "was"?'

'He died a few years ago. Both my parents are dead.'

'But your grandparents know you are here and have given their approval?'

'Oh yes!' She was in so deep that one lie more or less seemed unimportant.

Malkovic regarded her broodingly for a moment, then he rose to his feet. 'I promised you a reward. What shall it be?'

'I don't want a reward,' she answered. 'I saw someone's life in danger and I did what I could to save it. That is all.'

'At some risk to yourself,' he said.

She shrugged. 'I didn't stop to think about that.'

He gave her one of his rare smiles. 'So I saw. But courage and self-sacrifice should be rewarded. I won't insult you by offering you money, but perhaps something as a keepsake …?'

He crossed to a chest which stood at the side of the tent and opened it. It took him a few minutes to find what he was looking for. Then he turned towards her and held out a small dagger with a beautifully enamelled hilt. 'It's a toy, of course, not much use in a fight, but it is sharp so have a care.'

She took it from him with a hand that shook slightly. 'It's beautiful. I shall treasure it.' She looked up and met his eyes. 'A keepsake, as you said.'

For a moment his gaze held hers and she saw a small frown form on his brow, as if he was troubled by an elusive memory. It passed in a second and he turned away.

'You can go now. Thank you again for what you did.'

She went to the tent flap but, as she reached it, he said, 'There may be times when I need a Turkish interpreter. I may send for you again.'

Leo caught her breath. 'If there is anything I can do, sir, you have only to ask.'

He nodded dismissal and she went out into the dark.

Leo said nothing about the incident to Victoria and Luke when they returned. She was certain that Victoria would tell her she was mad to think that her deception could go undetected for very long. In her more sober moments she knew that that assessment was probably correct, but common sense was over-ridden by the feeling that she had embarked on an adventure that she must see through to the end. She spent the next two days in a ferment of anticipation, wondering if and when Malkovic would send for her.

Sometimes she asked herself why she was so anxious to see him again. He had behaved rudely when they first met, she reminded herself. He was condescending and arrogant. Yet the very knowledge that he was present in the camp and might send for her at any moment made the air electric with excitement.

The call came on the second afternoon. Leo was busy stitching a bayonet wound in a man's shoulder when she looked up to see the young Lieutenant standing over her.

'The colonel wants you.'

Irritation at the brusqueness of the request kept her excitement under control. 'I'm busy, as you can see. Please tell the colonel that I will come as soon as I have finished here.'

He hesitated, unused to having his superior officer's orders questioned. He looked down at what Leo was doing and she saw him blanch. He said curtly, 'Very well. I will tell him. But he does not like to be kept waiting.'

Leo finished the stitching, applied a dressing and settled her patient as comfortably as was possible in the circumstances. Then she washed her hands and, seeing that Draganoff was occupied, slipped out and headed for the Serbian tents.

She was prepared for Malkovic to be angry with her but in the event he looked up from the maps he was studying and said simply, 'Ah, you're here. Come in. I want you to help me interrogate a prisoner.' He strode to the tent flap and called to someone outside to bring in the prisoner, while Leo grappled with a sudden sense of unease. 'Interrogation' had a brutal sound. Suppose the prisoner had been maltreated, or that she might be expected to witness and condone ill-treatment?

To her relief, when the Turk was brought in, there was no sign that he had been harmed. He was a big man, with a flamboyant moustache and flashing dark eyes. It was apparent from his uniform that he was an officer and he carried himself with a haughty dignity that proclaimed a strong sense of his own importance. Malkovic rose to greet him and the two men saluted each other with formal courtesy.

Malkovic lifted the wine bottle. 'Ask him if he would like a glass of wine.'

The Turk did not need her translation. His head went back and his nostrils flared as if he had been insulted. 'He is a Moslem, sir,' Leo said hastily. 'Alcohol is forbidden by his religion.'

Malkovic struck the heel of his hand against his brow. 'Of course. How foolish of me. Ask him if he would care for a drink of water.'

The offer was accepted, the water brought and the Turk drank thirstily. Malkovic offered him a chair and the interrogation began. He wanted to know which regiment the prisoner belonged to, where they were stationed, what condition they were in. Did they have adequate supplies of ammunition? Where they expecting to be reinforced in the near future? How many of their men had deserted? To every question he received the same response. 'I will tell you nothing.'

Leo translated faithfully, on tenterhooks lest the continued refusal should spark a violent reaction. But Malkovic maintained the same level, courteous tone throughout the interview, though once or twice he sighed and passed a hand wearily over his face. She began to think that he saw the whole conversation as a waste of time. It was a relief when he brought it to an end and told his men to take the prisoner away.

'What will happen to him now?' Leo asked, wondering if he might be passed on to someone less scrupulous in his methods.

'He will be sent back to Lozengrad with the other prisoners, I imagine.' He must have seen the relief on her face because he said, 'You surely did not imagine that I would have him tortured?'

She felt herself blush. 'No, of course not ... except, you hear of terrible things being done in war and ...' Her words petered into silence at the injured look on his face.

'For one thing, he is a fellow officer and as such to be treated with courtesy. Moreover, I judge from his

expression that any attempt to coerce him would be
futile. He is one of those who cannot be browbeaten.
But—' he turned back to the maps on his table '—it
is a pity that I could get nothing out of him. There are
things we need to know, and time is running out. There
are rumours of an armistice, but before that is signed
we must know what the condition of the enemy is. If
he is weak, running out of ammunition, depleted by
sickness or desertion, then it is worth making a final
push which could carry us through to Constantinople;
and we do not want an armistice agreement before
that happens. On the other hand, if he is expecting
to be reinforced and preparing for a counter-attack,
then a quick agreement will allow us to hold on to
gains that we might otherwise lose.' He sat drum-
ming his fingers on the table, lost in thought, and Leo
shifted uneasily, not sure whether she should stay or
go. Abruptly, he looked up and seemed to become
aware of her and she realised that he had been talking
to himself rather than her. But now a new expression
came into his face, as if a decision had been reached.
He got up and came towards her.

'You are a resourceful and courageous lad. How
would you like to join me in an adventure?'

Leo swallowed. 'An adventure, sir?'

His face was animated and she saw a different
man. The sardonic sophistication had been discarded

and he appeared years younger, excited by the prospect of action.

'Listen. When it gets dark I am going to make an attempt to infiltrate the Turkish trenches. The two lines are so close that our saps are within feet of theirs. It would take hardly any time to break through from one to the other. Then, I should be able to get close enough to pick up some intelligence, even if it is only soldiers' gossip. It might give us an idea of morale, if nothing else. But I need someone with me who understands Turkish. Will you come?'

Leo felt dizzy with fear at the prospect. But he had called her courageous and she would not disappoint him. 'Tonight, sir?'

'No. I need time to prepare the ground. Tomorrow night. Be here when dinner is finished. Can I rely on you?'

'Yes.' She did not know as she spoke whether her courage would hold till then, but she nodded and said again, 'Yes. I will come.'

He grasped her shoulders and pressed down on them briefly. 'Good lad! Off you go, now. See you tomorrow.'

She went out into the night with his touch still tingling in her shoulders.

Chapter 12

Victoria and Luke came back later that day and as they walked up from the road Luke's arm was round Victoria's shoulders, but Leo made no comment. She had difficulty keeping her mind on the conversation over dinner and at bedtime Victoria said, 'Leo, is everything all right? You seem to be miles away.'

'Oh, it's just this place, that's all,' Leo said. 'You know, the mud, the noise of the guns ...'

'Then swap with me,' Victoria urged. 'You know you only have to say. It's your turn for a bit of a break. It'll do you good to get away.'

Briefly the tantalising prospect hovered before Leo's imagination. Tomorrow night she could be safe in Lozengrad, instead of facing unknown dangers in the Turkish trenches. But she knew that she could never accept the offer. Whatever happened, she was going with Sasha Malkovic and the thought came to her that she would follow that man anywhere if he called her, though she could not, for the life of her, explain why. 'No, really,' she replied, 'I'd rather stick it out here. Thanks for the offer, but I'm sort of settled here, and I'm learning a lot. I'll be all right. I'm just tired, that's all. Let's get some sleep.'

There was little sleep for her that night and the next day she had to struggle to keep her mind on her work. By dinner time her nerves were strung so tight that she could not eat. She presented herself at Colonel Malkovic's tent while he was still finishing his meal.

He looked up and wiped his mouth. 'You're early, good. Here—' he rose and threw her a bundle of clothes from the chest '—put these on. You'll never pass for a Turk in those English tweeds.'

Leo stared at the bundle in her hands. If she was forced to strip in front of him her secret would be discovered at once. She had sometimes wished for the kind of magnificent bosom that made some of her friends look so splendid in a low-cut evening dress but now she was glad that several weeks of sparse food and hard work had pared her figure down until her breasts hardly created a curve in her chemise, and she had long ago abandoned her stays. Nevertheless, without her tunic and breeches it would be obvious that she was not a boy. To her relief, he moved to the rear of the tent, where a curtain hid the sleeping quarters.

'I must change too. Be quick, I shall not be long.'

In fumbling haste she took off her clothes and pulled on those he had given her. They were made of rough brown serge, the kind of garment that might be worn by an ordinary soldier on either side, and she shuddered as she saw that the back of the tunic was stained with blood and realised that it had probably been taken from a corpse. She had just finished when Malkovic returned, dressed in a similar costume. He looked her over, then beckoned her to a corner of the tent where the bare earth was exposed.

'Rub some mud on your face. That fair complexion will shine like the moon.'

She obeyed and he smeared mud on his own cheeks and brow. Then he threw a uniform cloak over his disguise and handed her a similar one.

'Now, you know what I am looking for. Any hint of weakness, any suggestion of a retreat; or on the other hand any sign of reinforcements or a planned attack. Understood?'

'Yes, sir.'

As he led the way out of the tent the sentry outside came to attention and Malkovic said, 'If anyone wants me, I am sleeping and not to be disturbed under any circumstances. Do you understand?'

'Yes, sir.'

He beckoned and Leo followed him into the darkness. The rain had stopped at last and a crescent moon appeared fleetingly through the cloud wrack but the main light came from the innumerable fires that dotted the camp. Once a sentry shouted a challenge but Malovic answered, 'Colonel Malkovic, on my rounds,' and the sentry saluted and let them pass. Before long, they came to the first trench and climbed down into it. Leo had grown used to the smell in the dressing tent, but the stench here was of a different order and she put her sleeve across her face. The bottom of the trench was ankle deep in water and they waded along for what seemed to her a considerable distance. As they got nearer to the front line, they passed men clustered in little groups in dugouts burrowed into the side of the trench and then men on guard duty and others dozing on the fire-step. One trench led to another until Leo lost all sense of direction. Eventually, Malkovic led her up a side turning and came to a stop where a sapper waited, armed with a small lamp and his entrenching tool. Beside them, was the dark opening of a tunnel.

'All quiet?' Malkovic asked.

'Haven't heard a whisper since yesterday,' was the response. 'We've dug as close as we dared. It'll take no more than a minute to break through.'

'Right,' Malkovic said. 'Lead on.'

With a flutter of rising panic, Leo saw that they were going to have to crawl into that black hole. The sapper went first, Malkovic followed and Leo, clenching her teeth to suppress a whimper of distress, went after him. The tunnel was no more than three feet high, shored up at intervals with baulks of timber, and too narrow to turn round in. Panic threatened as she realised that it was impossible to go back. Since Malkovic's body blocked most of the light from the sapper's lamp Leo was left in almost total darkness, able to see only the soles of his boots ahead of her. The ground under her hands and knees was sticky with wet clay and her nose was filled with the stench of damp earth.

They crawled for what seemed miles, until Leo's muscles were throbbing with cramp. Then the moving shape in front of her came to a sudden halt and she almost collided with him. The sapper had come to a stop at a point where the roof was slightly higher and was holding up his lantern. 'Still!' Malkovic whispered. 'No sound!' Leo froze, straining her ears.

At length, the colonel whispered, 'Go ahead,' and the sapper struck the side wall of the tunnel with his entrenching tool. The noise seemed so loud that Leo felt it must carry to the Turkish trenches but at last there was a sound of falling earth and a blessed draft of cool air reached her face. The sapper worked for a moment or two longer, then wriggled out of the way and Malkovic squirmed through the hole he had made. Thankful to be out of that living grave, Leo followed.

They were in another trench, as wet and foul-smelling as the previous ones, but Leo assumed that they were now on the Turkish side of the lines. At that thought the full realisation of her own foolhardiness struck her. If they were to be captured, how long would she be able to sustain the illusion that she was a boy? And once her true sex was discovered what fate might await her? She tried to comfort herself with the recollection of the honourable and dignified behaviour of the Turkish officer she had helped to question. Surely, he would treat a woman with respect. But how long would it be before she was handed over to someone of his rank – if ever – and what might she have to suffer at the hands of the common soldiers before that? For a moment she was tempted to confess the whole deception to Malkovic, but already he was leading the way along the trench and she had no option but to follow. At a junction with a second trench he flattened himself against the wall and peered round. Leo could hear the low mumble of distant voices but after a moment Malkovic straightened up and moved swiftly and soundlessly across the junction and into the shadows beyond. Leo followed, getting a glimpse as she did so of Turkish soldiers sitting and standing along the other trench in similar attitudes to the Bulgars they had passed on the other side.

They moved on, away from the front line, along what Leo knew enough to recognise as a communication trench leading back to the area where the reserves were quartered. There was enough light from the stars to see a short way ahead, but the trench was deliberately built with frequent bends and dogs' legs, to prevent attackers from having a clear view. Suddenly, from beyond the next corner, Leo heard the sound of voices and the tramp of feet. A company of soldiers, marching in single file, appeared round the bend and bore down on them. Malkovic flattened himself against the side of the trench and she did likewise, but there was no way of avoiding the oncoming troops. The officer leading them stopped.

'I'm looking for Mehmet Pasha. Am I heading the right way? How do you find your way around this rabbit warren?'

The question was addressed to Malkovic, who simply shook his head and shrugged. Leo answered, 'Yes, straight on.'

The officer jerked his head at Malkovic. 'What's the matter with him? He should know dumb insolence won't be tolerated.'

Leo pointed her finger to her temple and rotated it, in the universal sign implying that her companion was an idiot. The Turk gave a brief grunt of comprehension and beckoned his men forward.

The file of men tramped past them, until one halted by Leo. 'What are conditions like in this shithole? As bad as they make out?'

'Pretty bad,' Leo agreed. 'Just arrived?'

'Yes. But we won't be here long. We'll soon send the infidels packing.'

'*Insh'allah!*' Leo responded piously.

Someone further back shouted, 'What's the hold up? Get a move on!' and the man grinned and nodded and plodded on.

Leo leaned against the side of the trench and realised her legs were shaking. Malkovic touched her arm and jerked his head in the direction they had been walking. He led on until the trench turned another sudden corner and they almost fell over three men slumped together in attitudes of sleep. One of them roused himself and muttered, 'Who's that? Mind your feet, can't you?' Malkovic froze and looked at Leo and she said softly, 'Sorry, brother. Go back to sleep.' The man grunted and settled back and Leo followed the colonel until they came to a wider trench running a right-angles. At intervals along this light spilled from dugouts burrowed in the trench wall. They could hear voices and there was a smell of cooking and tobacco smoke.

Malkovic stepped aside and gestured Leo forward. She crept closer to the first opening and listened, but the conversation going on inside was just the sort of soldiers chat that she had heard many times in the Bulgarian camp: complaints about the food; gossip about wives and girlfriends; dirty jokes. She shook her head at the colonel and moved silently to the next opening.

Peering cautiously round the corner she saw a small space, roughly roofed with straw matting, in which half a dozen soldiers were smoking and playing back-gammon. Malkovic looked at her and cupped his hand to his ear in a pantomime of listening. She pressed herself against the side of the trench, as close to the entrance as she dared, and strained her ears.

One man was grumbling. 'What are we doing sitting here? We've been here for two days and all we do is sit in a hole in the ground like rabbits.'

'Be grateful!' another chided him. 'After those forced marches I'm just glad to sit still.'

'But why are we here?' the other persisted.

'Stop grousing,' said another man, who from his tone Leo guessed to be the corporal in charge. 'You'll get enough action soon. We're here to drive the infidels out of the Sultan's territory and we move when we're ordered to and not before. My guess is it won't be long now.'

This appeared to put an end to the conversation. Leo looked at Malkovic and nodded back along the trench. When they were far enough away for their voices not to be heard he whispered, 'Well, what were they saying? Anything useful?'

'They are from the south,' she whispered in return. 'I recognise the accent. Somewhere around Ankara, I should guess. They have been marched here – forced marches – and they are waiting for the order to attack.'

She saw his eyes glitter in the reflected light from the dugout. 'Did they know when?'

'No. They have been here for two days and some of them are getting impatient. They expect it to be soon.'

He nodded and reached out to squeeze her arm. 'Well done. That's all I need. Come on. Let's get back.'

This time the three sleepers did not stir as they picked their way over their feet. It seemed to Leo that it was a long way back to the entrance of the tunnel. Excitement had kept the adrenalin flowing until now, but as it subsided exhaustion took its place. She began to fear that they were lost in the maze of trenches, but Malkovic led the way without hesitation and at last the black hole of the tunnel loomed up out of the shadows. It took all her strength to haul herself back to the Bulgarian side. The sapper was waiting for them and set to work at once to block up the hole he had made, while Leo followed Malkovic back to the camp.

Back at his tent Malkovic turned to Leo. 'So those men in the dugout had only recently arrived. What about the ones we met first?'

'They are new, too. But they seemed very confident that they wouldn't be staying long. I had the impression they expect to attack us very soon.'

Makovic nodded and said no more. Leo expected congratulations, but the colonel had other things on his mind. He shouted for his orderly and when the man appeared, rubbing his eyes, he ordered, 'Fetch Lieutenant Popitch to me, and then get me something to eat. I'm ravenous.'

The man went and Malkovic pointed to Leo's clothes, which she had left on the chest. 'Get dressed. I'll be back in a moment.'

She scrambled into her clothes, afraid to hear Popitch or the orderly returning, and she was still doing up her buttons when the lieutenant came in. He looked at her and raised an eyebrow and she was suddenly consumed with embarrassment at the thought of what interpretation he might put on the situation. But surely, she reasoned, Malkovic could not be suspected of anything like that. Or could he? He had shown her more kindness in her guise as a boy than he had shown to her as a woman.

Further thought was banished as Malkovic came back in his usual uniform. 'Michaelo, go and tell General Vasoff that I need to see him urgently. Wake him up if necessary. I'll be with you shortly.'

'Is something happening, sir?' the young man enquired.

'The Turks have been reinforced. It sounds as though they are preparing to make a counter-attack. For now they are resting the men after a long march but the attack could come at any moment. But if we can hit them first, while the new troops are still exhausted, we might break through. If not, then the sooner we get the armistice signed the better. Either way, we need to move fast. Go!'

Popitch left and the orderly came in with a tray carrying a bottle of wine, bread and cheese. At the sight, Leo stomach growled so loudly she thought Malkovic must hear, but he was already pouring himself a glass of wine. She shuffled her feet, hoping to attract his attention, and he put down the goblet and came over to her.

'You did well, my lion cub. Thanks to your ears, we have vital information. If you hear tomorrow that there has been a great attack and that we have broken through the defences and are marching on Constantinople, you will know that you have had a hand in the victory. If, on the other hand, you hear in a few days that the fighting is over and the armistice has been signed, you will have contributed to that, too. A good night's work, no?'

'Yes, I hope so, sir,' she said.

He squeezed her shoulder briefly. 'Now, off you go. Get some sleep. Goodnight.'

She turned away to the tent flap and paused to cast a last glance at the tray of food. He was already cutting a hunk of bread.

'Goodnight,' she said.

He waved a knife at her and responded, 'Goodnight,' with his mouth full. She went out into the darkness with an empty stomach and a jumble of emotions that refused to make any logical sense.

Chapter 13

While Leo was crawling through the Turkish trenches, Victoria and Luke were sitting at a long table in the mess at the Bulgarian Red Cross hospital in Lozengrad, eating the best meal they had had for a long time. They had arrived that morning with a new casualty to be greeted by the nurses on duty with a cry of 'Merry Christmas!'

'What?' Victoria exclaimed. 'It's not, is it? Do you mean today is Christmas Day?'

'Didn't you know?' asked Sylvia Wallace, a vivacious girl who had often raised the spirits of her colleagues at difficult moments.

'No, we had no idea. I've completely lost track of dates and there hasn't been any mention of it back at Chataldzha.'

'Well, there wouldn't be, would there?' her companion reasoned. 'It's Christmas for us but not for the Bulgars. They're Orthodox, and Christmas for them is thirteen days later than ours.'

'But we made up our minds to celebrate it anyway,' Sylvia said. 'We had a carol service last night and we even managed to make up little gifts for the men in the wards – just a few cigarettes mainly, but they appreciated it. They get so few comforts, poor creatures.'

'The funny part was,' the other girl broke in, 'the students who interpret for us found out what was going on and explained it to the patients. So when we walked into the ward this morning all the men sat up in bed and shouted "Melly Chissimas".'

'No, really?' Victoria laughed.

'Apparently, some of them were so worried about getting it wrong that they lay awake muttering it to themselves half the night,' Sylvia confirmed.

'How sweet!'

'I'm sorry we weren't here,' Luke said. 'We seem to have missed out on the fun.'

'No, you haven't,' Sylvia told him, 'Not the best bit, anyway. We are all invited to dinner at the Red Cross hospital tonight, and I'm sure that includes you.'

That evening the Director of the Red Cross hospital sent a small fleet of horse-drawn carriages to collect all the staff who could be spared and they were treated to a lavish meal of roast pork, the traditional Bulgarian Christmas dish, washed down with large quantities of wine and followed by many toasts to each other's countries and the co-operation between the two medical teams. After swallowing glass after glass of slivovitz Victoria had to admit to herself that she was more drunk than she had ever been before.

In the carriage on the way home she found herself alone with Luke. He had held back, politely allowing all the others to climb into the first carriages, until they were the only ones left. It was a clear night, with a sharp frost and a sky brilliant with stars. There was a cutting edge to the wind and when she felt Luke's arm round her shoulders her first instinct was to snuggle closer for warmth. Once she would have shrugged off such an advance with indignation but over the last weeks she had grown used to physical contact, which had seemed at first casual, almost accidental, but which she had come to expect and enjoy. After all, she reasoned drowsily to herself, this was different. Luke wasn't just any man trying his luck. He was a friend, a colleague – a comrade in arms. The thought made her giggle and he bent his head closer and asked 'What's the joke?'

She looked up at him. 'Nothing. Just a thought.'

Then his lips found hers and her body erupted with a volcanic explosion of desire. She let the pressure of his lips open hers and shivered as his tongue touched her own. After a moment he drew back enough to look into her eyes.

'I've been longing to do that. You know that, don't you?'

'Mmm,' she murmured, and sought his lips again.

This time the kiss was longer and more passionate. She felt his hand on her breast and could find no reason to remove it.

He whispered in her ear, 'I've got a room of my own in the place where I lodge. It's only small, but it's private. Will you come?'

Upbringing and common sense told her to refuse. Then an inner voice reminded her of what she had said to Leo. 'I thought you were supposed to be free of Victorian morality,' it said. 'You're a modern, progressive woman, a free spirit. What's the matter with you?'

She swallowed hard. 'Yes, all right.'

His room was a freezing garret at the top of an old house. He took her in his arms and murmured, 'I'm sorry it's so cold. We'll be warm once we're in bed.'

His fingers fumbled with the buttons on her dress. She felt she should help but did not want to break free of his embrace. When the last button gave and he pulled the dress down from her shoulders she had to draw back to step out of it. He let her go and turned his back to pull off his jacket and then his shirt. Victoria, shivering, shed the rest of her under-garments and he stayed with his back to her until she had scrambled between the sheets. Then he finished stripping and slid in beside her. In contrast to the cold, rough sheets his body was warm and his skin surprisingly smooth. She pressed herself against him and felt a quiver of ecstasy run though her nerves. He kissed her again, his thumb caressing her nipple, and she felt a sudden wetness between her thighs. Then, suddenly, he was on top of her, thrusting, panting hotly in her ear, and she was struggling against him. There was a sharp pain and then he drew back and looked down into her face.

'Jeez, Victoria! You're ... Was this your first time?'

She stared back at him. Anger had taken the place of desire. 'What sort of woman do you take me for? A common prostitute?'

'No! No, of course not. But I assumed ... you seemed to be a woman of the world. I never imagined ...'

'And I suppose you have a great deal of experi-ence in these matters.'

She saw the colour rise in his face. 'No ... no, I ... It was my first time, too.'

'I see. So you chose me to ... to induct you into the mysteries of sex.'

'No! It wasn't like that at all. I really love you, Victoria. I thought you felt the same about me.'

She rolled over to face away from him. She remembered Leo's warning and realised that she had been irresponsible, to say the least. Now she found herself in a situation she did not know how to deal with. She threw back the blanket and got up.

'What are you doing?' Luke said.

'Getting dressed. I have to get back to the nurses' home.'

'You can't! Not at this time of night. Come back to bed, please! I won't touch you, I promise.'

'I can't stay out all night and then walk into the hospital tomorrow as if nothing has happened. I have to go back.'

'Then I'll come with you.'

'There's no need.'

'Of course there is. I can't let you walk back through a strange town on your own at this time of night.'

They pulled on their clothes in silence and he followed her down to the street. Outside the cold struck through her clothes like a knife and she set off as fast as she could walk. He kept beside her but for a while he said nothing.

Eventually, when they were almost at the door of the house, he broke the silence. 'Victoria, I just want to tell you I'm sorry for what happened tonight. I really thought you knew ... well, knew what to expect. But I wasn't lying when I said I love you. Please don't let this make any difference between us.'

'I ... don't know,' she groped for words. 'I'll have to think about it. Just give me time.'

'Of course. You can take all the time you want. I'll wait as long as it takes. Just say you forgive me for tonight.'

'It was my fault, too. I must go in. Goodnight.'

'Goodnight.' He reached out to her but she opened the door and slipped inside before he could touch her.

Next morning when she woke every part of her body seemed to hurt; but in a few moments the pain concentrated in two places – her head, which ached sickeningly, and the area between her legs. Memory flooded back and with it a new anxiety. Suppose she was pregnant? She had heard that there were ways a man could protect a woman from conceiving, but she was hazy about the details. One thing she was fairly sure about was that Luke had taken no such precautions. The prospect of giving birth out of wedlock terrified her. She began to see that her brave boast of independence and modernity had severe limitations. The life she envisioned for herself had no place in it for a child; certainly not one rejected by society as a bastard and totally dependent on her for support. There was another possibility, of course. A married woman need have no such fears. But the prospect of marriage to Luke was equally at odds with her expectations. She recalled how she had boasted to Leo that she had no intention of allowing herself to be at any man's beck and call. She liked Luke and her reaction the previous evening had proved that she found him attractive; but if married life meant a repetition of what had happened at the climax of their love-making it was not something she could bear to imagine.

As she worried away at the problem a new thought occurred to her. Once, during her short career as a racing driver, she had heard an older woman telling a friend that there were doctors in London who would relieve a woman of the burden of an unwanted pregnancy, for a fee. Well, she had money. The solution was obvious. She must get back to England as soon as possible.

*

All day after her adventure with Malkovic, Leo waited for news of an attack but none came. In the evening Victoria and Luke returned from Lozengrad and she saw from their faces that something had happened. Luke looked uncharacteristically subdued and Victoria's vivacity seemed forced.

Victoria took her arm. 'Leo, what day is it?'

'Day? I've got no idea. All the days are the same here.'

'What date?'

'I don't know.'

Her friend leaned to her and kissed her cheek. 'Merry Christmas, darling.'

'Today?'

'No, yesterday. We arrived just in time to join in the celebrations. In the evening there was a dinner party at the Red Cross hospital and the doctors there had laid on a really good spread. You should have been there, Leo. You look as if you need a good feed. If you'd accepted my offer it would have been you instead of me.'

'Then you would have missed out,' Leo said. 'Don't worry. I don't mind.' She was thinking of how she had spent her Christmas night and deciding that she had no regrets. But there was something about the way Victoria and Luke looked at each other that made her very uneasy. She wondered if she should try to persuade Victoria to confide in her when they were alone but decided it was best left alone.

At midday, two days later, the guns suddenly fell silent and rumours began to spread that the armistice had been signed. So, Leo thought, the Bulgars had decided to hold onto their gains rather than risk another push. She waited for Malkovic to send for her, thinking that at least he would tell her the result of their adventure, but no summons came. That evening, when they returned from another trip to Lozengrad, Luke and Victoria confirmed the news. A peace conference had been arranged in London, under the chairmanship of the Foreign Secretary, Sir Edward Grey. The fighting was over.

'So what do we do now?' Leo asked, as they sat round the campfire that night.

'Go home,' Victoria said, and Leo heard relief in her voice. 'If there are no more casualties our job is over.'

'Yes, I suppose it is,' Leo said bleakly. 'We don't seem to have been here long, after all the trouble we had getting here.'

'Aren't you just longing for a decent meal and a hot bath and a comfortable bed?'

'I suppose so,' Leo repeated. Two thoughts sprang to her mind. One, that going home meant facing her grandma. So far, there had been no response to her letter so she had no means of knowing what sort of reception she could expect. The second, more pressing thought, was that if she went home she would never see Sasha Malkovic again. She asked herself why she cared. He had not even had the courtesy to offer her a glass of wine, after what they had risked together. And then there was the look Popitch had given her. What sort of man was it that she had allowed to capture her imagination to this extent?

'Leo!' Victoria's voice had an edge of impatience. 'You haven't heard a word we were saying. You seem to be in a world of your own these days.'

'I'm sorry,' Leo said. 'What were you talking about?'

'We were just wondering how much longer we should hang on here,' Luke said. 'After all, there are still casualties to be shipped up to Lozengrad. It's going to take some time to clear the backlog.'

'That's true,' Leo said. 'We can't go for a while yet.' She looked at him and wondered if he had his own reasons for not wanting to leave. But she had been told to mind her own business and she would do so.

Next morning, coming out of the mess tent after breakfast, Leo heard hoof beats. Turning to look, she saw the Serbian cavalry troop trotting away up the road, and at its head rode an officer on a grey horse. Sasha Malkovic had left without even sending for her to say goodbye.

Chapter 14

Tom was examining the cracks in the whitewashed ceiling above his head. They seemed to make a familiar pattern but he could not think where he had seen it before. A noise attracted his attention and with a great effort he turned his head to look for the source of it. A long row of beds stretched away from him and for a moment he thought he was back in the dorm at school. Then the noise came again and he saw that it came from a trolley, which was being pushed up the aisle between the beds by two nurses. It stopped at the end of his bed and one of the nurses ladled something into a bowl and brought it to him. She was a middle-aged woman, with a round, pale face and small, dark eyes that looked like two buttons pushed into a lump of dough.

Tom summoned all his strength and whispered, 'Where am I?'

The dough face became animated and she said something in a language he did not understand. She leaned over him and he smelt sweat and garlic but he let her heave him into a sitting position and prop him up with pillows. As she did so she spoke to the other nurse, who wheeled the trolley on up the ward, while Doughface sat on the edge of the bed and began to spoon-feed him from the bowl. It was some kind of soup and the taste seemed familiar. While he ate she kept up a running commentary, as if talking to a baby, cooing encouragement and tutting if he turned his head away. When he could eat no more she laid his pillows flat again and went away and he drifted back to sleep.

The next time he opened his eyes a man was standing by the bed. He wore a shabby white coat and had a stethoscope round his neck.

'Good afternoon, Meester Devenish,' he said. 'I am Dr Charalambous and I speak a leetle bit English. How you feel?'

'Not very good,' Tom whispered. 'Where am I?'

'You are in hospital in Salonika.'

'How long have I been here?'

'Two, maybe three weeks. You been very ill – double pneumonia. When your friend bring you, we thought you going to die. But now, see! Much better! Soon you will be well again.'

'My friend?'

'The American. He is, how you say? Journalist?'

'Max!' Tom groped in the fog of his memory. 'Max brought me here? Is he here?'

'No, he go – long time ago. But he left you letter. Here.' The doctor took an envelope from the pocket of his white coat and handed it to Tom. 'You read later. Now I listen to your chest.'

When the doctor had finished his examination and pronounced himself satisfied Tom opened the envelope.

Hey buddy!

They tell me you are making good progress, which is a relief because for a while there we thought we were going to lose you. I hung on as long as I could but my editor back home is getting pretty cheesed off and wants me back in Belgrade, so I'm going to have to leave you. I've been in touch with the British military attaché, so he knows you are here and will take care of everything.

I'm really sorry not to be here for you, but I guess you will understand. If you get back to Belgrade, make sure to look me up. I'll be at the same hotel.

One more thing. I made some enquiries about the possible whereabouts of your lady-friend. Some

Serbian officers at the Makedonia Palace Hotel remembered two young English women coming through back in November. They weren't sure where they went after that. Some thought they had taken a boat back to Italy but others seemed pretty sure that they had headed towards Adrianople. Of course, by the time you are well enough to read this, your Leonora may be back home and all your worries will be at an end, but I pass it on just in case it comes in useful.

Take care of yourself, old pal. And make sure you keep in touch.

Yours,
Max

Tom sank back against his pillows and closed his eyes. Slowly the recollection of his mission and the journey he had made with Max took shape, and with that came the realisation that some of the images that had haunted his brain during his illness were not nightmares but reality.

By the following day he was feeling stronger but when he attempted to get out of bed his legs buckled under him and his head swam. Doughface pushed him back onto the bed, tutting loudly, and proceeded to perform various humiliating but necessary procedures on his person. Shortly afterwards he woke from a doze to find another man standing by the bed, this time in the uniform of a captain in the Dragoon Guards.

'Sorry to disturb you, old man. Reggie Vincent, at your service. I'm the British military attaché, for my sins. We've been waiting for you to become *compos mentis*. It's good to see you looking better.'

'Thanks,' Tom murmured.

'I gather you got yourself mixed up in a spot of bother outside Bitola.'

'I'm afraid I don't remember much about it.'

'Well, according to the American chappie who brought you here, you were held up by the *cetniks* and had your car stolen and had to walk until you reached the Serbian camp. He brought you through the enemy lines on the back of a donkey. Had the devil of a time, by all accounts.'

'I didn't know,' Tom said. 'I probably owe him my life.'

'Definitely, I should say.' Vincent sat down on the edge of the bed. 'What I don't understand is, what you were doing there in the first place.'

Tom considered explaining about his quest but remembered Ralph's caution about publicity. He said, 'I'm an artist. I wanted to make some sketches of conditions out here, you know, the reality of war sort of thing – for the newspapers.' He had a sudden thought. 'My sketch pad! Where is it?'

Vincent opened the locker by the bed and rummaged for a moment. 'This it?'

'Oh, yes! Thank you. I wouldn't want to lose that.'

'Mind if I look?'

'If you like,' Tom said unwillingly. The pad was still in his visitor's hand and he could hardly snatch it away.

Vincent turned the pages and whistled softly. 'These are bloody good, if you don't mind me saying so. But some of them are … Was it really that bad out there?'

'It was terrible. That isn't the half of it.'

'Well, I take my hat off to you. I've heard of suffering for your art, but this goes beyond the call of duty.' He handed the pad to Tom and went on, 'Anyway, that isn't what I came for. What I need to tell you is that we found an address among your papers, so I've telegraphed your people back in England and let them know where you are. And I've got a couple of letters for you in reply.' He took two envelopes out of his pocket and laid them on the locker. 'Now, is there anything you need?'

Tom struggled to focus his mind. 'Something to read, perhaps? A newspaper? How long am I going to be in here?'

'A while yet, I'm afraid. I had a word with the medic and he says you won't be strong enough to be discharged for at least a week and then you will need several weeks' recuperation before you are fit to travel back to England. I can try to book you into a room at the Makadonia Palace when you are ready to be discharged, if you like. But quite frankly Salonika is not a good place for a convalescent at the moment. Food is very short for one thing. If I were you, I'd take the boat down to Athens as soon as you feel up to it, and recuperate there.'

'Thanks. I'll ... think about it,' Tom agreed.

'Right.' Vincent rose. 'I must be off. I'll pop in and see you tomorrow. Sure there's nothing else I can do?'

'No, really. Thanks very much for calling in – and for getting in touch with my family.'

'Think nothing of it. All in a day's work. See you tomorrow.'

As soon as Vincent had gone Tom reached for the letters on his locker. He had already seen that one of them was addressed in Ralph's handwriting. The other was from his mother. He opened Ralph's first.

My dear Tom,

*I can't begin to tell you how sorry I am to hear that
you are ill. But at least we know now where you are.
For the last few weeks I have been frantic with worry,
so the note from your father giving me the news was
welcome – to that extent at least. But I can't forgive
myself for sending you off on what has turned out to
be a wild goose chase, and putting you in such danger. I never dreamed you would end up in the thick of
it on the battlefield. How on earth did that happen?*

*And it turns out that it was all for nothing. We
received a letter from Leo the other day. It seems
she has joined up with a group calling themselves
'The Women's Sick and Wounded Convoy'. These
people have somehow got themselves to Lozengrad,
which is in the far eastern part of Bulgaria and was
a Turkish town until the Bulgars took it from them,
and they have set up a hospital there. I would never
have imagined Leo as a nurse! I thought this FANY
business was just an excuse to kick over the traces,
but she must have been more serious than I realised.
Anyway, she says she is safe and well and I suppose
we must take her word for it, though I still think it's
a most foolhardy affair. Lozengrad is well away from
the front line, so she should not be in any danger
from the actual fighting and presumably since she's*

*with other Englishwomen she should be protected
from ... what shall I say? ... local dangers.*

*As far as I can make out, the fighting has reached
a stalemate and there are rumours of an armistice.
Presumably, if that happens, these women will pack
up and come home, and Leo will come with them. So
there is no need for you to worry yourself, my dear
old chap. Just take it easy and get well again and by
the time you get home Leo should be here as well.
Trust me, when I see her I shall give her a good talking to and make her see what trouble she has caused
and what a debt of gratitude she owes to you.*

*Please write as soon as you are well enough and
tell me you forgive me for all I have made you go
through!*

*Your affectionate friend,
Ralph*

Tom lay back and closed his eyes. So it had all been
for nothing! He thought of Leo and supposed he
should be angry with her, but he found that in fact
he was more annoyed with Ralph for insisting that
he should go in search of her. He wondered how
she had managed to get to Lozengrad and whether
she had encountered any of the horrors that he had
seen. It struck him that in future they would have

a special bond because they had witnessed at first-hand things Ralph had only read about in the papers. Then it crossed his mind that if it had not been for her mad escapade he would have stayed at home, making pointless drawings of barges on the Thames or bland rural scenes. He should be grateful to her for dragging him out of that stagnant existence. He had seen things that would give him nightmares for the rest of his life, and he had been close to death if the doctor was to be believed, but he had lived more intensely in these last weeks than in the whole of his previous existence – and at last he had made some pictures that meant something.

His mind began to drift pleasantly. If there was no further need to look for Leo, he was free to do as he liked. He would go to Athens, as Vincent suggested, and draw some of the wonderful buildings and statues from life, instead of copying them from books. What a fool he had been not to travel before! When he was well enough, he would head for home by any route that took his fancy. He might go to Delphi, or to Mycenae where Leo's father had excavated. Then, when he had seen enough of Greece, he would take a boat to Italy and visit Venice and Florence and Rome; and after that he would make his way back through France and see some of the scenes that had inspired painters like Cezanne and Van Gogh.

He saw himself wandering in sunlit pastures, among vines and cypress trees.

His pleasant reverie was disturbed, at that point, by the recollection that Leo was supposed to be going home, to face her brother's lectures – and her grandma's wrath, no doubt. Should he try to get back as soon as possible, to shield her from the worst of it? Would she be ready now to accept his proposal of marriage? He contemplated the prospect with no great enthusiasm. But if he did not marry her, what were her prospects? She had no other beaux, to his knowledge, and there was no doubt that her reputation would have been injured by her escapade. Would she find someone else? And what would Ralph think of him if he let her down? Perhaps his duty lay in that direction.

The problem was too intractable and he soon shelved it by falling asleep.

Over the next week Tom made slow progress, gaining a little more strength each day. Vincent called in from time to time and took away the letters that Tom had made the effort to write, to Ralph and to his mother and father. One morning he arrived bearing a bottle of wine and a jar of cherry jam.

'Thought I should bring you a little something, seeing as it's Christmas.'

'Christmas!' Tom sat up in bed. 'It can't be!'

'I promise you it is. Of course, this lot—' indicating the other inmates of the hospital '—don't celebrate it for another couple of weeks, but today is the twenty-fifth. So, Happy Christmas!'

'Thank you very much.' Tom rubbed a hand over his eyes. 'I had no idea I'd been here that long.'

'You've been pretty ill. It's not surprising you've lost count of time. Anyway, I brought you these. I'm sorry I couldn't manage a roast fowl or something, but food really is very hard to come by. Most of the shops are still shut and the villages in the interior, that used to supply the city with meat and milk and vegetables, have been devastated and the peasants have fled to the mountains. So this is the best I can do, I'm afraid. But at least the jam will help that ghastly brown bread to go down.'

'It certainly will,' Tom agreed. 'I'm longing for something sweet. Open that bottle, why don't you, and we'll have a Christmas drink.'

So they had a glass of wine each and wished each other Happy Christmas and drank to absent friends.

Four days later, on the day that Tom was due to leave hospital, Vincent arrived with the look of one who bears good news.

'The armistice has been signed and there is going to be a big conference in London – not just the combatants but all the interested Great Powers; Russia, Germany, Austria-Hungary, and ourselves. I'm glad I'm not one of them. They are going to have to redraw the map of Eastern Europe.'

'The Ottomans are finished, then?' Tom queried.

'Undoubtedly. The Turkish Empire is a thing of the past. They will be lucky to retain even a foothold in Europe.'

'And do you think the armistice will hold? Will there be peace now?'

'I wouldn't bank on it, personally. For a start, they will have to get the Bulgarians and the Serbs to agree about the division of Macedonia. The Bulgars feel, with some reason, that ethnically it's part of Bulgaria. But the Serbs regard it as the spoils of war and a step towards a Greater Serbia. Already they are pursuing a policy of enforced Serbianisation – sacking Bulgarian officials, closing Bulgarian schools. It will take all Sir Edward Grey's diplomatic skills to keep those two from each other's throats. But still, at least the fighting is over for the present, so we can all go home.'

Tom nodded slowly and gathered up his few personal possessions. Leo would be going home and as for him ... he would go to Athens and when he felt strong enough he would consider his next move.

Chapter 15

It was a week before the last casualties could be moved from Chataldzha to Lozengrad. When they had been dispatched, Leo said goodbye to the men she had worked with and was gratified by the warmth of their good wishes. Dragonoff, particularly, seemed really sorry to see her go and thanked her warmly for all her hard work. She took a last look round, threw her bag into the boot of Victoria's car and climbed into the back seat. For the last time they set off on the long road back.

When they arrived at the hospital Mabel Stobart looked Leo up and down and said dryly, 'Very practical, no doubt, but I think you had better go and change into your dress before we have dinner.'

Leo slipped back into the routine of the hospital, but her fellow nurses commented on her lacklustre manner. 'You've been overdoing it, all on your own down there at the front line,' she was told and she often saw Victoria watching her with a worried frown. She could not tell her that her lack of sparkle was not due to overwork or too little food. It was the memory of one terrifying and exhilarating night and the fact that the man she had shared it with had gone away without a backwards glance.

It was another two weeks before the last patients were ready either to be discharged or transferred to the Red Cross hospital, which now had room for them. There was a sentimental leave-taking as the last ox-carts set off with the men who were still not able to walk. The British and Bulgarian national anthems were sung, hands were kissed and handker-chiefs waved and then it was time to prepare for their own departure. Some of the railway lines had been reconnected, so the plan was for the women of the convoy to travel by a roundabout route to Sophia, so that they did not have to make the gruelling seven-day trek by ox-cart through the mountains, which they had had to endure on the way out. From there, they would take the Orient Express back to Paris. It was suggested that Leo and Victoria should accompany them, but Victoria pointed out that they could not take Sparky on the Orient Express. She was very keen that they should drive back the way they had come, to Salonika, and Leo was not surprised when Luke said that he needed to get to Salonika too, to pick up a ship that would take him on his way to New Zealand. Mrs Stobart was not happy about the idea and tried hard to change their minds but Victoria was adamant. She refused to leave her beloved car behind.

As they packed Victoria remarked, 'You had better find your skirt, Leo. You can't go back to Salonika dressed like that.'

Leo sighed. She had accepted the necessity of changing into a dress while on duty in the wards but she had grown used to the freedom of her breeches and boots and was reluctant to encumber herself with a heavy skirt again. 'I suppose I must.'

When she unearthed the skirt from where it lay rolled up at the bottom of her bag, however, it gave off a strong smell of mould. It was still damp and caked with mud, with patches of fungus growing on it, and in spite of all her attempts to brush and sponge it, it became clear that, as a respectable garment, it was beyond redemption. So Leo took it out into the street and gave it to an old beggar woman whom she had seen shivering at the corner. The old lady seized upon it with glee and, instead of putting it round her waist, hung it from her shoulders like a cloak. Leo returned smiling at the thought that at least it would keep someone warm until the spring came, but Victoria was aghast.

'What are you going to wear now? You really can't go around in breeches and that linen dress isn't practical for outdoors in this weather.'

'I've got an ordinary skirt in the trunk in the boot of the car,' Leo pointed out. They had both packed some non-uniform clothes before leaving London but there had been no occasion to wear them and they had never been unpacked. 'I can put that on when we get near civilisation, but I think I'll stick to my breeches and boots until then. It will only get covered in mud and ruined if I wear it to travel in.'

With time on her hands at last, Leo begged the use of a mirror from one of the other women and inspected her impromptu haircut. The hair had started to grow again and the result was an untidy bird's nest that first horrified her and then sent her into a paroxysm of laughter. She collected a bucket of warm water from the kitchen and washed it as thoroughly as she could. Then she sought out the barber who often came in to shave the patients and cut their hair. He was scandalised at the prospect of cutting a lady's hair, but Leo told him to cut it just as he would a young man's. She left his little shop with a sleek crop that fitted her head like a bronze helmet.

Mabel Stobart shook their hands when they were ready to leave. 'You have both done sterling service and I thank you for it. I am sure that if it had not been for your efforts at Chataldzha, Leonora, and your indefatigable journeying too and fro, Victoria, many more men would have died. You have both shown great courage and determination. If there ever should be a national emergency requiring our services, such as a war, I feel sure that we have proved ourselves more than capable of playing a useful part and I should be very glad to have you two as part of my team. Do come and see me when you get back to London.'

They promised that they would and climbed aboard Sparky, with Luke sitting beside Victoria, and set off for the last time down the road to the south. It had snowed heavily since they travelled in the opposite direction and then frozen hard, so that the ruts made by the ox-carts had filled up and the surface of the road was like an ice-rink. It took all Victoria's skill to prevent the car from skidding into the ditch, but at least the snow had covered the worst horrors of battle. It also meant that they did not have to stop to push the car out of the mud, and they reached Adrianople in one day.

In spite of the armistice, the siege had not been lifted. The guns were silent but the armed camp was still there and the trenches made dark gashes in the covering of snow, which gleamed red around them. Leo thought at first that it was the reflection of the setting sun; but drawing closer she saw that the snow was stained with blood.

They left the car on the road and climbed up to the general's tent on the hill. General Dimitriev broke off a conversation with a junior officer to greet them.

'My dear young ladies! What a pleasure to see you both safe and well! But I thought you were in Lozengrad.'

'The hospital has closed,' Victoria explained. 'We are on our way home. When do you expect the next train from Salonika?'

Dimitriev spread his hands. 'I am sorry. There is no knowing when a train will come. We have been waiting now for days for new supplies, but it seems that now the armistice has been signed the authorities have other priorities. But it must come soon, and until then you will be very welcome to stay here.'

He did not offer them his own tent this time. Instead, they were given the use of one which had been occupied until recently by two junior officers, who had both been wounded. Luke had to share with two of the others.

As they left the general, Leo said, 'We'd better get our bags from the car.'

Victoria groaned. 'Oh no! It means slipping and sliding down the hill and then struggling up again, and I'm absolutely whacked!'

'It's all right,' Leo said. 'I'll get them. You've done all the driving. You go and have a lie down.'

She had almost reached the bottom of the hill when a voice hailed her. 'You, boy! Come here!'

Leo stood transfixed, her heart beginning to pound. So he was here! But now, surely, he would see through her deception and be furious with her. She turned, glad that the low winter sun was behind her and saw Sasha Malkovic sitting his grey horse some twenty yards away. She stood still and after a moment he walked the horse forwards and drew rein beside her.

'So, what are you doing here?' Something in his eyes told her that he was surprised but not displeased to see her.

'I'm on my way home,' she responded, as coolly as she could manage.

'I see.' She saw the familiar ironic curl of his lips. 'You have decided that you have discharged your duty to your grandparents' heritage, then?'

'The fighting is finished. There is nothing more for me to do.'

He jerked his head towards the hospital tent. 'I should have thought there was plenty of work there for you.'

'Perhaps. But it will get less now there are no more casualties.'

'You think so? What makes you think the fighting is over?'

'There is an armistice, and a peace conference, I have been told.'

'A conference that will go on for months without finding an agreement. This is a truce, no more. And meanwhile, the Turks are reinforcing their positions and men will continue to die here, on both sides of the line.'

'But surely the siege will be lifted now?'

He shook his head with a grim smile at her naivety 'Adrianople is too precious a bargaining counter to be yielded up until agreement is reached. The siege will last a long time yet.' He gathered up his reins. 'But if you feel you have done your duty then by all means go home. I am sure your grandparents are eager to welcome you back. I wish you a safe journey.'

He touched the horse with his heels and would have ridden away but Leo suddenly remembered something that had occurred to her on their first encounter at Chataldzha. With a rush of reckless daring she called after him.

'Colonel Malkovic!' He stopped and looked back and she caught up with him. 'May I give you a small piece of advice?'

His eyebrows shot up at her temerity. 'Advice?'

'Find yourself a different horse, one that is less noticeable. Greys always stand out from the rest and only an officer would ride such a magnificent animal. It makes you a target for snipers.'

He looked amused. 'So what are you suggesting? That I buy myself a pony and lead my men from behind, like others I could mention?'

She smiled in spite of herself. 'No, I can't imagine you doing that. But a different mount perhaps? A bay, like that one there.' She pointed to the horse lines where a number of the cavalry mounts were tethered. 'The second from the right.'

He looked where she indicated and nodded. 'I see you have an eye for horseflesh. But you are English, of course. I should expect that.' He smiled down at her. 'Well, I will consider what you said. But you see—' he stroked the arched grey neck '—I am very fond of Cloud and I believe he is of me. He would pine if I abandoned him.'

'He would pine longer if you were killed,' she said.

He pursed his lips and shrugged, as if accepting the inevitability of that. Then he smiled again. 'Thank you for your advice. Now I must be on my way. Goodbye.'

She watched him walk out of sight and then turned back to fetch the baggage from the car.

They were invited to dine with the general and his officers, and were treated with the same courtesy as before, though the signs of strain were apparent on the faces of their hosts and the food was inferior and served in smaller portions. Leo was relieved to discover that Sasha Malkovic was not among the diners. If he had seen her in the company of the Bulgarian officers, who knew her as a woman, her deception would have been at an end. It seemed the Serbs now had their own mess and she was reminded of the strained relations between the two so-called allies.

Next morning Leo suggested to Victoria that, as they were going to have to stay for a few days, they should go and see how Sophie and the others were getting on in the hospital tent.

'Must we?' Victoria groaned. 'I've seen enough of hospitals to last me a lifetime. Do we have to wait for the train? Why don't we drive to Salonika?'

'Because we haven't got enough petrol, for one thing,' Leo said. She was beginning to realise that her friend found the reality of nursing hard to face, but she was disturbed by the change in her normally cheerful manner. Over the last weeks she had become increasingly short-tempered and withdrawn. 'Come on,' she said, trying to sound encouraging. 'We can't sit around doing nothing all day. Let's at least see how Sophie and the others are getting on.'

When they entered the tent, with Luke behind them, Sophie left what she was doing and came hurrying over.

'Victoria! I am so pleased to see you again! How are you? And this is …?' She broke off and covered her mouth to stifle a giggle. 'It's you, Leonora! I thought it was a young man. But what has happened to your hair?'

'It's more practical like this,' Leo explained. 'And so are the breeches.'

Sophie caught her breath. 'You are so brave! I would not dare …' Then she saw Luke. 'But this *is* a young man, and I don't know him.'

Victoria made the introductions and when Luke greeted her in Macedonian she exclaimed, 'You speak our language. How wonderful!'

Luke began to explain his antecedents but Sophie had already turned to the two women and caught a hand of each. 'I am so glad to see you both. We are so desperately short-handed here. Some of the staff are down with a fever and everyday there are more patients to deal with. You have come back to help, haven't you?'

Victoria began to explain that they were only passing through on their way home but Leo was looking at Sophie. When they had first met, her face had been as smooth and rounded as a doll's but now her cheeks were hollow and there were dark shadows under her eyes. It was obvious that she was not exaggerating the need for extra help. Besides, Sasha Malkovic was in camp and she wanted an excuse to stay. 'Vita, I really think we should help out, if we can. Just for a day or two.'

'I don't understand why you are so hard pressed, Sophie,' Victoria said. 'Now the firing has stopped there are fewer casualties, surely.'

'It's the typhus,' Sophie explained. 'We have new cases every day.'

'Typhus!' Victoria clapped her hand over her mouth and took a step back. 'You want us to nurse typhus cases?'

'They need care, just as much as the wounded do,' Sophie said.

Victoria was shaking her head. 'No, I'm sorry. I volunteered to collect wounded men from the battle-field and give First Aid, not to nurse plague victims. I can't do it. I just can't …' She turned and hurried out of the tent.

Luke called after her, 'Vicky!'

Leo knew that Victoria hated that diminutive, but she had heard him use it before and she seemed to tolerate it from him. However, this time she turned back and snapped, 'Don't call me Vicky!' Then she was gone. 'I'd better go after her,' Leo said, but Luke put a hand on her arm. 'I'll go. Leave her to me.'

He went out and Leo was left with Sophie, who fixed a pleading gaze upon her. With a chill at the pit of her stomach, Leo said, 'What do you want me to do?'

Sophie handed her a bottle. 'It's paraffin. The disease is carried by lice. We're not sure that paraffin actually kills lice but it certainly deters them. Go and smear it all over your body. Then come back to me and I will give you an overall and gloves. Leave them here at the end of each shift and when you undress check your body and the seams of your clothing very carefully for lice. Do you understand?'

Leo shuddered. 'Yes, I understand.'

She went back to the tent she shared with Victoria and was glad to find it empty. Luke and Victoria had apparently gone off somewhere together. She stripped off her clothes, shivering, and smeared the paraffin over herself. Then she dressed again and made her way back to where Sophie was waiting. As soon as she was ready, Sophie took her on a tour of the ward, explaining what was wrong with each man. Some had wounds from bullets or shrapnel, but far more were suffering from frostbite incurred through long hours on watch in the trenches, up to their knees in icy water. Several had already had their feet amputated. At the far end of the tent a section had been divided off with a canvas curtain. Behind this were the typhus patients.

Sophie described the symptoms in dispassionate tones. 'The first indications are headache and inability to sleep. Then comes a high fever with intense thirst. The body is covered with mud-coloured spots and the tongue is coated with brown fur. Next the patient goes into a coma, which closely resembles death. Around the fourteenth day the crisis occurs. Temperatures fall to below normal and death usually follows.'

'Do none of them survive?' Leo asked.

'Yes, a few, the strongest. But not many.'

'So what can we do for them?'

'Very little. Give them drink, bathe them to reduce the temperature, try to get them to take some nourishment. That is about all.'

Leo looked at her. 'How can you bear it – to see them like that and not be able to do anything?'

Sophie gave her a grim little smile. 'We bear it because we must – because we are alive and their need is so great.'

Leo braced her shoulders. 'Tell me what you want me to do.'

When they congregated in the mess tent for the midday meal, Sophie came over to where Leo was standing, bringing with her a small, lean man with very bright eyes.

'This is Dr Iannis Nikolaides,' she said. 'He came from Gallipoli to join us.'

They shook hands and exchanged greetings, then Leo said, 'But isn't Gallipoli still under Turkish control?'

Iannis smiled. 'For the present, yes. But I wanted to help the Allies who are fighting to drive them out, so I slipped through the lines one dark night and came here.'

'That must have been very dangerous,' Leo said.

'He is a very brave man,' Sophie declared, laying her hand proprietarily on the doctor's arm. He smiled at her fondly and Leo realised that they were more than just colleagues. She was glad that Sophie had something to lighten the burden of her heart-breaking work but she felt a twist of envy. Victoria had Luke and Sophie had Iannis, but what hope was there that she might one day be united with her soul mate?

'You are Greek?' she asked Iannis. 'I mean, I would guess that from your name.'

'Macedonian Greek,' he said. 'As Sophie is Macedonian Serb. We are all mongrels, here in

Macedonia, but we all love our country in the same way.'

Luke had reappeared during the course of the morning but in answer to Leo's query about Victoria all he had said was 'Give her time. She needs a bit of breathing space.' He had offered his services as a stretcher bearer and general orderly and Sophie had been happy to accept. He joined them at lunch and Leo felt as they talked that a real sense of comradeship was developing between the four of them. She wished Victoria was there to be part of it.

When she returned to their tent that evening there was no sign of her friend and she was beginning to grow anxious when she came in, flushed and with her sleeves rolled up.

'Vita! Where have you been? What have you been doing?' Leo asked.

'You were right. I couldn't sit around all day doing nothing,' Victoria responded, 'so I volunteered to help in the hospital kitchen.'

Leo jumped up and went to hug her. 'Well done! I should have known you would find something to do.'

But Victoria backed away, gesturing Leo back. 'I'm sorry, but if you don't mind I think it would be better if we didn't get too close to each other, don't you?'

Leo retreated to her bed and sat down. It was sensible, she had to admit, but she felt rejected and unclean. Victoria made a conciliatory gesture. 'I'm sorry, Leo. Honestly, I admire you for what you are doing . . . but I just can't bring myself to do it. At least at Lozengrad everything was kept clean, but here . . . the filth and the smell make me feel sick. And to be honest with you, I don't see why we should risk our own health. Dying in a car crash or by a stray bullet is one thing; but not like that!'

'It's all right,' Leo responded. 'I understand. We all have things we can't cope with. We must each do what we feel able to.'

For some days they both continued to work at their chosen stations, but Leo felt that Victoria had withdrawn emotionally as well as physically. She was uncomfortably aware that she watched with distaste as she examined her body for lice every night, and she kept all her clothes and other belongings well away from anything of Leo's. One day as they worked together in the ward she mentioned her disquiet to Luke.

'I think she's just about at the end of her tether, to be honest,' he said. 'She's a strong person and she's a tiger behind the wheel of a car, but she needs a rest.'

'I can't seem to get through to her anymore,' Leo said. 'It's as if she's cut herself off.'

Luke's face tightened. 'Yeah. I know what you mean.'

He said no more but later that evening, sitting by the campfire, Leo saw him talking to Victoria in the shadows just beyond the firelight. She could not hear what they were saying but she saw him reach out to put his arms round her and saw her shrug him off and turn away. Is this the end of the affair, she asked herself, or just a temporary hiccup? Perhaps she's got herself involved and now she's regretting it. Well, I tried to warn her. Hard on that thought came a moment or ironic self-awareness. Who am I to warn others about love affairs, when I'm pining my heart out for a man who thinks I'm a boy and believes women should stay in the kitchen?

Next day a column of ox-carts bearing wounded arrived with the news that the Turks were attacking in force around Gallipoli. The truce had broken down. The same evening they learned that fighting had begun again on the Chataldza front.

Luke looked at Victoria. 'Looks to me as if we could be back in business.'

'You don't mean back to Chataldzha?' she asked. 'It's a long way from here and anyway, the hospital at Lozengrad has closed down.'

'I was thinking of Gallipoli,' he said. 'If they are bringing the wounded here from that front there must be a need for the kind of ambulance service we were running before.'

'You're right!' Victoria said, and Leo saw her face brighten for the first time in days. For a moment she was inclined to be angry. The breakdown in the truce had to be bad news for all concerned, but to Victoria it was a chance to get away from the squalor and drudgery of the camp and do what she did best. Leo decided she could not be blamed for preferring that.

Chapter 16

Luke and Victoria left at first light the next morning. The distance to the battle front was greater from here, and there was no possibility of making a return journey in one day, so Leo knew she would not see them until the following evening. She was making her own way towards the hospital tent when she heard hoof beats approaching and saw Lieutenant Popitch, Colonel Malkovic's aide-de-camp, cantering towards her, leading a second horse. She stood still, her pulse quickening. She had seen Sasha Malkovic at a distance once or twice since that first day, but there had been no contact.

Popitch dismounted beside her. 'The Colonel needs your help. Will you come?'

His tone was so different from the peremptory order he had delivered the first time that she wondered if Malkovic had told him to tread carefully. 'What does he need me for?' she asked.

'He requires a translator. It is urgent, I believe.'

Leo hesitated a moment longer. Sophie would be expecting her in the ward, and she had her duty there, but she could surely be spared for an hour. And it must be important for Malkovic to send for her. She nodded. 'Very well. Where is he?'

'I'll take you to him. Can you ride?'

'Of course.'

She thanked heaven as she mounted that she had been taught to ride astride. It was good to be in the saddle again. They cantered back through the camp to the point some distance from the rest where the Serbian contingent had its base. Outside the largest tent Popitch took the reins from her and said, 'He's inside.'

Malkovic was talking to two other officers and Leo had a moment of terror at the thought that one of them might be Milan Dragitch, who would certainly recognise her; but they were both strangers.

Malkovic looked round and said, 'Ah, here is the young man who will translate for us. Leo, we are about to meet with some Turkish officers for an important discussion. I need you to translate but what you hear must remain absolutely confidential.'

'Of course,' Leo responded.

Malkovic pulled a watch from his pocket and looked at it. 'It's time. Let us go.'

Leo followed him and the other two through the lines of trenches until they came to the no man's land between the foremost Bulgarian trench and the first Turkish one. The halfway point was marked by a line of tattered white flags, grubby against a new fall of snow. There was no sign of the Turks and the four of them stood around, stamping their feet and blowing on their hands. 'Patience, gentlemen,' Malkovic said. 'It is a point of honour with the Turks to keep us waiting. Our best response is to behave as if time was of no importance.'

Leo was wearing only her tweed jacket and breeches. She had a fur-lined cape in her tent, but as she had only intended to walk from her tent to the hospital she had not put it on. Now she soon began to shiver, although she did her best to conceal the fact. Malkovic was not deceived.

'Our lion cub is shaking. Is it cold or fear?'

'Cold, sir,' Leo replied through chattering teeth.

'Don't you have a coat?'

'Not with me.'

He swung the cloak off his own shoulders and put it round her. 'I need you to be able to speak clearly. The Turks will not understand you if your teeth chatter so.'

She huddled into the cloak, feeling the warmth of his body enfolding her. Just then two Turkish officers strolled out to meet them, magnificently accoutred and fiercely moustached. The winter sun glittered on polished sword hilts and reflected from rows of medals and swags of gold braid. Greetings were exchanged in what seemed to Leo a surprisingly cordial manner, in view of the circumstances, and then the business of the conference was broached. The gist of what she translated was a proposal from the Turks that they should surrender the city to the Serbs in return for a safe conduct for them and their men. The Serbs would then hold all the key points in Macedonia, and leave the Bulgarians empty-handed. Malkovic thanked them with formal courtesy for their offer but intimated that he had no intention of betraying his allies. The discussion ended with mutual compliments and Leo followed the three Serbs back to the colonel's tent.

'Divide and rule,' he said when they reached it. 'That was the objective. They must be getting pretty desperate in there.'

The two officers were dismissed and Malkovic shouted to his orderly to bring warm wine. A brazier smouldered in the middle of the tent and he pointed Leo to a chair beside it. 'Sit and take some wine. You look as if you need it.'

The orderly appeared with a speed that told Leo he had anticipated the command and Malkovic poured two goblets of the steaming liquid. Leo sipped and felt the warmth spread through her body. 'You told me you were going home,' Malkovic said.

'I realised there was work to be done here.'

'You are working in the hospital tent?'

'Yes.'

He frowned. 'There is typhus there, I'm told.'

'Yes. There is an epidemic. That is why I stayed.'

'You should not be risking your life doing such work.'

She looked at him but his expression was inscrutable. 'I take no more risk than anyone else. Someone has to care for those men.'

'Not you. You are not involved in our war. I was wrong to tease you about your duty to your heritage the other day. You have done enough – more than enough. You should go home to England.'

'I will, soon,' she said and wondered what his reaction would be if he knew that the only reason she stayed was to be near him.

The guard who stood outside the tent put his head in through the flap. 'Excuse me, sir. There is a messenger here with a letter for you.'

'Send him in.'

The man who entered was plastered from head to foot with mud, his face pinched with cold. It was obvious that he had ridden from some distance away but Leo could not at first identify his uniform. Then she remembered that it was Greek. He handed the letter to Malkovic and said, in broken Serbian, 'For you, sir, from General Todorov.'

Malkovic tore open the envelope and then threw the contents down on his table in frustration. 'What use is this to me? I don't read Greek!'

The messenger looked nonplussed. Leo said, 'I can read it.'

Malkovic swung round. 'You know Greek as well as Turkish?'

'Yes, sir.' She had sworn to herself that she would stop using the subservient 'sir' but somehow it seemed to come naturally in the role she had assumed.

'Translate this for me.' He indicated the chair behind his table and pushed a sheet of paper and a pen and ink horn towards her. 'Write it down.' He gestured to the messenger. 'Tell him to get himself a hot meal.'

Leo worked in silence for some minutes. Translating the Greek was easy, but rephrasing it in Serbian was more of a problem. When she had finished, she handed the paper to Malkovic. It contained a plea from the Greek general for him to abandon his position with the Bulgarians and join up with his forces in Salonika in expectation of a future conflict with their former allies.

Leo said, 'It seems everyone wants you to turn traitor.'

He gave her one of his sudden, ironic grins. 'Now the main battle is over, the wolves are fighting over the corpse. Will you write a reply for me?'

'Of course.'

He dictated an answer, which informed the general that he felt it was important for the moment to remain where he was, so that Serbia had a stake in the conquest of Adrianople, which would be a valuable bargaining counter in any future settlement. But if the time came when they had to resort to arms, the general could count on his support. Leo transcribed his words into Greek and he signed the letter. It struck her that he had no way of knowing that she had translated him faithfully, and was gladdened by this evidence of trust. She addressed the envelope, and when she looked up she found he was leaning against the central pole of the tent with his arms folded and his eyes fixed on her.

Her heartbeat quickened. Had he seen through her at last? But instead he said, 'You told me once that you wanted to join the Bulgarian army but they turned you down. How would you like to join the Serbian army?'

'What?' Leo said, aghast.

'I need a secretary who can speak and write Greek and Turkish. I could give you the rank of Cadet Ensign. What do you say?'

Leo stared at him, dry-mouthed. For a brief moment the tantalising possibility of working with him every day flashed before her imagination. Then common sense reasserted itself. How could she sustain the deception she had practised if she was with him every day? Under what conditions would she be expected to live? Would she, for example, be expected to share a tent with some of the junior officers? And there was her duty to Sophie and the others in the hospital tent. She was needed there far more than here. And yet, she could not quite relinquish the dream.

'I'm very honoured, sir. I should like to work for you, very much. But ... but I do not think it would be ... appropriate for me to become a soldier in your army. As I said, I must go home soon and if I was to accept your offer I should not be free to leave. The fighting is over, more or less. At least the battle that I wanted to take part in, to expel the Turks, is over. But if I can be of service to you while I am here you have only to send for me. You know where to find me.'

He frowned at her and she knew that he was not used to being refused, but after a moment his face cleared. 'You are probably right. I will send next time I require your help. Now, you had better get back to your other duties.'

Leo rose, regretfully. For a short while she had felt closer to him than ever before. Now, she knew, the relationship had cooled, just as the wind that met her as she left the tent cooled her body. But what else could she have done? She walked back towards her own tent beset by moods that varied wildly between euphoria and despair – euphoria because she sensed that Malkovic wanted her company and thought he had found a way to keep her near him; despair because nothing could ever come of it. If he was attracted to her, it must be for the wrong reasons and once he knew the truth their relationship would be at an end.

Her thoughts were interrupted by a sound at once familiar and unexpected – the whistle of a locomotive. Looking across the snow-covered plain to the west, she saw the puffs of steam from an approaching train. She quickened her step. In the hospital tent there was a new sense of purpose and optimism.

'The train will take many of our patients back to Salonika, to the hospitals there,' Sophie said. 'Things will be easier from now on.'

During the rest of the day, wagon trains plodded backwards and forwards, unloading the provisions and ammunition for the besiegers. Leo wondered how much the starving people inside the city could see of what was going on, and pitied the anguish the sight must provoke for them.

Next morning, she and all the rest of the staff were busy from daybreak, preparing their patients for the journey, and soon the ox-carts were on their way again, carrying the wounded men down to the train. Leo went with them, trying to ensure that each man was made as comfortable as possible. It took until midday to transfer all the casualties and Leo was just plodding wearily back towards the hospital tent when she saw a car coming fast along the road from Gallipoli. Victoria and Luke hoping to catch the train with an urgent case, she guessed.

The car stopped by the train, as she expected, but then after a short wait it pulled away again and came racing towards the camp. Victoria jumped out and ran up the slope towards their tent.

'Leo! Are you ready? For goodness sake, tidy yourself up a bit. We haven't got much time.'

She hurried into the tent. Leo followed, and found her throwing her belongings into a bag.

'What are you doing?' Leo asked, aghast.

'What do you think? We're catching that train. Grab your things.'

'You can't! You can't just leave like that.'

'Can't I? You watch me!' She turned briefly to look at Leo. 'Think about it! How long have we waited for this train? God knows how long it might be before the next one. Don't be a fool, Leo! Get your things together. I've arranged for them to take us and Sparky.'

'But …' Leo struggled for words. 'What about Luke? You can't leave him behind. Where is he?'

Victoria jerked her chin over her shoulder. 'Back there, at Gallipoli.'

'Why? Why have you come without him?'

Her friend did not reply immediately. Then she said, 'The idiot proposed to me. He wants me to marry him and go back to New Zealand with him.'

'But Vita, that's wonderful, isn't it? I mean, it's obvious he's in love with you, and I thought you were with him.'

Victoria turned towards her. 'Can you see me, living on a farm in some Godforsaken backwater at the far end of the earth? Anyway, I told you, I never intend to marry.'

'But did Luke know that?' Victoria shrugged and returned to her packing. Leo persisted angrily. 'I told you, I tried to tell you, that this is what he would expect. He's a good man, Vita, and you have led him on and broken his heart.'

'It was an affair, that's all,' Victoria said. 'He should have realised that.'

'Have you … have you slept with him?'

'It's none of your business. It's up to me to choose whether I sleep with someone or not.'

'How could you be so heartless?'

The train whistle sounded and Victoria picked up her bag. 'Are you coming? The train won't wait.'

'No,' Leo said, 'I'm not.'

'You can't stay here, all alone.'

'I won't be alone. There's Sophie, and Iannis. And Luke when he gets back. I won't run off and leave him, even if you do.'

'Suit yourself.' Victoria moved to the entrance. In the opening of the tent she turned and her expression changed. 'I can't do it any more, Leo. I can't face the dirt and the squalor and the suffering, and I'm frightened of getting ill myself. I don't want to die out here! I'm sorry. I can't stay any longer.'

She turned and ran down the slope to the car. Leo stood still, straining her eyes towards the train, and saw the car loaded onto one of the flat-bed wagons that were used to transport field guns. She glimpsed Victoria getting into one of the carriages, but she did not look back. The whistle blew again, there was a clank of couplings and a volley of escaping steam from the engine and the train began its slow journey towards Salonika. Leo watched with a growing sense of panic. She should have gone with Victoria. What was she thinking of? By now she could have been on her way home; back to all the things her friend had listed – hot baths and comfortable beds and good food. Back, also, to her old life and any restrictions her grandma chose to put on her liberty; back to Ralph's mockery and the pressure to marry Tom. And away from any chance of seeing Sasha Malkovic again. She took a deep breath and walked back to the hospital tent.

Sophie saw her and ran over. 'Leo, what are you doing here? I thought you had gone on the train.'

'Gone?' Leo said. 'Why? What made you think that?'

'I just assumed ... I saw the car being loaded. Has Victoria gone?'

'Yes.'

'And left you behind?'

'It was my choice. I could have gone with her.'

Sophie looked around the tent and for the first time Leo realised that it was virtually empty. Sophie said, 'Oh dear! You know, you should have gone. You can see there are hardly any patients left. There will be more, of course, but we can manage. I should have said this yesterday ...'

In the distance the train whistle sounded once more and Leo forced a smile. 'It's all right. It doesn't matter. There will be another train.'

Sophie hugged her impulsively. 'Of course there will – and Iannis and I will be glad to have your company for a little longer.'

Back in her tent Leo sat for a long time on the edge of her bed, staring at the ground. Had she been a fool? She was stuck here now, with no real function and who could say when the next train might arrive? Sophie and Iannis were kind, but no substitute for Victoria. Then it came to her. With Victoria gone and her help no longer needed in the hospital tent, she was free to accept the position Sasha Malkovic had offered her. Not on a permanent basis, of course, but perhaps part-time. As long as she continued to live in her own tent, in the Bulgarian camp where she was known as a woman and able to use the facilities provided for the female nurses, it should be possible to maintain the deception. It was a risk, of course. A mad gamble. But after all, what could happen if she was discovered? She would be dismissed, but that was all. It was a gamble worth taking, and for a few days or weeks she could keep her dream alive.

Chapter 17

Tom Devenish took a sip of gritty coffee and raised his face to the winter sun. He had been in Athens for almost a month and was feeling perfectly healthy. In fact, he felt better than he had done for a long time. The last month had been pure enjoyment, as he wandered round Athens with his sketch pad, wondering why on earth he had set his face against foreign travel until now. Now he was contemplating his next move. He had almost decided to go to Delphi and then across the Gulf of Corinth to Patras, from where he could take a boat to Italy. He would do what he had dreamed of in the hospital, and take his time making his way home via Venice and Florence and then through France. There was no hurry. Leo would be safe at home now and he had admitted to himself long ago that he was not in love with her, nor she with him. The best thing he could do, for both of them, was to keep out of the way. She would find plenty of suitors once he was off the scene.

It meant, of course, that he would not see Ralph for a long time. Already they had been apart for a longer period than at any time since they had first met at the age of twelve. At school they had been inseparable, often staying in each other's homes during the holidays, and later, when Tom was up at Oxford and Ralph in the army, they had still managed to meet regularly. When Ralph had suggested that Tom would be an ideal husband for Leo, the idea had seemed wonderful at first, and for months Tom had allowed himself to entertain a dream in which the three of them all lived together. He knew that what he really wanted was something quite different but he had closed his mind to it as being too shameful to consider. Now, after so many weeks away from Ralph, he was beginning to feel like a recovering alcoholic, aware of a vacancy at the centre of his being but also experiencing an unfamiliar sense of freedom.

The waiter came out onto the terrace, carrying a newspaper and a letter. His usually bland face was animated and he waved the paper under Tom's nose.

'See, *kirie*? It is as I told you. The truce has broken down. Those treacherous Turks are attacking on Gallipoli.'

Tom waved the paper away. He'd had enough of wars and it was no longer his concern. Besides, he had recognised the handwriting on the envelope and had felt at once the old, familiar tingle of pleasure and excitement. 'You know I can't read Greek, Dimitrios. Is that a letter for me?'

'*Ne, kirie.* For you, from England.' He presented the letter with a flourish, gathered up Tom's cup and went back inside.

Tom slit the envelope. He had telegraphed to Ralph to let him know where he was, but this was the first reply that had reached him. He read:

My dear Tom,

I was delighted to get your telegram and to know that you are now on the way to full health. I am sure you will find Athens a very congenial place to convalesce. Sadly, I have two pieces of bad news to impart. First, my grandma died a few days ago. She had a stroke last week and never recovered consciousness. The funeral will take place next Tuesday. It is a great loss, of course, as she was the only close family I have, apart from Leonora.

Which brings me to my second item, one which concerns you more closely. Leo has not returned as we expected. The Women's Sick and Wounded

279

Convoy arrived back two days ago and I managed to arrange an interview with Mrs Stobart, their self-styled commandant. She told me that Leo and Victoria did not board the Orient Express with the rest of the group. Instead, they chose to return via Salonika in order to accommodate Victoria's car. (It seems they took it with them all that way, via Marseilles, so it's not surprising you found no trace of them on your journey.) They intended to find a ship to take them back to Marseilles, or some other port from whence they could drive home.

Of course, they may still be at sea but I have not had any word from Leo and I am afraid that she may never have reached Salonika. Two women travelling alone in that lawless country would be a tempting prey for any bandits.

Dear Tom, I hardly dare ask this of you, after all you have been through, but could you possibly nip back to Salonika and find out if they ever arrived and if so, which ship they boarded?

Tom lowered the letter and thumped the table in irritation. 'Nip back' – typical of Ralph! As if it was as simple as walking round the corner. He read on:

Now that Grandma has gone, I am, of course, Leo's legal guardian, so I have a double duty to find out what has happened to her. I have been moving heaven and earth to get myself posted as a military attaché to the Serbs, and it finally seems that my efforts may be about to bear fruit. Of course, if Leo and Victoria are already on their way home I shall be leaving just as they return – but by then perhaps you will be here to keep an eye on Leo. The sooner you two get married the better!

Whatever happens, I shall not have a moment's peace of mind until I know where she is, so please, dear friend, try to find out for me.

I remain, as always,

Your affectionate friend,
Ralph

Tom put the letter back in the envelope and sat gazing unseeingly at the Parthenon, which seemed to float against the pale blue of the sky above him. So, that was the end of his dream of a Grand Tour. He must go back to Salonika, if not for Ralph's sake then for Leo's. Even if he had rejected the idea of marriage he still had an obligation towards her. He was not in love with her but he was very fond of her and her safety mattered as much to him as it did to her brother. Ralph would never forgive him if he failed in this duty, but he did not relish the prospect of explaining to him that he no longer intended to marry Leo. With a sigh, he got up and went inside to prepare for his departure.

It took him the best part of a week to reach his destination and his first act was to call on Reggie Vincent, the British military attaché.

'Good lord,' Vincent exclaimed, 'I thought you'd be back in England by now. What are you doing back in this godforsaken hole?'

Tom cleared his throat. 'I'm afraid I wasn't entirely honest with you when we first met. I told you I was out here in order to make sketches for the newspapers. It's true that I had been drawing battleground scenes and some of them have been published by papers back home. But that wasn't my principal reason for being here. When I tell you that it touches upon the honour of a lady, you will understand why I was less than frank. The fact is, I am engaged, or about to be engaged, to a young lady called Leonora Malham Brown. She is a very independently minded girl, and she took it into her head to run off without telling anyone to join something called The Women's Sick and Wounded Convoy in Bulgaria.'

'I've heard of them,' Vincent interrupted. 'Done sterling work, by all accounts. But I think they've gone home now.'

'So I understand,' Tom said. 'But Leo isn't with them. It seems she and a friend are driving and were intending to come here to find a ship to take them and the car home. Have you, by any chance, heard of two young English women looking for passage on a boat heading for France or Italy?'

'Good God! What an amazing coincidence!' Vincent exclaimed. 'I had a girl in here a couple of days ago, asking me to help her find exactly that.'

'Oh, thank God!' Tom felt almost weak with relief. 'A tall girl with reddish hair?'

'No, 'fraid not. This one was dark.'

'Oh, well that would be Victoria, Leo's friend. Did you find them a ship?'

'Well, I did. But here's the thing. According to what the girl said, she was on her own.'

'On her own!'

'That's what she said.'

'When did her ship sail? Is there any chance she is still here?'

'Wait a minute, I wrote it down somewhere. Yes, here it is. She sails today. Oh God! What's the time?' He looked at the clock on the wall and rose, grabbing his cap. 'Come on. We might just catch her.'

Tom followed him down to the docks. He would have been completely at a loss in the general hubbub and confusion but Vincent led him through it at a run, brushing aside hawkers and beggars and dodging donkey carts and piles of crates. They reached the right pier just as a Greek-registered cargo ship was casting off, and on the deck Tom saw a battered and mud-covered car. Beside it stood a young woman in what he recognised as FANY uniform.

'Victoria!' Tom bawled at the top of his lungs.

He saw her turn, searching the dock for the source of the voice. Then she saw him.

'Tom Devenish! What are you doing here?'

'Where's Leo?' he yelled.

The ship was drawing away from the quay and Victoria's voice only just carried to him. 'She's at Adrianople. At the Red Cross hospital. She's nursing typhus patients.'

'Why isn't she with you?'

If she heard him her reply was drowned by the noise of the ship's engines. Tom turned to Vincent. 'Is there any chance of stopping the ship? Or could we get on board somehow?'

'Not a hope,' Vincent replied. 'Even if we could persuade the customs chaps that there was a good reason to detain her, she would be miles away before we got through all the red tape.'

Tom stood panting for a moment, then he said, 'Where's Adrianople?'

'Some distance away, I'm afraid. Over to the east. The Bulgarians have been besieging it for months. I assume your lady friend is working with them.'

'Nursing typhus patients,' Tom reminded himself. 'Is she out of her mind?'

'She must be a remarkable young woman,' Vincent commented.

'How can I get there?' Tom asked.

'It won't be easy, I'm afraid. There's no regular train service but they do send out reinforcements and supplies from time to time. They don't go as regularly as they might, because the Serbs control this end of the operation and there's no love lost between them and the Bulgarians. But we could go to the station and see if anything is scheduled.'

At the station, after being referred from one official to another until Tom's temper began to fray, they discovered that a train was due to leave in five days' time. When Tom asked if he could travel on it, however, he was told it was for military personnel only. There was some discussion in broken Serbian between Vincent and the official and at length the Englishman turned to Tom.

'He says he wants to see your passport. Which I take to mean that if he happened to find a few crisp bank notes nestling inside it he might be prepared to stretch a point.'

Tom remembered how Max had got them into the country, it seemed a long time ago now. He turned his back, took out his wallet and slipped what he thought was a generous amount between the pages of his passport and handed it over. The official grunted, pocketed the money without comment and laboriously filled in some kind of docket, stamped it and handed it to Tom.

First thing in the morning, five days later, he arrived at the station to find no sign of imminent departure. After hanging around for several hours he was told that there had been an unforeseen hold up but the train would go tomorrow. Eventually, at midday the following day, the engine wheezed and clanked into motion and they were on their way. Tom sat back and gazed bleakly out of the window. He was not sure what he hoped to accomplish. Leo would almost certainly refuse to come back with him, but at least he could tell Ralph he had done his best.

*

Luke Pavel stood on the heights overlooking the battle lines on the Gallipoli peninsula and gazed towards the white flecked waters of the Dardanelles. To his right he could just make out the line where the

Adriatic met the horizon, and to his left was the Sea of Marmara. Between the two, stretched across the neck of the peninsular, were the trenches, Bulgarian nearer to him, Turkish further away, and in the no man's land between lay the bodies of hundreds of men. He could see the Turkish ships standing off the coast but not the beaches where the troops had landed. They had come storming out of the trenches, wave after wave of them, screaming 'Allah! Allah!' and had been mown down by the Bulgarian guns on the higher ground. It was the first time he had understood the terrible destruction that these new machine guns could inflict.

An icy wind was blowing from the mountains to the north and sky and sea were slate grey against the white of the snow-covered landscape. It was a monochrome landscape, without colour or life, and without mercy. It reflected precisely the inner landscape of Luke's heart.

Chapter 18

On the morning after Victoria's departure, Leo presented herself at Malkovic's tent. He was in the middle of giving orders for the day to his aides-de-camp and his only reaction to her appearance was a quizzically raised eyebrow. When he had finished and dismissed the men, he sat back and looked at her with that steady, inscrutable gaze that she found so unnerving.

'I didn't send for you.'

'I know. The train took most of the patients from the hospital so I am no longer needed. So I am at your service – if you need me.'

'But you still refuse to accept a commission in the army?'

'Yes. As I said, I may have to leave soon and I must be free to go when the time comes.'

He continued to look at her broodingly. She had hurt his pride with her initial refusal and now she was afraid he would send her away. Finally he said, 'As you wish. I don't know how often I shall require you, but you can stay if you like.'

'Thank you!' She felt she had been holding her breath.

Maybe it was her heartfelt tone that touched him. His face relaxed and he said, with an almost mischievous smile, 'But if you are going to be part of my entourage we really must find you some other clothes. Those English tweeds are very serviceable, no doubt, but they are really appallingly dirty.'

Leo looked down at herself and realised for the first time how mud-spattered and stained her clothes were. She also recalled, with a jolt, that everything else she possessed apart from a change of underwear was in the trunk in the back of Victoria's car. Not that that would have been any help to her in the present circumstances.

She said, 'It's all I have.'

He got up and stretched. 'I have no doubt that we can find something. Suppose I were to ask the quartermaster to fit you out with a Serbian uniform, but without any badges or insignia. Would that serve?'

Leo was seized with a wave of panic. If she had to undress to have a uniform fitted she would undoubtedly be discovered. 'I doubt if he has anything that would fit,' she said, catching a straws.

He grinned. 'What? Do you think you're the only skinny lad in the army? He'll find you something.'

Before she could think of any further objection he strode to the tent entrance and shouted for his orderly. The man appeared at once and was instructed to conduct Leo to the quartermaster's tent and tell him to fit her out. 'Officer's quality!' Malkovic called after him as they left. All the way, Leo racked her brains for a way of getting out of the dilemma, but short of a sudden attack of vomiting she could think of nothing. It crossed her mind how easy it would have been if she were not masquerading as a man. As a woman a fainting fit would have been easy to simulate, but in her present guise no such stratagem was open to her.

In the event, she need not have worried. The quartermaster looked her up and down, grunted, and disappeared into his store to return with a bundle of clothes.

'This is as near as I can get. Got your own boots? Good. I've got nothing that small. Right, off you go.'

Leo took the clothes back to her tent and tried them on. The basic uniform was not so different from what she had been wearing, consisting of breeches and a tunic in brown serge. They were at least a size too large and she had to use a belt to hold the breeches up, but that was all to the good, as they concealed what feminine curves remained to her. The serge was rough against her skin, but at least it was clean. The best part of her new outfit was the overcoat, which came down almost to her ankles and was split up the back of the skirt for riding, so that it felt much like her old FANY uniform. At least now she could keep warm. The whole ensemble was topped off by a round cap trimmed with black astra-khan. Thus accoutred, she made her way back to the colonel's tent.

Malkovic was on his feet and she had the impression he had been pacing restlessly. He stopped when she entered and looked at her, with a slow grin form-ing on his lips.

'Well, well. Quite a handsome young fellow. What a pity I can't persuade you to accept a commission. But at least you look less of a ragamuffin than you did.'

Popitch looked into the tent. 'The horses are ready, sir.'

'Good.' He was moving towards the entrance. 'You can ride, I take it?'

'Yes, sir.'

'Then you may as well join us. Tell them to saddle Shadow, Michaelo.'

He led the way outside. A soldier was holding his big grey, and others, ready mounted, waited in attendance. A moment later another man ran up with a coal black gelding whose delicate legs and pretty head proclaimed his Arab blood.

'Take Shadow,' Malkovic said. 'He's a good horse but he doesn't take kindly to too firm a hand on the reins, so have a care.'

He vaulted on to Cloud and Leo swung herself into the black horse's saddle. Followed by the escort they trotted through the camp. Malkovic led the way and Shadow jogged and danced in the grey's wake, his ears flicking backwards and forwards, ready to spook at any sudden sound or movement. Leo sat still, letting her hands move with the horse's head, and little by little she felt him relax. Once clear of the camp they were out on the open plain. There had been fresh snow the day before, but it had not frozen and the horses paced through a white carpet that was almost fetlock deep. Malkovic glanced round, raised an arm and gestured forward, then touched his heels to his mount's flanks and Cloud sprang forward in a fast canter. Shadow surged after them and showed an inclination to make it a race. Leo quickly understood the warning Malkovic had give her. As she tightened the reins, the horse put his head down and bucked, almost unseating her. She eased the pressure and he settled into a power-ful stride. She found that by gentle touches on the reins she could control him just enough to keep him level with Cloud. Malkovic glanced at her and gave Cloud his head. Side by side they flew over the plain, the snow scattering behind them, the wind whipping their faces, and Leo threw back her head and laughed aloud. It was so long since she had enjoyed a gallop like this and she had missed it more than she realised.

Eventually the horses slackened speed of their own accord and Malkovic drew Cloud back to a walk. They looked at each other and she saw that his cheeks were flushed and his eyes sparkled like a boy's.

He said, 'Well done. Shadow is not usually so ready to accept a strange rider.' And she knew that she had been tested and not found wanting.

They returned to the camp at a more sober pace and handed the horses over to the soldier-grooms. Entering his tent, Malkovic flung his cloak onto the chest and shouted to his orderly to bring warm wine. The man appeared, carrying a steaming flagon. Malkovic poured two goblets and threw himself into a chair by the brazier.

'Sit.' He pointed to a second chair and she drew it closer and sat opposite him. He handed her a goblet and raised his own.

'Your health, lion cub.'

'Yours, Colonel.'

He sat back and stretched his legs to the heat, and she thought she had never seen him so relaxed. The brooding look had vanished from his eyes and his smile, as he looked at her, was no longer sardonic. For the first time she gave words to the feelings that had beset her all these weeks, though only in her silent thoughts. 'I am in love with this man. He is the only man I shall ever love.'

'So,' he said, 'explain to me how the grandson of a poor Macedonian peasant comes to possess the accomplishments of a gentleman.'

This was close enough to her own history for her to reply with confidence. After all, her real grandfather had risen from lowly beginnings. 'My grandfather may have been poor, but he was a clever man. When he reached England he saw that there were many opportunities for trade. He began to import goods from Macedonia and Greece – olive oil, herbs and spices, dried fruits – and his business prospered. He bought his own shop, then another and another and in the end he was able to purchase a small country estate and to send his only son to a good school. And in due course he sent me there, too.'

'Which school?'

'It is called Harrow School,' she said. The wine and the warmth after the ride had made her daring.

'Indeed, I am familiar with the name.'

That brought her to her senses. She knew enough about the school from Ralph to speak of it with some familiarity, but she could only pray that he did not know someone who had actually been there.

'With the name only?' she hazarded.

'Sadly, yes. But I hear it has an excellent reputation.'

'Oh, yes,' she agreed and took the opportunity to change the subject. 'May I ask you a little about yourself? Do you have a family?'

'A mother and two sisters, one older than me and married, the other still a young girl of seventeen – your age, I think you said.' Was there a hint of mischief in his eyes?

'You have no father?'

'He died ten years ago.'

'I'm sorry. So we are both fatherless.'

'And do you have brothers or sisters?'

'I had a sister, but she died.' Why had she said that? It had seemed to come unbidden to her tongue.

'You said your father assisted with the excavations at Troy. Tell me about that.'

Now she was on safe ground and for some time she talked about the treasures her father had helped to unearth. Malkovic showed an easy familiarity with the legend of the fall of Troy and a keen appreciation of how the discoveries made by the archaeologists had turned that from myth into history. She began to understand that, although he had always been destined for a career in the military, his education had been much the same as her own.

'Did you mind going into the army?' she asked. 'Would you rather have done something else?'

'Mind?' He frowned, as if the question was one he had never considered. 'I took it for granted. It had always been my family's duty and honour to defend our homeland.'

'Defend?' she said. 'Against whom?'

He gave a grim smile. 'It is hard for you to understand. Your grandparents may have been Macedonian but you have grown up in a country which is one of the Great Powers, safe on your island behind the protection of the Royal Navy. For us it is very different. For centuries we were dominated by the Ottomans. It was only in 1878 that we gained our independence. Now we are squeezed between two great empires, the Ottomans to the south and east and the Austro-Hungarians to the north. That is why our army is so important to us.'

'I see that,' she said. 'But, Sasha ...'

His eyebrows flew up. 'Only my immediate family call me that – to my face, at least.'

Leo dropped her gaze. She had clearly overstepped the mark. 'Forgive me. That was presumptuous.'

He regarded her in silence for a moment and that look was back in his eyes, as if he was trying to work out a puzzle of some sort. Then he said, 'Well, why not? You are not subject to military discipline. But only when we are alone, not in front of my officers. You understand?'

'Yes, I will remember,' she promised. 'Thank you!'

She was more careful after that, remembering that intimacy could only lead to her discovery. It still amazed her that he seemed to accept her so easily as a boy; but it occurred to her that perhaps the whole notion of a girl who might dress as a man and do the things they had done together was so foreign to his concept of femininity that it never crossed his mind to doubt her.

At midday the orderly came in with soup and bread and cheese. There were few luxuries available, even after the arrival of the supply train, but he had brought enough for two and it was obviously assumed that they would eat together. When the meal was over Sasha (as she now permitted herself to think of him) rose and took up his cloak.

'I must go on my rounds. You are at liberty until this evening. Stay here, if you wish, or go, as you choose.'

The tent was warm, and she had a full stomach and they had drunk more wine with the meal. The prospect of an afternoon of leisure was too tempting to resist. She returned to her chair by the brazier, put her feet up on the other one and allowed her thoughts to drift. It was the first real rest she had had since they disembarked at Salonika and it was only now she realised how worn out she was. Thinking back over her conversation with Sasha she remembered her response to his question about siblings. Why had she told him she had a sister who was dead? To deny the existence of Ralph was perhaps sensible, to avoid future complications, but why a dead sister? Then it came to her: *Twelfth Night*. It had been lurking at the back of her mind for weeks.

'*My father had a daughter loved a man, as it might be, were I a woman, I should your lordship.*'

'*What's her history?*'

'*A blank, my lord, she never told her love.*'

'*But died your sister of her love, my boy?*'

'*I am all the daughters of my father's house, and all the brothers, too.*'

Poor disguised Viola, hopelessly in love. Exactly like herself. On that thought, she drifted off to sleep.

She roused herself when the orderly came in to light the lamps and went back to her own tent to wash her face and comb her hair. When she returned to the Serbian camp she found she was to dine with Sasha and his officers. Used to the formal courtesy with which the Bulgarian officers had treated her in her female guise, she almost gave herself away by sailing into the mess tent ahead of the others. A hand gripped her arm fiercely and she found herself looking into the angry face of Michaelo Popitch.

'You may be the colonel's pet,' he hissed, 'but don't give yourself airs. You rank below everyone else here.'

She apologised and dropped back to follow the others, taking a place at the far end of the table. 'The colonel's pet!' Is that how she was seen? If so, did that mean he was known to have favourites, and had she supplanted Popitch? What exactly had he meant by the expression? And what did that reveal about Sasha himself? She watched him all through dinner, but she could see nothing that suggested he was other than a man among men. It was a new experience, to see how men behaved with each other when there were no women present, and she paid careful attention, for future reference. But there was nothing in their behaviour to explain Popitch's remark.

The next morning she reported to the Serbian camp again and was again invited to ride out with the colonel. In the afternoon she made her way to the hospital tent, guessing that Sophie must be wondering what had become of her. Sophie and Iannis laughed uproariously at her new outfit and teased her that she would turn into a boy if she was not careful, but they did not seem to find her new role particularly strange.

'It is good that you have found something to do away from the hospital,' Sophie said. 'We were very grateful for your help but I should never have forgiven myself if you had contracted typhus.'

Over the next days Leo learned that conducting a siege is primarily an exercise in boredom, especially when the fighting has stopped but peace negotiations have reached a stalemate. She sensed that Sasha was desperate to get away but when she asked why he did not take his Serbians home and leave the siege to the Bulgarians he told her that it was vital to maintain a Serbian presence. She sensed, too, that he was glad to have her company, though she wondered what he saw in her that his officers lacked. She found the clue in their long conversations. They shared many interests in common, and the discussions ranged widely. He was well-read, not only in classical literature but in the works of Shakespeare, which he read in translation, and of German poets like Goethe, which he read in the original. At the other end of the spectrum, they shared a love of the countryside and of country pursuits; particularly anything to do with horses. The morning ride became a regular routine, and in the afternoon, when Malkovic had carried out his inspection, they passed the time playing cards with some of his officers. Sometimes Sasha dictated letters for her to translate into Greek for the commanders in Salonika, but it seemed to her that there was very little in them of much importance and she wondered if it was just a way of justifying her presence.

In the evenings, after dinner, they sat round the campfire and listened to the gusla and the epic songs that retold the history of Serbia. Most of them centred round the reign of King Dusan the Strong, when Serbia had been a proud and independent nation, and the subsequent defeat in 1389 by the Turks at Kosovo Polje, the Field of the Blackbirds. The poems had the power of myths and Leo began to understand their importance in connecting the men around her to a heroic past and justifying their desire to recreate it.

One morning, returning from their ride, she saw that the train of ox-wagons had just drawn up in the road below the hospital. She nudged Shadow alongside Cloud and said, 'A friend of mine is probably with that convoy. Do you mind if I go and talk to him?'

'A friend?' he queried. 'Another Englishman?'

'No,' Leo said, deciding not to embark on an explanation of Luke's origins. 'Just someone I worked with in the hospital at Chataldzha. He's a stretcher-bearer.'

'Very well, I'll see you at luncheon.'

Leo wheeled Shadow away and trotted down to the hospital tent, arriving just as Luke was helping to carry a stretcher inside. She tethered the horse and waited for him to come out. He would have walked past her if she had not called, 'Luke, wait a minute. I want to talk to you.'

He swung round and she was distressed to see how bleak and haggard he looked. For a moment he stared at her, then his jaw dropped.

'Jeez, Leo! What have you done now? I didn't recognise you.'

'I'm sorry,' she said. 'I'll explain later. Why don't you come up to the tent? The others can finish off here.'

He looked round, then nodded and followed her up to her tent. Inside, he said, 'Where's Victoria?'

With deepening distress she realised that Victoria had not told him of her intentions. 'She's gone, Luke. A train came in from Salonika with supplies and took most of the patients from the hospital back. You didn't know? Victoria went with them.'

His face brightened. 'Oh, then she'll be back?'

'No, I'm afraid not. She took the car and she was intending to find a ship to get her home. I'm so sorry, Luke.'

'Did she tell you what happened?'

302

'She said you proposed to her and she turned you down. It was unforgivable. I tried to warn her, weeks ago, what would happen. I knew you were in love with her and that you would assume she felt the same way. She wouldn't listen.'

He shook his head sadly. 'I guess I'm too simple for a sophisticated girl like Victoria. I should have known better than to expect her to marry me.'

'She should have known better than to lead you on like that.'

He was silent for a moment, then he said, 'And she went off and left you behind.'

'That was my choice. She would have taken me with her if I wanted.'

'Why didn't you?'

'I … I was happy here. I didn't want to leave.'

'Happy?' He looked at her, frowning. 'What's going on, Leo? You look as if you've joined the army.'

'No, I haven't done that. I'm working for Colonel Malkovic as a sort of secretary. You may have seen him at Chataldzha.'

'Tall guy on a big white horse?'

'That's him.'

'So what's the big attraction?'

It was Leo's turn to drop her head. The urge to confide was almost overpowering. 'He's … I just …'

He leaned forward and touched her arm. 'Are you in love with him?'

'Yes, I think I am.'

'So why are you dressed up as a boy?'

'Because he doesn't approve of women anywhere near the front line. If he knew who I was he'd send me away.'

He shook his head at her. 'I can't see much future in that arrangement.'

'Nor can I,' she agreed sadly.

He heaved a deep sigh. 'What a pity you and I didn't fall for each other. We could both have been so much happier.'

She forced a smile. 'Yes, you're right. But these things don't happen to order.'

'You're right there!'

'But we are friends, aren't we? I should be sad to lose that.'

'Of course we are. Don't worry. Victoria's decision doesn't make any difference to that.'

'I'm glad. What will you do now?'

He shrugged. 'Go home, I suppose. The fighting seems to have died down again at Gallipoli. There isn't much work to do. You don't fancy a trip to New Zealand?'

'I'd love to, one day. But not now. I don't know what I'm waiting for, but I know I have to make the most of this time. You will keep in touch, won't you?'

'Of course I will. Except I don't know how. I don't have your address. I can't really address it to "the girl with the chestnut hair who dresses like a boy c/o Adrianople".'

Leo laughed, relieved to see him recovering something of his old spirit. 'And I can't address mine to "the tall, thin red-headed man who lives in New Zealand". I'll give you my home address and you can give me yours.'

She found some paper and wrote her address in Sussex Gardens, then tore it in half and told him to write his on the blank piece. In the hospital mess below a bell rang, summoning the staff to eat.

Leo stood up. 'My boss will be expecting me back, and you should get some food.' He stood up too and they looked into each other's faces. 'It's been lovely to know you, Luke. I wish it hadn't ended like this.'

'It isn't your fault,' he said. 'It's been good to know you, too. I wish I could see a happy ending for you, at least.'

'I'll survive,' she said. 'So will you.'

'I imagine I will.' He took her hands and kissed her on the cheek. 'Take care of yourself.'

'And you.'

It wasn't quite the end, because outside the tent he paused to admire Shadow and, remembering their common interest in horseflesh, Leo said, 'I'll come and inspect your animals one day.'

'Make that a promise!' he said, and walked away down the slope. She watched him out of sight and wondered if she would ever fulfil the pledge.

Chapter 19

Two days later, riding back to camp, they saw the train from Salonika steaming in.

'More supplies!' Sasha said. 'Excellent!'

Back in his tent the orderly had just come in with the warm wine when the guard on duty outside put his head round the tent flap.

'Excuse me, sir. You've got a visitor.'

'Send him in.'

Malkovic was removing his cloak and Leo was pouring wine with her back to the entrance when a voice behind her caused her to slop it onto the tray.

'Forgive me for intruding on you. My name is Thomas ...' Leo whirled round and Tom's words dried in his throat. He gaped at her and she saw him turn pale, as if he was seeing a ghost, or a vision. Seizing the advantage, she did the first thing that came into her head. She marched across the tent and slapped Tom jovially on the shoulder.

'Good Lord! Tom! What are you doing here, old friend?' Then in the same tone, remembering that Sasha spoke no English, she continued, 'Don't say anything. If you give me away I shall never forgive you. Let me do the talking.' Turning to Malkovic she went on in Serbian, 'Sasha, this is an old friend of mine, all the way from England. His name is Thomas Devenish.'

'Indeed?' Malkovic's eyes had the guarded look she had seen when they first met. 'Please tell him he is welcome.'

'Tom,' she said, reverting to English, 'this is Colonel Aleksander Malkovic. He has been kind enough to give me a position in his entourage. He asks me to say you are welcome.'

'I don't understand,' Tom croaked. 'What are you doing dressed like that?'

'Never mind that for the moment. Just be polite to the colonel.' She was careful to keep her voice light, as if they were exchanging pleasantries.

Tom advanced as if in a dream and extended his hand. 'How do you do, sir? I hope you will forgive me for intruding without an introduction.'

Malkovic shook hands with him and greeted him in his own language, adding, 'Will you have a glass of wine?'

Leo handed Tom a goblet and out of force of habit he raised it to Malkovic. 'Your health, sir.'

Sasha looked past him at Leo. 'What has he come for? To take you home?'

'Oh, no!' she replied. 'He is here out of concern for me, to make sure I am all right, that is all.' She turned to Tom. 'Did you come on the train? I expect you're tired.' His pallor and look of confusion gave credence to the assumption.

'Yes, but ...'

She cut across him, turning back to Sasha. 'My friend is not strong. He's exhausted after the journey. Is there somewhere he can rest?'

Malkovic lifted his shoulders. 'Why not in your tent?'

'Of course,' Leo said hastily. 'Will you excuse us? I think he should lie down at once.'

'As you please.' He turned away to his table. 'I have work to do, anyway.' Leo looked at him and knew that he was suspicious of this newcomer, and possibly jealous as well. That was something she could try to sort out later. For the moment, Tom was the priority. She took him by the arm.

'Come with me to somewhere we can talk.'

He nodded and put down his goblet, and they left the tent. Outside he erupted furiously, 'Leonora, what is going on? Why are you dressed like this?'

'Don't call me Leonora! I'm known as Leo here. What are you doing here, Tom?'

'Looking for you, obviously.'

'Why now? I've been gone for months.'

'And I've been looking for you for months. Have you any idea of the trouble you have caused? I've traipsed round half of Europe looking for you. I've been arrested and nearly shot as a spy. I've been through hell on the battlefields in the west. Have you any conception of what things are like around Scopje and Bitola? I saw horrors I'll have nightmares about for the rest of my life. And I've been ill. If it wasn't for an American journalist I'd be one more corpse rotting in the mud outside Bitola. And then, just when I was recuperating in Athens and thinking you were safe home and I was free to get on with my life, I get a letter telling me you haven't gone home and asking me to go back to Salonika to find out where you had got to. And now I find you here, like this!'

Taken aback by this furious tirade from a man who had always seemed to her so lacking in spirit, Leo could only say, 'I'm so sorry, Tom. I never imagined you would come after me. I thought my grandma might inform the police and I might be stopped at a frontier somewhere, but I never imagined this.'

He said nothing and they walked in silence for a few minutes.

Then Leo said, 'What made you think I was safe at home?'

'I had a letter from Ralph. He had seen that Mrs Stibbert ...'

'Stobart?'

'Yes. And he found out that you had not come back with the other women. She told him that you and Victoria were planning to travel via Salonika, so he asked me to go there and find out which ship you were on.'

'Yes, well, we changed our plans. Victoria went home without me.'

'I know.'

'How?'

'She told me.'

'You saw Victoria?'

'After a fashion. She was on board a ship that was just setting sail. We yelled to each other from the deck to the dock. She told me you were here but she said you were nursing typhus patients.'

'I was when she left. I'm ... doing something different now.'

'That much is apparent! Well, I suppose it is something to be grateful for. At least you are away from the danger of infection.'

'How did you know where to find me?'

'I asked at the hospital. They directed me to Colonel Malkovic's tent. But what on earth has got into you, to dress like this?'

They had reached her tent. 'Come in,' she said, holding the flap aside. 'Sit down and I'll try to explain.'

He sank onto the bed that had once been Victoria's and she sat opposite. In the close confines of the tent their knees were almost touching.

'Is this where you sleep?'

'Yes.'

'Not with him?'

'Of course not! What sort of a man do you take him for? He thinks I'm a boy.'

'Precisely my point!'

She laughed suddenly. 'Oh, come on, Tom! Think about it. It isn't possible.'

He ran his hand over his face. 'Of course. I'm sorry. I'm just confused. Dear God, Leo! When I first saw you just now I thought you were Ralph. Not Ralph as he is now, but as he was seven, eight years ago, when we were at school. I felt as though I had stepped into a time machine.'

'Poor Tom!' she said, smiling. 'No wonder you looked stunned.'

'I'm still stunned. Please explain!'

Leo drew a deep breath. 'It started when I was working in the field hospital at Chataldzha, before Christmas. My skirt got so muddy and wet it was impossible to wear, so I left it off and just wore the tunic and breeches. I wasn't trying to look like a man, just to be practical. And I cut my hair because I couldn't get it dry and I was afraid of catching cold. One day Sasha came riding by and he mistook me for a boy. I didn't disillusion him because I knew that he has very strong views about women anywhere near the front line. He found out I could speak Turkish and asked me to help him interrogate a prisoner. Then, when I got here, he found out I could write Greek as well and offered me a position as a sort of secretary.'

'And you have never told him who you really are?'

'I've told you, he would send me away if he knew. And I'll never forgive you, Tom, if you give me away!'

For a moment their eyes met and she saw that her vehemence had shocked him. Then he shrugged. 'Well, it's immaterial now. Get your things together. If we are quick we can catch the train before it leaves for Salonika.'

'Leaves!' She stared at him. 'I'm not leaving, Tom. You can go, if you like, but I'm staying here.'

'Don't be ridiculous! I've come to fetch you home.'

'I'm not a child! I don't need to be fetched. I'll make my own way home when I'm ready.'

'But why? Don't you want to go home?'

'Why should I? What have I got to look forward to when I get home? Grandma will probably lock me up. The best I can hope for is to be sent off to Cheshire, with someone who will watch me like a ... like a criminal ... in case I try to escape again.'

His expression softened. 'Leo, there's something I must tell you. It's bad news, I'm afraid. Your grandma is dead.'

Leo swayed as if he had struck her. 'Dead? When? How?'

'A few weeks ago. I only found out from Ralph's letter. It was a stroke.'

She ran both hands through her hair. 'Was it my fault? Was it because of what I did?'

He shook his head and took her hands. 'No, I really don't think so. It happened so long after you left. She was an old lady, Leo. It was just ... the natural order of things.'

'But now I shall never see her again. Never be able to explain ... never be able to tell her I'm sorry.'

Her tears fell on his hands and he leaned forward and kissed the top of her head. 'Don't cry, my dear. She's in a better place and, who knows, perhaps she can look down and see that you are contrite.'

'But I'm not,' Leo wept. 'I'll never regret what I've done and she would have stopped me doing it. So why am I crying?'

'Because, for all the arguments and cross words between you, you loved her. And she loved you.'

'I suppose so, in her way.'

'Well,' he said, 'look on the positive side. It means that Ralph is now your legal guardian. That's good, isn't it?'

'Ralph!' She jerked upright and stared at Tom. 'No! No, it isn't good. It's worse.'

'What on earth makes you say that?'

'You know how pompous and self-important he has become. All that matters to him is his "honour", his reputation. He hated me being in the FANY. If I go home now he'll make my life a misery.'

'Oh, come on now! I think you're being unjust.'

'Am I? You saw what it was like when Victoria and I wanted to go to camp. He'd have stopped me if he could.'

She saw that he remembered and understood. 'But what do you propose to do?' he asked. 'If you don't go home, I mean.'

She shook her head sadly. 'I don't know. Stay here until the siege ends. It can't be much longer now. And then ... I'll be twenty in a week or two, Tom. In another year I shall be of age and my own mistress. I've been working as a nurse in the hospital here. I expect the doctors could find me a job somewhere.'

'You would rather do that ... that menial work ... than come home?'

'It's not menial, Tom!' she responded with a flash of anger. 'It's hard and sometimes very distressing, but it's useful and important. I would rather do that than sit at home twiddling my thumbs.'

He gave her a look as if he was seeing her for the first time. Then he said, 'I think I can understand that – and I admire you for it. But what is it about what you are doing right now that is so important? Is it Colonel Malkovic?'

She met his eyes and saw that he had guessed her secret. Emboldened by his look, she said, 'Yes. I know it's foolish but I can't help myself.' She gave him a wry smile. 'It looks as though we are both fated to pine for something we can never have.'

The colour rose in his face and for a moment she thought he was going to repudiate the suggestion. Then he sighed and nodded. 'I'm afraid you're right.'

She leaned forward and pressed her advantage. 'Tom, you must see what would happen if I go home now. Ralph will be more determined than ever to see us married. Neither of us wants that. It would be misery for both of us. But as long as I am dependent on him it will be very difficult to resist. Isn't it better for me to keep out of his way as long as I can?'

'That's all very well,' he said, 'but if I go back without you how am I going to explain it to him?'

'Tell him I refused point-blank to come with you. After all, you have no authority over me. Short of binding me hand and foot and kidnapping me, you can't make me come. You go home, Tom – or go wherever it was you were planning to go. Tell Ralph you found me and I'm in good health and not in any danger and I'll find my own way home when … when I'm ready.' She reached out and touched his hand. 'Give me these few days, Tom. It matters so much. Please!'

He squeezed her fingers. 'Poor Leo. How is it all going to end? Why don't you explain to him, as you have to me?'

She shook her head. 'He would think I had deceived him, which I have. He would be furious. He is a proud man and he could not bear to think he had been taken in like that.'

'So what do you expect to happen?'

'I don't know. I just want to make the most of it while it lasts.'

'All right. But I'm not going to leave you here. I'll stay, if Malkovic will let me.'

She considered. 'I don't suppose he will object. Hospitality to visitors is a very important part of the culture here – and he will probably enjoy having someone new to talk to. But what will you do with yourself? You'll be bored to death. There's nothing to occupy you here.'

'Yes, there is. When I was travelling through those battlegrounds I started drawing what I saw along the way, no matter how terrible it was. There must be plenty of things I can sketch here, to add to what I have already. I should be grateful to you. I was vegetating in London, living in a dream, and you forced me to get out into the world and face reality. When I get home I plan to have a small exhibition, or perhaps produce a book. I have already had a few pictures published in the papers back in England. I want people to see the horror of war, so perhaps they won't want to rush into another one.'

Leo leaned forward and grasped his hands. 'Tom, I am so pleased! It's exactly what I want, too, but your pictures will be far more powerful than anything I could say. You'll stay, then, for a while?'

'For a while,' he said, and smiled suddenly. 'I don't know, Leo. You've led us all a merry dance, but I take my hat off to you. I couldn't do what you've done.'

'Yes, you could, if the need arose,' she said. 'It's surprising what one can do, if pushed. Now, why don't you get some rest? I know what that train journey is like.'

He stretched. 'Yes, perhaps I will.

Leo rose. 'I must go back to Sasha. Somehow I've got to explain you turning up out of the blue like this.' She got up. 'You can use that bed, and Victoria's sleeping bag. She left it behind in her rush to be off. I'll come and collect you later.'

'But, Leo!' he expostulated. 'We can't both sleep in this tent. It wouldn't be decent.'

She gave him a wry grin. 'I don't think we have any choice, Tom. But don't worry. We'll find a way to preserve our modesty somehow. Anyway, for now you have it to yourself. Sleep well.'

When she got back to the colonel's tent he was already eating. He sat back and gave her one of those searching looks. 'So, your friend is resting?'

'Yes.'

'He seems a good deal older than you. It must be an unusual friendship.'

'We were at school together. He was in his last year when I arrived there. I was his fag. You know what that means?'

'A system of institutional slavery, as I understand it.'

She managed a smile. 'Something close to that.'

'But is it not unusual for such a relationship to result in a lasting friendship?'

'He is a family friend. He came on behalf on my grandparents.' The lie caught in her throat and she swallowed hard. He looked at her more keenly.

'Something is wrong. What is it?'

'My grandma is dead. She died of a stroke a few weeks ago. I shall never see her again.'

He got up and came to her, putting his hands on her shoulders. 'Poor lad! For you it must be like the death of a mother. I am sorry.'

She longed to lay her head against his chest and weep, but she knew if she did they would be a woman's tears so she choked them back and rubbed her hand across her face. 'Thank you, but I must be strong. After all, what is one death among so many? Thousands must be weeping, even now.'

He nodded and patted her shoulder and then turned away. 'Come and drink some wine. Have you eaten?'

Towards evening she fetched some warm water from the kitchens and woke Tom. When he had dressed and washed, they walked back towards the Serbian camp.

'You will be careful, Tom,' she begged. 'Don't call me Leonora.'

'I'll try to remember. But it's not going to be easy keeping up this charade, you know.'

'Oh well,' she said, 'there's one comfort. Sasha doesn't understand English, so if you make a slip he won't notice.'

In the mess tent Malkovic insisted that Tom sit next to him, and called Leo to his other side to translate. The conversation was laborious, but focussed mainly on Tom's experiences in his search for Leo. He told them about his arrest in Belgrade, which provoked some hilarity among the officers listening, and then about what he had seen along the road, which was greeted very differently. By the time the meal was over Leo felt that Sasha was less suspicious of him, and had even begun to like him.

Back in Sasha's tent later, Tom brought out his sketches and told him what he intended, asking his permission to make more drawings in the camp.

Malkovic nodded gravely. 'I applaud your intentions. I am a soldier by profession, but I have seen too much cruelty in the last months. Let us pray that the conference in London comes to some conclusion soon, so we can all go home.'

'Amen,' said Tom. But Leo turned away and was silent.

Chapter 20

The snow melted, revealing the camp in all its filth and squalor. A cold wind dried the mud to dust and sent it blowing into faces and food and clothing, but they discovered on their daily rides that the plain was studded with tiny wildflowers, crocuses and orchids and pale pink cyclamen. It was during these rides that Leo began to learn a little more about Sasha's background and to understand the sardonic reserve with which he masked his real feelings. She also discovered that he was younger than she had thought, less than ten years older than herself. His father had died when he was just eighteen, and he had been left with the responsibility of looking after his mother and his two sisters, together with the family estates.

'How did your father die?' she asked.

He pursed his lips and for a moment she thought he was not going to answer. Then he said, 'Do you know anything about how our last king, King Aleksander, met his end?'

Leo trawled her memory. 'Wasn't he assassinated?'

'Yes, he was. In many ways it was necessary. Aleksander Obrenovic was an arrogant fool who had married a woman, Queen Draga, who was little better than a streetwalker. She was unable to bear him children, so the next in line to the throne were her two brothers, who were universally hated. But it was when she persuaded him to turn on the army and purge all those who disliked her and her family that some of the officers decided the situation had become intolerable. Led by a man called Dragutin Dimitrijevic they burst into the palace one night with drawn swords, intent on slaughtering the king and queen in their bed.' He paused, his brows drawn together. 'My father was captain of the Royal Guard. They confronted the assassins in the main courtyard. He had no liking for Draga and her brothers, but he had sworn an oath and he knew his duty. The conspirators cut him down and went on to murder the king and queen.'

'That must have been terrible for you and your family,' Leo said. 'But you must be proud of him.'

'Proud? Yes. But I found myself caught between the two factions. I had just joined the army and my sympathies were mainly with the conspirators. Yet my father had behaved honourably and I could not disown him.'

'I see now why you had to be careful. But you are obviously trusted by the new regime, or you would not be in command here.'

He inclined his head with a slight smile. 'It is true. King Petar Karadjordjevic is a sensible, pragmatic man, who rewards loyalty where he sees it and has done much to make our army the force it is today. I have reason to be grateful to him.'

Tom often rode with them, and although Leo never felt quite able to relax when the two men were together, it seemed that a kind of friendship had been established. In the afternoons Tom wandered about the camp with his sketchpad, making friends with the ordinary soldiers. He even began to learn a little Serbian. Sometimes Leo went with him as interpreter. As the days passed she pitied the people trapped inside the city more and more, yet, to her shame, she could not wish the siege to end. Every added day was precious.

They continued to share a tent. Tom smoked a cigar outside every evening until Leo called that she was in bed, and then she was careful to lie with her face turned away until he had undressed and got into bed in his turn. After that, they often lay chatting companionably and once he was asleep she found it comforting to hear his steady breathing. She had missed Victoria and now she felt she had a friend who was almost a brother.

One day in early March a messenger arrived with the news that Prince Aleksander of Serbia was on his way to inspect the Serbian detachment at Adrianople and would arrive the following day. The news triggered a flurry of activity. Drills were held on a bit of level ground between the camp and the trenches. Boots were cleaned and buckles polished and the few luxuries the kitchen could muster were prepared and laid out in the officers' mess tent.

About midday the sentry posted on the hill overlooking the road reported that three cars were heading towards them. Watching from the front of the mess tent with Malkovic, Leo and Tom saw a group of officers descend and walk up the hill to where General Dimitriev was waiting.

'Going to pay his respects to the Bulgarians first,' Sasha commented. 'Correct protocol, as the general is the senior officer here.'

Shortly afterwards the visitors emerged from the general's tent and Sasha went to meet them. The troops, apart from those on guard in the trenches, were drawn up ready on the improvised parade ground. Sasha had suggested that it would be better for Leo and Tom to remain in the background until after the inspection, promising to introduce them at the reception later. Tom was keen to draw a picture of the parade, so they moved up to a point on the hillside where they had a bird's eye view of the proceedings.

'Isn't that a British army uniform, in among the prince's entourage?' Leo asked, screwing up her eyes against the sunlight.

'That'll be a military attaché,' Tom said. 'I wonder if it's Reggie Vincent. He was very helpful to me in Salonika.'

When the inspection was over they returned to the mess tent and withdrew to a corner to await their opportunity to be presented. Footsteps and voices approached and Malkovic ushered in a tall, good-looking man in military uniform decorated with medals and with a sash across his chest. The officers of his entourage crowded in behind them. Sasha beckoned Leo and Tom forward.

'Your highness, may I present two English gentlemen, who have risked their lives in the Serbian cause? This is Mr Tom Devenish ...'

His voice was drowned by a shout from one of the accompanying officers.

'Leonora! What in the name of God ...?'

Everyone swung round to look at the speaker and Leo found herself face to face with Ralph. Speechless and paralysed by shock she could only stare at him. For an instant nobody moved. Then Ralph lunged forward and grabbed her by the wrist.

'What do you think you are doing?' he demanded, in a voice hoarse with fury. 'Have you no shame?'

At the same moment, Sasha exclaimed in Serbian, 'Who is this fellow? What is going on?'

Prince Aleksander, who obviously understood English, intervened with a commanding gesture. 'Gentlemen, gentlemen, please!' Turning to Ralph, he went on in English, 'You have some argument with this young man? What is the problem?'

'This is not a young man, sir!' Ralph responded in a desperate undertone. 'This is my sister! My sister, I am ashamed to say!'

The prince looked at Leo. 'Is this true?'

Almost choked with tears, Leo could only nod her head. To her surprise, she saw amusement twitch the corners of Aleksander's mouth. He turned to Sasha and reverted to Serbian.

'My friend, it seems you have been the subject of a masquerade. This young gentleman is not a man at all. She is a woman.'

'What?' She saw the colour drain from Sasha's face. 'Is this true?'

Weeping now, she whispered, 'I'm sorry! I'm so sorry! Please don't be angry.'

Ralph dragged at her arm. 'Come away! You are making a show of yourself.'

'Who is this man?' Sasha demanded. 'Your husband?'

'No! No, my brother.'

'Tell him to get you out of my sight and lock you up! You are a disgrace to your family.'

'Sasha!' she pleaded.

The colour had come back to his face now and he spoke in the low tones of a man struggling to control himself. 'How could you? How dared you deceive me like this? If I were your brother I would beat you for shaming me in such a way.' Then, with an effort, he resumed the mask of formal courtesy and turned to the prince. 'Forgive me, sir. This is most unseemly. Will you take a glass of wine?'

Aleksander looked from one to another and apparently decided in favour of tact. 'Thank you, no. I must be on my way. We have a long journey to make. I congratulate you, Colonel, on your tenacity in this situation. You and your men are a credit to the army and Serbia is grateful.' He turned to Ralph, who had not relaxed his grip on Leo's arm. 'If your sister wishes to return with us, I am sure we can find room for her in one of the cars. I am going to say farewell to General Dimitriev. You have a short time to arrange your affairs.' Then, to Sasha, 'There is no need for you to see us off, Colonel. You have more urgent matters to attend to.'

The prince led his entourage out of the tent, leaving the four of them alone. Ralph looked at Leo.

'For God's sake, make yourself decent. Haven't you got a skirt to put on?'

Tom spoke for the first time. 'Don't be too hard on her, Ralph ...'

Ralph turned on him. 'You! I trusted you. How could you let this happen?'

Sasha cut in. 'You have no further business here. You can continue your argument outside.'

Ralph looked at him blankly and Leo said, 'He wants us to go.'

Ralph looked at Sasha and then at her. 'What is there between you? If he's laid a finger on you ...'

'Oh, don't be stupid, Ralph.' Anger overcame distress for a moment. 'None of this is Sasha's fault. I deceived him. He has acted honourably.' She turned to Sasha and broke into Serbian. 'Please, Sasha, don't think too badly of me. I didn't set out to deceive you. You mistook me for a boy and I didn't tell you the truth because I knew if I did you would send me away. I only wanted to be near you. That's all I am guilty of.'

His face was unyielding. 'I trusted you and you have made a fool of me. I cannot forgive that. The sooner you leave the better.'

She contemplated a further appeal but knew it would be useless. She turned back to her brother. 'All right, Ralph. Let's go. There is nothing more to say here.'

At the entrance to the tent she looked round, but his back was towards her and he did not turn.

Outside Ralph said, 'You can't walk through a camp full of soldiers dressed like that. Where are your proper clothes?'

'They won't notice anything unusual,' she replied. 'They think I'm a boy.'

'But you must have a dress somewhere. Where do you live?'

'In a tent over there. We're going there now.'

'Then hurry and change. We mustn't keep the prince waiting.'

'I can't,' she said woodenly. 'I don't have any-thing else to wear.'

'Why, in heaven's name?'

'My FANY skirt got too stained with mud and other things to wear. And all my other clothes are in a trunk in the back of Victoria's car. She took them with her when she left.'

He stared at her. 'What are we going to do? I can't take you back to Salonika dressed like that.'

She shrugged wearily. 'I've got a long cloak. That will cover me for the time being.'

They had reached her tent. 'Get your things, and be quick,' he instructed.

When Tom made to follow her in, Ralph caught his arm. 'Where are you going?'

'To get my things. You weren't going to leave me behind, were you?'

'You mean you two have been sleeping together?' Leo thought that in other circumstances Ralph's expression would have been comic.

'We have shared a tent, but nothing more.' Tom spoke with greater dignity than she had ever heard him employ when talking to her brother. 'I assure you, we have been like brother and sister. Leo's honour is perfectly safe.'

'Her honour!' Ralph exploded. 'She has no honour! After this we shall be the laughing stock of Europe.'

Leo ignored him and went into the tent. Tom came after her and put his arms round her. 'Poor Leo, I'm so sorry it ended like this.'

She sniffed. 'I knew it couldn't last for ever. But I never imagined the end would be as bad as this. What am I going to do, Tom? I can't go back to London. Do you think Ralph will throw me out?'

'Of course he won't. If he tries he'll have me to answer to. Come on, put a brave face on it. Don't let the prince and his hangers-on see you humbled.'

She looked up at him and murmured, 'Dear Tom. I've never really appreciated you properly. Thank you.'

He gave her a handkerchief and she dried her face and packed her few belongings into her bag. Then she straightened her shoulders and went out to join Ralph. As they walked down to the cars she contemplated asking if she could go and say goodbye to Sophie and Iannis and the rest but she knew that the permission would be refused. Perhaps it was just as well. What could she have said about her sudden departure?

Prince Aleksander must have been watching for them, because he came out of the general's tent almost immediately and they all got into the cars. It was a tight fit, and Leo was jammed between Ralph and Tom. Tom took the opportunity to grasp her hand and squeeze it and she was grateful for the comfort. As the engines started she craned her neck to look back towards the Serbian camp, hoping that Sasha might have come out to watch her go, but there was no sign of him.

As they bumped over the uneven road, she whispered to Ralph, 'Where are we going?'

'Salonika first. Then back to Belgrade.'

'Not London?'

'No. Not London. I have been appointed attaché to Prince Aleksander and I must go where he goes, which is currently to Belgrade. And since I am now your legal guardian, God help me, you will come with me. I am not going to trust you on your own again. So make the best of it.'

Leo sat back and closed her eyes. Belgrade! At least she would still be in Serbia, and while she was in Serbia there was always a chance of encountering Sasha Malkovic.

*

Belgrade was *en fête*. To all intents and purposes the war was over and for Serbia it had been a great success. They had overrun large parts of Albania and most of Macedonia and now had an outlet to the Adriatic at Durrazzo and to the Mediterranean proper at Salonika. The final outcome of the London Conference was yet to be announced, but no one doubted that it would be in Serbia's favour.

There were to be no celebrations, however, for Leonora. Ralph had taken a suite for them at the Hotel Moscow, only recently opened and proclaiming its modernity with a flamboyant art-deco facade. In Salonika he had gone out himself and found a dress shop and returned with a plain, respectable grey dress that more or less fitted her. On arriving in Belgrade he came into their sitting room and sat facing her with a frown.

'You must understand that I have my duties here, and those duties include social ones. There are many invitations that I cannot refuse without causing offence. Obviously, you cannot appear in society. The story of your extraordinary behaviour will have gone the rounds and you would be a laughing stock. Anyway, I suspect no hostess would wish to include you among her guests. Fortunately, we have a ready excuse. You are in mourning for our grandma.'

'And you are not, I suppose,' Leo said.

'That is beside the point. I have already explained my position.'

'But what am I supposed to do with myself? I can't sit in this room all day, twiddling my thumbs.'

He stood up. 'That is up to you. I suggest you take up a hobby or read some improving books.'

Tormented by the memory of Sasha's bitter look, Leo took refuge in laughter that verged on the hysterical. 'Oh, Ralph, you should see yourself. What have you been reading? Are you studying to be a Dickensian paterfamilias?'

He glared at her. 'I am struggling to redeem the reputation of this family, which you have dragged in the dust. However, I appreciate that you cannot be confined to the hotel altogether. I have engaged a ladies' maid for you, a respectable woman who will accompany you for walks and shopping. She will also take you to a dressmaker who will provide you with a suitable wardrobe.'

Leo continued to giggle. 'So I am to have a duenna? How hilarious!'

'I don't regard it as a joke. And get something done about your hair. You will have to get a wig.'

Sobering, she shook her shorn head. 'There's no need. I still have the switch of my own hair that I cut off. A competent hairdresser will be able to make it up into something suitable.'

'Very well.'

'And how am I supposed to pay for these suitable clothes?'

'The account can be sent to me.'

'What about my allowance? I haven't touched that since last October. I must have a useful sum saved up.'

'That will remain in your bank account in London. You will not need it here.'

Leo looked at him. 'Ralph, you are my brother. We played together as children. Have you no feelings for me? No sympathy?'

'Sympathy!' His lofty manner faltered. 'What sympathy did you have for me, when you decided to disappear without warning? What sympathy did you have for Grandma? And then you compound the fault by making yourself a public laughing stock.'

She lowered her head. 'I deserve that. You are right. I have no claim on your affection.'

For a moment his manner softened. 'Leo, I shall always love you as my sister. But you must understand how badly you have behaved. Maybe, in the long term, all this will be forgotten and we can go back to being as we were before. But for now, you must comply with my request and keep yourself out of the public eye. Will you do that?'

She sighed deeply. 'Very well. What does it matter now? What does anything matter?'

*

Tom took the first opportunity on his return to Belgrade to look up Maximillian Steinfeld at his hotel. The American greeted him with open arms.

'Hey, buddy! It's good to see you. How are you? You look a damn sight better than you did when I last saw you, that's for sure.'

'I'm well, thank you,' Tom replied. 'And I understand I owe my life to you. They told me in the hospital that you brought me through the enemy lines on the back of a donkey.'

'Sure did! And a more ornery, cussed creature you could not find anywhere. And the donkey was pretty obstinate, too. I'm joking! You were in a bad way. I couldn't just leave you.'

'Well, I'm grateful,' Tom said. 'If there is ever any way I can repay you, you only have to ask.'

'There's no need. I'm just glad to see you up and about again. So, what have you been doing since we last met?'

Tom related events from his recovery up to the point where he found Leonora. Then he paused.

'You found her?' Max said. 'Well, that's just great! What was she doing?'

'Well,' Tom said, 'this is where the story gets a bit ... a bit sensitive.' He went on to tell his companion what he had learned from her about the work she had done at Chataldzha and Adrianople. The one thing he omitted was the fact that she had dressed as a boy and the reason behind the deception.

When he finished Max whistled. 'So this little lady worked single-handed nursing wounded men at Chataldzha, nursed typhus sufferers at Adrianople, and acted as interpreter between a Serbian officer and the Turks. Jeez, Tom, what a story! You wait till my readers get this. Is there any chance of an interview with the lady?'

Tom frowned. His plan was working, but he still had to tread carefully. 'I doubt it. She is here in Belgrade but her brother, who is also her legal guardian, has instructed her to be discreet. He is afraid that it will damage her reputation if the story gets out.'

'Damage! When people read what she has done she will be the toast of Belgrade. Can't you arrange for me to have a few minutes with her?'

'I don't know … Her brother is my friend and I should not want to offend him.' This was not strictly true, since Ralph had hardly spoken to him since they left Adrianople, and then only in terms of frosty civility. He let Max see him coming to a decision. 'Very well. I will ask her to see you. But it will require the greatest discretion on your part. I do not want to be drawn into this.'

'I understand,' Max said. 'You can rely on me.'

*

Leo took little persuasion to grant Max an interview. Her confinement to the hotel and the constant, oppressive presence of Magda, the ladies' maid, who seemed to conceive her role as closer to that of a strict governess, were driving her to distraction.

Two days later the *Baltimore Herald* carried a eulogistic article, detailing her adventures. The story was rapidly taken up by other American papers and then by papers all over Europe.

Ralph stormed into her room one morning, carrying a sheaf of papers.

'What have you been saying? Who have you been talking to?'

'What about?' Leo asked innocently.

'About your antics in Bulgaria! Did I not ask you to be discreet? What were you thinking of?'

Leo rose to her feet. 'An American journalist picked up the story from somewhere and came to see me. I am not ashamed of what I did, even if you are, so I told him he could print it. Can I see what he has written?'

Ralph snatched the newspapers out of her reach. 'No, you can't! God knows what people here are going to think. How am I going to explain all this to my superiors when the word gets back to England? Really, Leo ...'

He was interrupted by a knock at the door. A page-boy stood outside.

'A message for Miss Malham Brown, sir.'

Ralph took it and handed it to Leo. 'I imagine this is some sort of reaction to the article in the paper. You had better read it.'

Leo opened the envelope and drew out a card. Then she began to laugh.

'What is it?' her brother demanded.

'Baroness Levinski requests the pleasure of my company at a reception this evening.'

Within days, Leo was inundated by a flood of invitations to receptions and balls. Ralph's instruction to her to order dresses and have the bill sent to him rebounded on him, as he found himself paying for yet another ball gown, or afternoon dress, or riding habit.

Leo floated through the firmament of Belgrade's beau monde like a visiting comet, admired and wondered at but unreachable. In spite of Tom's discretion, rumours spread by the officers who had been with Prince Alexander at Adrianople and had witnessed the denouement of the story began to spread. But this only added a titillating sense of the exotic and made her more sought after than ever. When it became known that there was no formal engagement between her and Tom, she was ardently courted by six or seven eligible men and received their attentions with a cool indifference that only strengthened their passion. She was glad to be out of the hotel and able to meet people and the adulation she received was some balm to her wounded spirit but none of it seemed real. She had the impression that she had left her real self behind outside Adrianople and was unlikely ever to be reunited with it. She was haunted by the thought that one day soon Sasha would return to Belgrade and she dreaded the prospect of another encounter, yet at the same time it filled her dreams.

One evening at a reception her hostess came towards her, bringing a tall, handsome girl of about seventeen, whose dark hair and eyes proclaimed her relationship before the introductions were made.

'Leonora, this is Adriana Malkovic. She has been longing to meet you.'

'Indeed I have,' the girl said, impulsively. 'Ever since I read that you were at the siege of Adrianople. I wonder, did you meet my brother Aleksander?'

Leo had had time to prepare herself and she answered calmly, 'Yes, I got to know him quite well.'

'How is he?' Adriana's eyes were wistful. 'It is so long since we saw him.'

'He was well when I left. I have no reason to think that has changed. He is very ... resilient.'

'I envy you so much!' the other girl exclaimed. 'To be able to go out there, to be near him and to do such wonderful work.'

'I was not the only one,' Leo said. 'There are many women there still, nursing the sick and wounded. Perhaps if you were to train as a nurse ...'

Adriana rolled her eyes. 'Sasha would never hear of it. He believes women should stay at home.'

'I know.' Leo felt a sudden warmth of fellow feeling for her. 'Brothers! I have one too.'

'I have met him,' Adriana responded. 'But he is charming.'

Leo looked across the room to where Ralph was being charming to two other young ladies. He turns it on like a tap, she thought. She turned back to Adriana. 'Whereas your brother is not, because he has no need to charm. He has other, more admirable, qualities that bind people to him.'

Adriana held her eyes. 'I see you do know him quite well.'

After that, Leo was not surprised to receive an invitation to take tea with the Dowager Countess Malkovic and her daughters, at the family's town house. As she rang the doorbell it crossed her mind to wonder what she would do if Sasha was inside, and how he would react to her arrival. Of course, he was not there and she passed a pleasant enough afternoon, although she had constantly to guard her tongue while they questioned her about him. It was clear from the start that they all adored him and were hungry for every detail.

From that day on, she and Adriana became close friends. They went walking and riding together and met constantly at the opera, or concerts or balls. But for all the frenetic gaiety of the city, there was a growing undercurrent of anxiety. If the London Conference did not end with a conclusion agreeable to Serbia, then it would not be accepted and there would be no peace. If it decided in Serbia's favour and awarded her most of Macedonia, then there would almost certainly be war with Bulgaria. And over all was the looming threat of the mighty Austro-Hungarian Empire, which had already annexed Bosnia-Herzegovina and resented Serbia's growing influence in the region, and particularly her access to the sea via the port of Durazzo. After the euphoria of victory, the future was looking increasingly uncertain.

One morning when Leo was sitting at her writing desk, replying to invitations, Tom came in. After a few general remarks he said, 'Leo, I'm worried about Ralph.'

'Ralph is perfectly capable of taking care of himself,' Leo responded tersely.

'On a physical level, perhaps. He's strong and brave and a match for anyone. But he's not as clever as you, Leo, and he doesn't always choose his friends very wisely.'

Leo put down her pen and turned to face him. 'What do you mean?'

'Have you ever heard of Dragutin Dimitrijevic?'

'The leader of the regicides? Yes, I was introduced to him the other day. No wonder his friends call him

Apis, after the Egyptian god. I've never seen anyone who looked more like a bull.'

'He's the leader of a society that calls itself "Unification or Death", otherwise known as the Black Hand. I came across some of them at Skopje and I didn't like what I saw.'

'What do they want to unify?'

'As far as I have been able to discover, their aim is a Greater Serbia, united with Bosnia and Croatia and independent of Austria-Hungary, and they are prepared to use any means to achieve it.'

'How do you know all this?'

'Partly from Max. He keeps his ear pretty close to the ground. And from gossip I've picked up over the billiard table. The Black Hand is supposed to be a secret society but everyone knows who they are.'

'Surely they are not contemplating another regicide?'

'I wouldn't put it past them, but King Petar has done what they wanted and made the army the most important element in the state. Max thinks he's safe enough, but he wouldn't be surprised if they are planning some act of provocation that will trigger a war with the Austrians.'

'And you think Ralph is mixed up in this?'

'I've seen him with Apis, and one or two of the others. I can imagine them appealing to Ralph.

They have this heady mixture of intense patriotism and military glamour that would really catch his imagination.'

'What can we do?'

'The ideal would be to get him back to London and out of harm's way. But as long as he's attached to Prince Aleksander there's no chance of that.'

'Can you talk to him?'

'He won't listen to me any more.'

'Or me.'

'Then there is nothing we can do, except hope that his own common sense prevents him from getting mixed up in anything really dangerous.'

Leo sighed and shook her head. 'I'm not sure that common sense is one of Ralph's most obvious characteristics.'

As Tom said, there was nothing they could do except watch and hope. But that evening Leo decided to tackle her brother on another subject.

'Ralph, I should like to ask you something.'

'What about?' he responded truculently.

'Why are you so hard on Tom?'

'Hard on him! I ought to have called him out and beaten him to a pulp after the way he behaved. He betrayed my trust.'

'Oh, nonsense, Ralph!' She had intended to remain calm and submissive, but it was not in her

nature. 'The only thing Tom is guilty of is not showing me up publicly, like you did.'

'What was I supposed to do? Let that ridiculous
charade continue?'

'It would have avoided a nasty scene! But that
isn't the point. Let me explain why Tom acted as
he did. I begged him to let me continue for a few
days, or weeks longer. I wanted to stay until the
siege was over. We all thought it couldn't last much
longer. He wasn't happy about it but I blackmailed
him into it.'

'What do you mean, blackmailed?'

'I told him that if he gave me away I would
never even consider marrying him.' She had prepared the lie carefully and it slipped glibly off her
tongue. It had the desired effect. For the first time
Ralph looked disconcerted. She pressed home her
advantage. 'Ralph, have you any idea what he went
through to find me? Has he told you his story? He
was arrested the first time he came here to Belgrade
and nearly shot as a spy. He saw things on the battlefield around Kumanovo and Bitola that still give
him nightmares and then he got ill and nearly died.
And after all that, when he was recuperating in
Athens and planning to travel to Italy, he got a letter from you asking him to go back into the lion's
jaws to look for me again. And he went, because

you asked him to. How can you possibly say he betrayed you?'

'Why didn't he at least write and let me know you were safe?'

'How could he? The only letters that went out from Adrianople were military despatches. Anyway, you wouldn't have received the letter if he had written. You had already left England.'

'And that was why he kept quiet, because you threatened not to marry him? I'm surprised he still wanted to.'

'He did it because he cares for both of us. No one could be more loyal. And look how you have repaid him.'

Ralph folded his arms and walked away from her. The clock on the mantelpiece struck the half hour and he looked round. 'Shouldn't you be getting ready for the concert tonight?'

Leo knew she had done as much as she could. She got up and left him to brood over what she had said.

*

Later that night when Tom was preparing for bed Ralph tapped at his door.

'I'd like a few words, if you don't mind.'

'Not at all. Come in.'

Ralph closed the door but he seemed in no hurry to broach whatever the subject was he wanted to discuss. Instead he wandered over to the dressing table and stood with his back to Tom, fiddling with items on the polished surface.

At length he said, 'I'm surprised you are still here. Wouldn't you prefer to go back to London?'

'I'm here for Leo's sake,' Tom replied. 'I think she needs a friend.'

'I should have thought you would just want to get away from her, after the way she's behaved.'

'I don't see that she has behaved badly at all. And I'm certainly not going to throw her over after I chased half way across Europe to find her – at your request, if you remember.'

'Are you still in love with her?'

Tom looked at him in silence. It seemed neither the truth nor a lie would serve him at this juncture. In the end he said, 'You know I am extremely fond of both of you. It distresses me that there is this rift between you, and I certainly have no intention of walking out on either of you.'

Ralph turned to look at him, then came across the room and laid a hand on his shoulder. To his amazement, Tom saw a tear at the corner of his eye. 'You're a loyal fellow, Tom, and I've treated you badly. I should be thanking you.' He held out his free hand. 'Will you accept my apology?'

Tom took the offered hand and resisted the temptation to pull him closer and put his arms round him. 'Yes, on one condition. You must make it up with Leo, too. She really is a wonderful girl, you know.'

When Ralph had gone Tom sat down on the edge of his bed and put his head in his hands. He was trembling. Once, back in Athens, he had thought he was free of the enchantment that had held him in its sway for so long; but the moment Ralph had appeared in Malkovic's tent he had understood that he could never release himself. When Ralph had turned on him and accused him of betraying his trust, it had felt as if a sharp blade had severed some essential internal ligament that held his personality together. Since that day, he had existed as two separate individuals; one who went about his duties as Leo's friend and escort and made conversation and even friendships among the young Serbian officers he met; the other a pathetic, shivering creature shut away to starve in darkness. He had begun to hope that one day, deprived of light and nourishment, it would die and leave him with the outer shell that carried on so painlessly with the business of living. But the prison door had been opened and the creature had seized upon the crumbs of comfort offered and now he would never be free of its demands.

*

Leo never knew what had passed between the two men, but two days later came news that put the whole matter out of her mind. Adrianople had surrendered at last. The siege was over and the troops were coming home.

Chapter 21

Leo lived on tenterhooks for the next week. Then she received a note from Adriana telling her that Sasha was home but had decided to spend some time relaxing on the family estate before re-entering Belgrade society. There was a promise that she would be invited out to the estate to meet him, but she was not surprised when no invitation arrived. A month passed until one night at a reception, when she was languidly fending off the attentions of one of her suitors, which were becoming more pressing as the days passed, she looked across the room and saw him being greeted by their hostess. The shock was so great that she froze in mid-sentence and her companion had to say her name twice before she responded. In panic she rose to her feet, trying to think of an excuse to leave the room; then she sat down again, aware that she was more likely to attract his attention by moving. He was with his family and his elder sister's husband and was immediately surrounded by well-wishers and people wanting to claim acquaintance with one of the heroes of the campaign and Leo was almost sure he had not seen her. Ralph, however, had seen him and came over.

Brusquely excusing himself to her cavalier, who withdrew with bad grace, he grabbed Leo's wrist. 'Come on, we're going home.'

'Why?' she asked, pretending innocence.

'That man is here! I won't have you meeting him, after the way he behaved last time.'

That was enough to strengthen Leo's resolve. 'You were the one who behaved badly,' she told him. 'Anyway, I have no intention of going home. I'm not going to give people the impression that I am ashamed to meet him. That really would be a cause for gossip.'

Ralph glared at her for a moment longer and must have seen in her eyes that she meant what she said and any attempt to remove her would result in a public fracas. Then he turned and stalked away.

Leo drew a deep breath and stood up, her chin held high. Let Malkovic see what had been hidden under the disguise of a scruffy boy! She was wearing a dress of onyx-green silk, with a low-cut, square neck decorated with a deep band of silver embroidery. Since leaving the privations of Adrianople she had put on a little weight and for the first time had no reason to feel ashamed of her *décolletage*. Her hair had begun to grow, but in addition she had had the hank of hair she had cut off at Chataldzha made up into a chignon. As a final touch she wore a necklace of moonstones, from which hung a single splendid emerald. Ralph, ashamed to see his sister without jewels among the glittering beau monde of Belgrade, had sent to England and instructed his bank to send out her grandma's jewellery by special courier. Most of it was hopelessly old-fashioned but this one item, Leo knew, really suited her. Tom had told her earlier that evening that she looked beautiful, and these days when Tom paid her a compliment she believed it. Abandoning her air of indifference, she turned to her suitors and gave them a smile that rocked them back on their heels.

As the evening progressed, she watched Sasha moving round the room, shaking hands, bowing, smiling, beset as she was by admirers but always gravely self-possessed; never, as she had predicted to Adriana, making an effort to charm. She saw him glance her way once or twice but he made no effort to approach her and she was careful to keep her distance. But at length the effort of trying to appear gay and insouciant became too much and she sought out Tom, who had retreated to the billiard room with some of the men.

'I'm feeling tired, Tom. Would you mind taking me home?'

'Of course not. Get your cloak. I'll wait for you in the hall.'

Leo went upstairs to the room that had been set aside for ladies to remove their cloaks and prink themselves, before making their entrance. She picked up her cloak, glanced at herself in the mirror and went to the door, to find Sasha Malkovic waiting in the corridor.

For a moment neither of them spoke, while he looked her up and down with the familiar sardonic smile. Then he said, 'So, the lion cub is actually a lioness.'

'More deadly than the male, if we are to believe Mr Kipling,' she replied, determined to play him at his own game.

He bent his head in acknowledgement of the riposte. 'At any rate, not a domestic cat. I confess I am a little at a loss. I expected that skinny youth I knew at Adrianople to metamorphose into a young girl. But you ... are a woman.'

'I lied about my age,' she said.

'I realised that. But I thought you were younger, not older.' He came a few steps closer and she saw that his face had lost some of the fine-drawn, hollow-cheeked appearance that she remembered. He said,

'When I saw you across the room this evening it was some time before I could believe the evidence of my eyes.'

Leo felt as if a hand was at her throat, restricting her breathing. 'I hope you are not disappointed.'

'On the contrary,' he said, 'I am vastly relieved.'

'Relieved? Why?'

From below they heard women's voices approaching, then Tom's. 'Excuse me, ladies, would you see if Miss Malham Brown is nearly ready? I am waiting for her.'

'I must go,' she said, and he stepped back to allow her to pass. She hesitated a moment. 'I expect we shall meet again, now you are here in Belgrade?'

'Inevitably,' he responded. Then, as she passed him, he added, 'I missed you after you had gone.'

The two ladies reached the top of the stairs and one said, 'Ah, here she is! Your escort is getting impatient, my dear.'

'Thank you. I am ready now,' Leo said. She looked behind her once and caught his eyes, then she ran down the stairs to where Tom was waiting.

It was three days before she encountered Sasha again. This time it was at a ball. As soon as she arrived, on Tom's arm, she was besieged as usual by young men wanting to put their names down for a dance. She saw him on the far side of the room, but he made no effort to approach her and her dance card was filling up fast. She saved the last dance before the supper interval, pretending that she had promised it to Tom, but by the time the orchestra struck up the first waltz it was still blank and she feared it would remain so. Tom, always mindful of his obligations although he hated dancing, led her onto the floor and she made up her mind to give the impression that she was completely carefree. Tonight she was wearing midnight blue velvet, with her grandma's sapphire earrings, and she knew Sasha was watching her. She watched him, too, and saw that he danced with the same poise and mastery as he rode.

She had danced three dances before she saw him crossing the floor towards her. He bowed and wished her good evening and she responded in the same manner.

'I suppose it is too much to hope that you might have a dance left for me,' he said.

For a moment she had an impulse to tell him that his assumption was correct. Instead she said, 'I was saving the supper dance for Tom Devenish, but I am sure he would be happy to retire in your favour.'

'Then I shall be very much obliged to him,' he replied. The orchestra struck up the next dance and he made a gesture of apology. 'I am engaged for this one, but I shall return to claim you for the supper dance.'

When the time came and he took her hand to lead her onto the floor she was aware that they were the focus of all eyes. The titillating gossip about their previous relationship had spread all through the close-knit group that made up Belgrade society and she could appreciate why he had hesitated at first to be seen with her. But as soon as they reached the dance floor and he took her in his arms she forgot the rest of the world. His right hand was firm in the small of her back while his left held hers with a gentle pressure and as he whirled her into the waltz she felt as if her feet flew across the floor without touching it.

The Viennese waltz requires stamina and leaves little breath for conversation, but when the dance ended he gave her his arm and took her into the room where the supper was laid out. A sumptuous buffet had been prepared. Hams glistened under the candlelight and barons of beef glowed pink and succulent, while pride of place was occupied by a whole roasted piglet. There were mountains of pastries, whose origin testified to Serbia as a place where two great empires met: baklava dripping with honey sat next to rich, dark Sachertorte and dishes of sweetmeats included the traditional *slatko*, a fruit preserve made from plums and cherries.

As they filled their plates he said, 'Next week we are celebrating my family's slava day. If I send you an invitation, will you come?'

'A slava day?' Leo said. 'What is that?'

'Every family in Serbia has one. It celebrates a momentous occasion in the extended family's history – usually their conversion to Christianity.'

'And how do you celebrate?'

'We entertain our friends and neighbours to a feast. And there will be musicians, dancing, that sort of thing. Will you come?'

'I should like that very much.' She thought a moment and added, 'It might be best if you invited Ralph and Tom as well. Otherwise I may not be able to accept.'

'Of course,' he said. 'I will ask Adriana to send you all invitations.'

The Malkovic estate was an hour's drive outside Belgrade and Sasha sent a car to pick them up. It was May, and for the first time Leo saw the full beauty of the Serbian countryside. They drove through meadows where sleek cattle and horses grazed. Orchards of plum and cherry shed their blossom on the road as they approached the rambling house with its stables and outbuildings. Tables had been set out in a courtyard, shaded by trellises supporting more vines, and Sasha stood at the entrance with his mother, the countess, and his sisters, to receive their guests. He had changed out of his uniform and wore the traditional loose white tunic, caught in with a belt of tooled leather, over baggy black breeches, and Leo thought she had never seen him looking so relaxed.

While they ate spit-roasted lamb and spicy goulash, red with paprika, a man played the gusla and began one of the interminable chants that took Leo back to many a night around the campfire at Adrianople.

After it had gone on for some time Ralph leaned across to her and hissed, 'How long is this cater-wauling going on?'

'Ssh!' she reproved him. 'He is telling the family history back from the year dot. It is terribly important to them.'

When the meal was over and the song was finished a flute and a violin struck up and Sasha rose and stepped out into the clear space in the centre of the tables. He stretched out his arms and immediately his brother-in-law came to his side, laying an arm across his shoulders. Another male relative joined in on his other side and he was followed by other men of the family and brother officers until the circle was complete and they began to trace the steps of the 'kolo'. This way and that the circle rotated, the steps growing faster and more intricate but never losing the sense of solemn ritual. The kolo, Leo had learned, was never light-hearted. However fast the dancers moved, they never leapt or skipped but kept their feet firmly on the ground, as if affirming their oneness with their native soil.

After the dancing the guests dispersed around the grounds of the estate, strolling in small groups in the May sunshine. Adriana tucked her arm through Leo's, saying, 'Come, I want to show you the garden.'

They wandered past formal beds, the air heavy with the scent of wallflowers, along pleached alleys of fruit trees, until they came to an arbour with a rustic seat shaded by honeysuckle and rambling rose. And there, a few yards away, was Sasha, chatting casually to two elderly ladies. Seeing them, he made his excuses to the ladies, who wandered away to rejoin the rest, and came over.

'Adriana, mother was looking for you.'

'I'll go to her,' the girl said immediately. 'Leo, you won't mind if I leave Sasha to entertain you, will you?'

Leo shook her head, smiling at the transparency of the stratagem, but feeling at the same time that constriction at her throat that his close proximity provoked.

He indicated the seat. 'Shall we sit down?' She sat and he went on, 'I was surprised to find you in Belgrade. I thought you would have gone back to England.'

'Been sent back, you mean,' Leo said wryly. 'But you see, my brother has to stay here and, as he is my legal guardian now my grandma is dead, I have to stay with him. He doesn't trust me to behave if I am out of his sight.'

'What about your grandfather?' he asked.

'My grandfather? I never knew … Oh, I'm afraid I made him up.'

'I see. And I suppose the fact that your grandparents knew where you were and had given their permission was also a fiction.'

'Yes, I must confess it was.'

'And your Macedonian ancestry?'

'Another myth, I'm afraid.'

'But why? I mean, why are you here? What made you come to the Balkans if you have no connection to this part of the world?'

Leo looked at him. 'You won't approve if I tell you.'

'Try me.'

She paused, ordering her thoughts. 'Very well. There are people in my country, men as well as women, who believe that women have more to contribute to society than just their role as wives and mothers.'

'Ah, the suffragettes. I have heard of them. The whole idea seems to me extraordinary.'

'Why?'

'Why would women who, as society is currently organised, are cared for and protected by men, wish to exchange that for the trials and dangers that men are accustomed to face on their behalf?'

'Because we feel we can offer more, can do more. I have seen women surgeons operate on the wounded with just as much expertise as male doctors and a great deal more compassion. If women can be doctors and lawyers and teachers, why should they not also have a say in how society is organised and how their country is governed?'

'Because ultimately it is we men who have to deal with the consequences, who have to, if necessary, take up arms to defend the country. And to endure the hardships and dangers that follow from that.'

'Yes, and that is why I am here now.'

'I don't follow you.'

'There is a remarkable Englishwoman called Mabel Stobart who believes that, if women wish to have an equal share in government, they must first show that they are prepared to endure the same dangers and privations that men face.'

'Surely you are not saying that you think women should become soldiers?'

'No. Mrs Stobart is very clear about that. Our role is to preserve life, not to take it. But that does not mean we cannot serve in our own way. It was to prove that that she set up a hospital in Lozengrad, staffed entirely by women.'

'I have heard about that, and I have read your story in the newspapers, but did it require you to dress up as a boy?'

'No.' She looked into his face. 'Please believe me, I never set out to deceive you. I discarded my skirts because at Chataldzha they became so heavy with mud and filth that I could hardly walk in them. And I cut my hair because I could never get it dry. When you saw me and mistook me for a boy I did not disillusion you, because I knew that if you guessed I was a woman you would send me away.'

'As I certainly should have,' he agreed. 'But what I find hardest to forgive is that you let me take you on that mad escapade into the Turkish trenches. Suppose we had been captured? The consequences are unthinkable. Weren't you scared?'

'Terrified,' Leo agreed. 'But it was the most exciting thing I have ever done.'

He laughed. 'You are a most extraordinary woman!'

'I don't think so,' she replied. 'I think there are many other women who would like to do what I have done, given the opportunity.'

He looked at her, shaking his head in disbelief. After a moment she went on, 'That evening, when we first met at the reception, you said you were relieved to discover I was a woman. What did you mean?'

'Surely you can guess.'

'No.'

'Why do you think I found excuses to keep you with me? Why did I take you riding every morning?'

'Lieutenant Popitch said I was the colonel's pet.'

'Did he indeed! Well, he would no longer be *Lieutenant* Popitch if I had heard him! But he had some justification. Did it never seem strange to you?'

'I have to admit that I sometimes wondered if … if you made a habit of choosing favourites.'

'Never! Never before. But that is the point. Don't you see? I was developing feelings for you that made me question my own manhood. That is why I was relieved to discover you were a woman.'

Leo's breath was coming fast and shallow. He was very close, his arm resting along the back of the seat behind her, his eyes holding hers as if he wanted to hypnotise her.

Her brother's voice jerked her back to reality. 'Leonora!' He was standing a short distance away with two more ladies. 'Come here, please. These ladies would like to meet you.'

She exchanged one brief, wry smile with Sasha and got up. The moment was past.

Next day rumours began to circulate that the London Conference had finally come to an agreement. Ralph returned from duty to the hotel grim-faced.

'It's exactly the sort of fudge we've been expecting. Albania gets full independence, which means that, after all the sacrifices the Serbian army made to get there, they lose access to the sea at Durazzo. And nothing concrete has been decided about Macedonia. The Serbs are determined to hang onto it as compensation for losing Albania and the Bulgarians think it should be theirs in recognition of the losses they incurred fighting the Turks in the east. Neither side is going to compromise. It's a recipe for another war.'

The following morning Leo received an invitation to take tea with Adriana at the Malkovic's town house. She went with a raised pulse and a fluttering in her stomach. It was no surprise to find Sasha waiting in the drawing room. Over tea the three of them discussed the settlement, and Sasha's estimation of the result was the same as Ralph's. Then Adriana rose to her feet.

'I know Sasha wants a few private words with you, Leo, so I'm going to leave you alone. I'll be in the garden if you want me.'

Leo's heart was pounding as the door closed behind her. This, surely, must be the logical conclusion to their interrupted conversation in the garden. Sasha had got up and was standing by the empty fireplace, his expression unreadable.

'You realise that the present situation means that I could be recalled to my regiment very soon, within days quite possibly. Before that happens there is something I must say to you.'

'Go on,' Leo said breathlessly.

'I have not behaved honourably towards you. I have allowed the relationship we had at Adrianople to cloud my better judgement.'

She shook her head. 'I don't understand.'

He moved quickly to sit beside her on the sofa. 'The other day I spoke of feelings I had developed for you, and my relief at discovering that you were a woman. I think you know what those feelings are. I have never loved a woman. I mean with my heart. I have known lust, but never love. Women have always seemed to me alien, unknowable. But with you I feel I have found my perfect partner, someone whose spirit blends with mine as if we were two halves of the same whole. I believe you feel the same.'

Unable to speak, she could only nod.

'If circumstances were other than they are,' he went on, 'I would at this moment be asking you give me the greatest happiness I can imagine by agreeing to be my wife. But I am not free. That is why I have behaved dishonourably in ever allowing you to imagine there might be anything between us.'

'Not free?' The words were forced from a tight throat.

'Let me explain. You know how turbulent the history of my country has been. It has been plagued for centuries by blood feuds and factions. It is the case with my own family. For generations there has been enmity between the Malkovices and the Kableshkovs. It is a history of raids, murders and pitched battles that weakened both families. When I was fourteen, my father and Todor Kableshkov decided to put an end to the feud once and for all. Todor has a daughter, Eudoxie, who was then three years old. We were formally betrothed as a pledge of good faith between our families. She is now eighteen. The marriage cannot be delayed much longer.'

Leo, struggling to assimilate what he had told her, seized on the most obvious fact. 'I have not met her.'

'No. Sadly she is not strong. She has a weakness in the chest that makes breathing difficult. She spends much of her time in her own room and goes out very little.'

'But that is not right for you!' Leo cried. 'How can you be forced to marry a girl like that, a girl who could never make a suitable wife for you?'

He shook his head miserably. 'If I were to renege on the agreement now the consequences for both families would be incalculable. For a start, one of her brothers would feel obliged to call me out and in the subsequent duel I should probably kill him. So the blood feud would start up all over again. For the sake of my mother and my sisters, and their children, I must go through with it.'

Tears were standing in her eyes but she refused to let them fall. What he required from her now was courage, not hysteria. She drew a deep, shuddering breath and said, 'Then what must be, must be.'

He caught her hand and raised it to his lips, then rubbed his cheek against it. 'Oh, my dear, brave girl. How well you were named! If only you and I were joined, we could face the world together.'

'But now it seems we must both face it alone,' she whispered. 'Before we part, may I ask you one last favour?'

'Anything!'

'Will you kiss me once, so that I have that to remember?'

He took her in his arms and his lips found hers and parted them. She had never kissed a man before and she lost all awareness of the world beyond his embrace, as every nerve in her body responded. At last he drew back and looked down into her eyes. She reached up and put her arms round his neck with sudden fierce intensity.

'Let me stay with you! I don't care about marriage. I don't care what society says, or the church. I will stay here and you can come to me whenever you are able. That will be enough for me.'

Very gently he disengaged himself. 'I will not allow you to do that to yourself. My honour, and yours are at stake. You will leave here and one day you will forget me. Or at least you will find someone who makes the memory of me irrelevant. We both have our duty and our different fates. It is useless to fight against it.' He reached into his pocket and withdrew a small case. 'Will you take this, as a memento of our time together?'

Inside the case was a gold locket and when she opened it she saw that it contained a twist of black hair.

He said, 'One day, you will take out that hair and put in its place a lock taken from the head of your firstborn child.'

'Never,' she replied. 'I shall keep this always and nothing will ever replace it.'

He fastened it round her neck and she slipped it inside her dress. Then he got up and said, 'I will leave you alone to compose yourself. When you feel ready, ring the bell and Adriana will come to you.'

When the door closed behind him she got up and went to the mirror over the fireplace. Her eyes and her lips were red and swollen. She took out her handkerchief and rubbed at them, and tidied her hair as best she could. Then, unable to face Adriana's sympathy, she went out into the hall, where a footman stood ready to open the front door. In a moment she was in the street.

At breakfast the next morning, she said, 'Ralph, I have decided I should like to go home.'

'Why?' he asked. 'I thought you were enjoying yourself here.'

'I was, but now I am tired and I think I need a little peace and quiet.'

He shook his head. 'You can't possibly go home all alone. If you're tired, just don't accept any more invitations.'

'You know it isn't as easy as that. Anyway, why can't I go home? I wouldn't be alone. The house is still there, presumably, and the staff.'

'I let some of them go. But Beavis is there, and Mrs Sanders and one or two of the others.'

'Then I can go to them. I don't need a nursemaid.'

He looked at her, chewing his lip as he did at moments of indecision. 'Leo, I don't want you in London, where I can't keep an eye on you.'

'Oh, for goodness sake! What do you think I am going to do?'

'Who knows? You will probably chum up with that Langford woman, for a start, and those FANYs. God knows what sort of mad scheme you might get yourself involved in. I'm sorry, Leo, but I just don't trust you to be sensible.'

Leo glared at him. She had cried herself to sleep the previous night and had no more tears to shed but in her extremity she felt she could hurl the cups and saucers and the cutlery at his head. Instead, she forced herself to be calm and to employ the last stratagem at her disposal.

'Would it make any difference if I were engaged to Tom?'

He looked stunned. 'Engaged? You mean you have finally come to your senses?'

'I believe so, yes.'

'And what makes you think Tom will still have you, after the way you have treated him?'

'The only one of us who has ill-treated Tom is you. He has never blamed me for what happened, or if he did he has forgiven me. I think he would be prepared to give me his name.'

Ralph's face cleared. 'You know nothing would please me more than to see you two married. If Tom is willing to go ahead with the engagement I see no reason why you shouldn't go back to London together.'

Three weeks later the *London Gazette* published the following paragraph.

'The engagement is announced of Miss Leonora Malham Brown, of 31 Sussex Gardens, London, to Mr Thomas Andrew Devenish, only son of Sir William Devenish, Bart., of Denham Manor, Hertfordshire.'

The following day, the Bulgarian General Savov launched a surprise attack on Serbian forces in Macedonia. The two former allies were at war.

*

Back in England Leo took refuge from the congratulations of friends and acquaintances and the inevitable invitations to attend social functions with her new fiancé by retreating to Bramwell, the family estate in Cheshire. Here, under the care of James and Annie Bartlett, the estate manager and housekeeper who had always treated her like one of their own children, she had time to reflect and recover. It was clearly understood between her and Tom that their engagement was simply a matter of expediency and was not to lead to marriage. The question she had to answer now was how she intended to use the rest of her life. She could not imagine finding a new love, and the idea of marrying for convenience, to secure her place in society, was abhorrent to her.

Whatever her grandma had thought of Leo's behaviour, she had not changed her will, which left her a generous settlement. That, together with her father's legacy, meant she was well provided for financially, so she had no worries on that score, but she urgently needed to find some purpose powerful enough to distract her mind from the contemplation of her loss. The newspapers were full of increasingly hysterical assertions of German aggressive intention and war seemed inevitable. Leo's one consolation was the thought that she had shown that she could be of use on the field of conflict and it seemed likely that before long she would be called on to prove her courage and ability again.

Author's Note

These books are not romantic fantasies but are based on solid historical fact. They were inspired by the lives of two remarkable women, Mabel St Clair Stobart and Flora Sands. Stobart, who features as a character in this book, was the founder of the Women's Sick and Wounded Convoy in 1912. She led a group of nurses to care for Bulgarian soldiers during the First Balkan War and returned to help the Serbs during World War One. She gave an account of her experiences in her books *Miracles and Adventures* and *The Flaming Sword in Serbia and Elsewhere*.

Flora Sands was the daughter of a clergyman and an early member of the FANY – the First Aid Nursing Yeomanry. In 1915 she volunteered to go to Serbia with Stobart, was separated from her unit and joined up with a company of Serbian soldiers, with whom she endured the terrible hardships of the retreat through the mountains of Albania. She later returned with them to Salonika and took part in the final advance which ended the war. She was the first women ever to be accepted as a fighting soldier and ended the war with the rank of sergeant. Though she does not appear as a character in these books, much of the action is derived from her experiences, which are recorded in her own memoir *An English Woman Sergeant in the Serbian Army* and by Alan Burgess in *The Lovely Sergeant*.

Make sure you read the rest of the
Frontline Nurse series

Can she find the courage to do her duty?

When war breaks out in 1914, Leonora Malham
Brown and her best friend, Victoria, head to Calais
to volunteer with the First Aid Nursing Yeomanry.
Determined to see her sweetheart, Colonel Malkovic,
again Leonora soon decides to return to the Front.

But once there, Leonora gets caught up in the
danger and chaos of the battlefields and she loses
hope of ever finding Sasha. Alone and in danger,
Leonora must put into practice the very best of her
nursing training if she is to return safely home.

When war comes, friendship will seem them through the tough times

In the midst of the First World War, Leonora Malham Brown is a volunteer with the Red Cross, while her best friend, Victoria, is a nurse at the Front in Calais. Despite the hardships of war, Leonora is delighted to be reunited with her sweetheart, Colonel Malkovic.

Before long, Leonora falls pregnant but she daren't tell Sasha for fear he would send her home. But when she finally plucks up the courage to tell him, tragedy strikes and he is reported missing in action. Heartbroken and now a new mother all alone, Leonora must turn to her friends back in England to help her …